BLOOD ONCE SPILLED

JOHN T. WAYNE

T̶ ̶G̶A̶ ̶G̶HT BOYS (series)

THE NEW S̶ ̶ ̶ ̶ D IN WESTERN FOLKLORE!

BLOOD ONCE SPILLED

JOHN T. WAYNE

THE GASLIGHT BOYS (series)

THE NEW STANDARD IN WESTERN FOLKLORE

Mockingbird Lane Press

Blood Once Spilled
Copyright © 2017 John T. Wayne

Mockingbird Lane Press—Maynard, Arkansas

ISBN: 978-1-6353526-2-7

Library of Congress Number in publication data

0 9 8 7 6 5 4 3 2 1

www.mockingbirdlanepress.com

Cover art: Jamie Johnson

I love the south; a man can still get away with telling the truth in the south!

---John T. Wayne

This book is dedicated to tireless servants, the missionaries all around the world who labor daily to bring the true word of God to those in remote places. I never thought I would see the day when America would also be known as a fertile ground for missionaries, but her time has come. We have forgotten our heritage, our contract with God and we no longer recognize evil. May God help us!!!

THE GASLIGHT BOYS

From 1861 – 1865 a storm rolled through our nation and in its wake left behind a path of death and destruction. Over 100,000 children lost everything they had come to know including both parents. This tragedy took place during the Civil War and sadly for years after; during a period known as Reconstruction. What became of those children? How were they instrumental in shaping the future of our society? These questions are answered in my series of books called, "The Gaslight Boys." Charles Dickens is credited with being the original Gaslight Boy, but there were many other Gaslight Children created by the war. The Gaslight Boys series brings to life the hardships, the conditions and individual struggles buried and /or forgotten by time.

These are the stories of the young men and women who grew up to become great in their own right, men and women of the great society. Some of them became great, some became outlaws, and some died short of the chance. The Gaslight Boy novels are their stories.

---John T. Wayne

Authors Note

In old Louisiana there is a tradition which came over with the Creole slaves, the African Diaspora or French speaking population. Voodoo is not a religion which stands on its own in Louisiana, but a religion that is augmented by Christianity. In other words; Voodoo has evolved, or Christianity has evolved into something a bit more perplexing; a people who have more than one ace up their sleeve. Together these two religions create a force like no other, (for them that believe).

All religions are based upon one thing, BELIEF! Nothing happens unless you first believe! You can accomplish nothing unless you first believe! The Lord put it succinctly in Mathew Chapter 8 verse 13; "Go thy way and as thou hast believed, so be it unto thee."

You can't operate outside of how you see yourself, or what you believe about yourself, not for very long anyway. Therefore, what we believe about ourselves is the most important dynamic we as humans face on a daily basis. *Blood Once Spilled* examines the relationship between Voodoo and Christianity in the heart of Louisiana just after the Civil War, a time when the blood of men still spilled from a human vile for reasons unprecedented.

Chapter 1

I was what most folks would call a sensitive child. My pa died when I was three so Ma had seen to it I knew the Bible. This was something she would have done whether Pa was around or not. Then Ma died when I was six years old. Yellow fever claimed her and there was nothing I could do to bring her back. I cried for days.

The pastor at our church, Brother Xzious Teeter had seen fit to take me in, only I wouldn't stay in. What I mean to say is, every time he turned around I was at my mother and father's grave weeping. Now this behavior went on until I forced his hand, whatever that meant. The best I could figure was I had left him no choice but to hand me down.

I was handed over to Mr. and Mrs. Whipple who were good Christian people and they continued to teach me in God fearing ways, but I was no longer in New Orleans. The handoff meant I was living in Iberville Parish, Louisiana.

My big problem seemed to be I was mad at God for what he'd done. Every time somebody said, "God had a pre-determined time for calling everyone home," I got mad clean through. Not at folks for telling me, but at God for his pre-determined plan for taking both my parents at such an early age as to leave me an orphan. While my adopted mother Mrs. Nancy Whipple saw fit to teach me to love and respect God, I didn't have much faith in my maker back then.

Now let me explain about orphans. Even good God-fearing Christian folk wanted nothing to do with orphans prior to the Civil War, less so afterward. Consequently, I was part of a generation of children who received a cold shoulder from normal folks. I was a down-and-outer. I ate lunch by myself because parents of normal children didn't want me to contaminate their offspring. All the other children seemed to want to do was make fun of me anyway they could, at school, at church or anywhere else.

On the playground at school, I was mocked. After church I was made fun of and laughed at. While some of the mothers would rein their children in at church, I was on my own when I set foot on the school ground. As a result, I ate my lunch at my desk, not outside with the other kids. When recess was called I developed a habit of staying at my desk to study. The play was no fun for me anyway. Many times Miss Anna Belle Arbuckle would sit in with me at recess and tutor me on a particular subject until it was time for the other children to return to class. I'll forever be thankful to her for the extra time she devoted to me, because if not for her attention I would have believed no one on earth cared one lick about me.

Whenever I got picked on, I would get real mad and whip up on two or three boys at once; however many they felt necessary to sic on me. I was a quick learner in that respect. At first I didn't want to fight, but as time went on the attacks against me became more frequent so I began to fight back. One particular afternoon the situation came to a head. I was ten at the time.

I was walking home from school minding my own business when five of the boys from school jumped out onto the dirt road in front of me and I didn't need nobody to tell me what for. I got mad clean through, mad that they felt I didn't belong, and mad they didn't have enough confidence among them to confront me with a more reasonable number.

"We're going to whoop you good this time," Butch Abernathy claimed. He was the one who hated me so much he would always sic the other boys on me. He wasn't man enough to do his own dirty work, that's why he needed all that help. He was a silver-tongued devil and used his talent to goad others into doing things he was too chicken to tackle himself, so I dropped my books with a thud and hit him right smack in the kisser with everything I had. I didn't wait for him to sic the other boys on me this time; I wanted to teach Butch a lesson. He landed in a heap in the middle of the road and before he could figure out what happened to him I was on top slugging for all I was worth. I beat his face to a bloody pulp. He'd jumped me for the last time, and when I landed on top of him I instantly pinned his arms beneath my knees. From that moment I began wailing away. The other boys were yelling and screaming, but I was too enraged to make out anything anyone was saying. I just kept hitting him. Right then I was no better than a miserable low down pole-cat, because I possessed a one track mind.

When I stopped, his eyes were practically swollen shut, and the rest of his face was a bloody hideous looking mess. I stood up and looked at the other boys who now wore a look of shock and horror on their evil little faces.

"All right, which one of you devils is next?" I challenged, huffing and puffing.

None of them were able to mask their horror. As one they began to back off, not wanting to risk becoming the next casualty.

"I'm waiting," I screamed with my own blood dripping from my raw lacerated knuckles.

"If any one of you ever set on me again, what I just did to Butch is nothing compared to what you'll look like when I get through with you," I vowed.

"He's going to need a doctor," Darnell put in. Darnell Blankenship was built much like Butch, only he was more level-headed. He was bigger than me by at least six inches, but Butch was four inches taller than I was, and look what happened to him.

"You get him some help and in the meantime you remember what happened here today. I'll fight again and again if I have to. The next one of you who makes fun of me at school or church is going to find himself worse off than Butch."

My opponent was beginning to moan and beg for help so I took it as a sign and gathered my things. Suddenly I remembered I was not alone. I did a bad thing right in front of the Townsend girl. She was a six-year-old who was forevermore asking me to carry her books for her, always complaining they were too heavy. I headed for home with Virginia Townsend tagging right along.

"You sure showed them," she said as she skipped along beside me. "Can I be your girlfriend," she asked after a minute.

"No you can't be my girlfriend, now be quiet." Just what I needed, a six-year-old girlfriend who still played with dolls, I thought.

"Will you carry my books for me, they're getting heavy," she whined.

"No, now be quiet," I repeated.

On the way home I began to realize the extent of what had taken place. All those months of being mad at God, getting madder all the time; when those boys saw fit to ridicule me, why it all just come to a head. I could no longer hold in my rage. It looked like I was no longer going to be able to withdraw inside myself. From then on I was going to confront situations head on right up until the day I died. All my aggression had been pent up inside me and Butch Abernathy was the sole benefactor of all my anger against God and the world.

I shuffled my feet in disgust at the situation I'd been forced into, so I took the long way home, said goodbye to the Townsend girl and continued on. As I came walking into the yard I knew there was trouble on the horizon. All I did was defend myself. The horse and team in front of the house belonged to Butch's father. I went to the front door and paused, able to hear loud talking in the parlor.

"The boy has got to go, Whipple. I was willing to go along with you when you took him in, but there has been nothing but trouble from my boy Butch since then. My own son is becoming ruined in order that you might save one child. I happen to know others who feel the same as I do. Now Doc Webster is dressing my boy's wounds and tells me he'll likely be scared for life. His nose is broken, his eyes are swollen shut, and he has a broken jaw with two teeth knocked out. It's unfortunate the boy lost his parents, but I can't sacrifice my only son to try and save a boy who seems a lost cause."

"Carl, I know tensions are high right now, but let's not pass judgment on the boy before he has a chance to speak for himself. I happen to know he is a tender and sensitive young man," Mr. Whipple countered.

"Tender and sensitive? The boy is nothing but trouble. His current circumstances are his own. Don't go laying them at my doorstep."

"Now you know I'm not doing that Carl, I'm simply saying let's be rational."

"I see. Well I'm not too rational at the moment. My son was almost killed on the way home from school today."

I didn't wait to hear anymore. I pushed open the door and entered the house. Dropping my books in the chair beside the front window I walked over to the parlor door and stood looking at my accuser who sat in a chair directly across from Mr. Whipple. I didn't figure to ever get a fair shake from the man so I just laid into him directly.

"You're just like your boy! You have to be the big talker, the devil with how others may feel. Well Mister, your son has picked on me for the last time. I don't think he'll be doing it any more, and if he does, he'll get what's coming to him. I never start any of the fights I end up in, I just finish them," I shouted.

"You hear that Whipple? The little whelp is threatening me!"

"All the boy is doing is standing his ground. And I, for one, am proud of him," Mr. Whipple answered back.

"Well, I can see I'm getting nowhere with the two of you. You're absolutely smitten by the little mercenary," Carl said as he stood. Picking up his hat he added, "I can see I'll have no satisfaction in the matter, so henceforth I'll not be in services on Sunday morning. Do me a favor and tell the preacher for me."

With that he stormed by me and out the front door. Mr. and Mrs. Whipple just sat and stared at me, then my adopted mother saw my dried bloody hands and took immediate action.

"Land sakes young man, when you stir up the pot, you stir it up. Let me see those hands," she said as she grabbed them and pulled them upright, palms down.

"If you don't beat all. Husband, we're going to have to go and see Doc Webster ourselves. Le Roy's hands are a complete mess. Look how swollen they are," she said holding them out further for him to see. They were covered with blood, mine or Butch's I didn't really know, but as I later learned at Doc's office it was a little of both. I wore my knuckles raw while beating on my adversary. As a result I had broken both hands in multiple places.

That was many years ago. Much time had passed since then. I became a man grown, a man who didn't take to funning very well. I had little use for folks who weren't serious about their business. A man only has a limited amount of time to get anything accomplished in this life, so I had little respect for those who thought they were on a schedule which allowed horse play or laziness.

Hard maybe, but that was the man I became.

One thing I learned long since was the fact all men were created equal, ends at birth, there's no two ways about it. We might all be born equal, but we all begin to grow at a different pace, mentally, physically and spiritually. There is no such thing as two equal human beings and any government who tries managing equality to keep people equal is doomed to fail. A man or woman is responsible for their own life, their own destiny, dreams and actions. No government can effectively manage a person's day to day quality of life. I had heard about some places around the world trying to, but the people in those countries were always rioting and fighting. That was the blessing of being born American.

Chapter 2

Recently I'd become a traveling man, a man headed for home. What kind of home I had no idea. I had been orphaned at an early age and now that the Whipple's were gone I discovered quite unexpectedly they had left their entire property in Louisiana to me. To that point, it was the only home I could remember.

The Whipple's had been a lonely couple, unable to bear a child of their own, so when I became available they took me in. Yet, from the beginning I had been trouble to them, not because I was trouble, but because I drew trouble from others like flies to a dead carcass. I never asked to be picked on, I never asked to be ostracized, yet those situations set upon me like the plague because of my orphan status.

I reckoned my problem to the likes of a family. As a child you don't get to pick your family, you get what you get and it usually isn't any great shakes of a deal for some folks. Family can do some strange things to you I learned. Whether you were adopted or you really were part of a family, those you considered loved ones, often as not, found ways to offend you. I recognized the fact I didn't have to worry about such offences any more. I had no family left, not even my adopted one.

Now, as I neared home a steady soaking rain settled in around me. The letter in my saddle bag said the estate was to become mine according to the will left by Mrs. Whipple. In the ten years since leaving I had accumulated no personal belongings except a rifle, a pistol and a Missouri mule named Regret. I became a drifter, a studier of life, but my studies had been self-perpetuating. I didn't need anyone and I liked my life just that way. The last thing I wanted or needed was to be responsible for anyone else.

Stepping down from ol' Regret I gathered pine boughs to create a shelter. When my shelter was finished, thatched heavily on the roof I unsaddled Regret, rubbed him down with pine needles and crawled inside. I pitched my saddle to the back corner and sat down to start a fire. I kept it barely big enough to put inside my hat, because anything bigger would burn down what I had just built and I couldn't carry anymore kindling in my saddle bag. I was cold wet and miserable from traveling in bad weather, and now it was time to get warm and cozy beside a comfortable fire.

I was going home, but to what? I hadn't been home in nearly ten years. A grown man now, I never felt like I had a real home. I traveled now like I traveled for the last ten years, alone and empty with caution born of abuse. Everybody I met seemed as if they were disposed to prove they were better than me somehow. This led to all sorts of trouble, causing me to leave more than one man dead back along my trail.

Hunger follows a man who was always riding point, and when you travel alone, you're always riding point, picking up the drag and watching everything in between, otherwise there is a good chance you might die.

I was soaked to the skin by a fall I'd taken back in the swamp with ol' Regret, yet I kept my fire small for I had now returned to a place where the pathways of my youth predetermined my present day destiny. Most of my memories were black or mudded with evil, so the last thing I wanted was to alert anyone to my presence before I was able to at least reach the home place and research my surroundings.

Folks in Iberville Parish endowed me with nothing in those days, nothing but bad thoughts, worse treatment and the desire to become a man somewhere else; anywhere else. They had kindly offered me nothing, and I'd offered them a good deal less. Likely the only recollection they possessed of me would include violence, trouble and anger. In all honesty, this was where I learned to fight; Iberville Parish, Louisiana. A place where the devil came to deal his cards to see how many souls he could pick up along the way. Thinking of that brought me to the conclusion I should saddle up right then and ride straight back out west, but I wanted to see home, the only home I could remember.

I kept my fire small, for I had come home by the back trails, not wanting to attract any attention until I had a chance to take a gander around the old place and witness the lay of the land. It would do little good to show up unannounced, claim my inheritance then fight just to stay alive. My best effort would have to be a diplomatic one. Anything else I might try would no doubt be a dangerous move on my part. It was in the back of my mind those other boys from class would be just as big, maybe even bigger than me now.

The cypress and pine trees which thrived in this part of Louisiana were my shelter, a hideout of sorts located deep in the swamp. From time to time a large raindrop would find its way through the pine boughs and drip into my fire. This was the only sound I heard for a good long while; the hissing of the rain as the fire quenched its thirst, yet after a time I seemed to discern another sound in the depths of the forest. With the rain falling slightly, the swamp truly became a liquid forest worthy of its name and reputation.

When I did hear a sound, it was insignificant at first, but then mysteriously drew closer. This was not a sound of the forest, the rain or even an approaching storm. It was not the sound of a bird or wild animal, for I had known these all of my life back to my boyhood. The sound was that of horses, two horses to be exact. They were coming down the road riding my back trail, so I hunkered down and waited, more certain than ever it was nobody I wanted to see, not now, not when I was so close to home.

That's why I placed my lean-to over the knoll away from the avenue, hidden deep among the trees in Pig Wallow Swamp. I wanted to be nowhere near the road. The swamp I traveled in was called such because it was a haven for wild boar in these parts.

I watched the two mounted horsemen round the bend in the distance and I heard them when they reined in their horses where I could no longer see them. They halted right where I left the road a few hours earlier to build and get beneath my shelter. In another thirty minutes it would have been dark and they would have ridden right by. As things stood, the two unknown riders were now looking at my freshly made mule tracks. I knew there had not been sufficient rain to erase them. I cursed my luck and waited for them to make a move.

I heard some mumbling as they began to ponder who might leave the road in such a place, and for what reason. Regret lifted his head and I motioned for him to be quiet. Now I don't know if my mule understood me or not, but I believed that he did and sometimes what you believe is all that's important. That was what a man lives by, what he dies by, what he believes whether he knows it or not. Often times I've noted that too many men don't have any idea what they believe, leaving them exposed to all sort of chance and circumstance, vulnerable to the Devil's schemes and vices.

Cautiously I crawled out of my lean-to and stood up. I listened as the rain trickled its way to the ground. I heard another drop hiss in my fire then all was quiet. While I could not see them, I could picture them in my mind. The two men on horseback were studying the situation over without saying a word. They had not moved one inch since stopping.

A rain drop dripped off the tree above me and landed on my head, for I was holding my hat in my hands. As I stood there in my hastily acquired clothes, I struggled to picture in my mind just what this encounter would mean.

There was no one local who would remember me favorably beyond the fellow named Andrews who had been building a plantation next door and he would likely not care one whit about a boy he hadn't been seen in ten years. John Andrews began construction on Belle Grove Plantation ten years before the war, but if he were there now, it was anybody's guess.

Beside me Regret pitched his head at a right angle and pricked his ears toward the silence. He, too, was listening. I started to get irritated then; irritated by the fact anyone would care enough to stop because of a silly mule track. Who were these men anyway? I wasn't going anywhere for a few days, not because I didn't want to, but Regret was starting to struggle of late and he needed a good rest. The fall we took back in the swamp was a sign of exhaustion. Maybe these men were twitching my stubborn bone by acting like I was some kind of a wanted criminal and all, but the truth was I'd come home to stay, whether folks in Iberville Parish liked the idea or not!

Standing there I adjusted my position so I could see across the small knoll I used to conceal my camp. The place I'd chosen to get comfortable had been picked for a reason. I could see several spots along the roadway because my position on the concealed hammock commanded a view of my back trail at certain intervals through the woods and the swamp. I reached down and picked up my .56 Spencer and slid it from its sheath.

My narrowed eyes watched them as they sat their mounts studying the mule tracks on the ground before them. They rode as men ride. Something in the behavior of one of those men gave me the idea he was someone familiar. Their hat brims were pointed down covering their faces as they studied the tracks. Maybe it was their manner, maybe it was their clothes, but when one of them looked up I knew I'd be all right. The other fellow was barefoot.

"Darnell Blankenship, if you weren't recognizable you'd be a sitting duck," I accused.

He looked at me then, not sure exactly who I was. He studied me long and hard. I stepped out to greet them and set my Spencer .56 at my feet holding the barrel with my left hand.

"Don't tell me you don't recognize me."

"Am I supposed to know you," Darnell asked with caution.

"James Le Roy Ware," I answered.

"Le Roy Ware. We figured you for dead by now," Darnell said.

"The war was a little bit rough on me, but I did what I had to in order to survive."

"We heard you got killed at Shiloh," Darnell insisted. He studied me top to bottom as if he couldn't believe what his eyes were telling him.

"You gonna believe what you hear or you gonna believe what you're looking at?" I'm afraid my frustration jumped out at him. The look on my face couldn't have been very flattering at that point.

"What I'm looking at, but why didn't you come home soon as the war was over?"

"I decided to drift. You remember what it was like for me around here in those days. I would have ended up dead, or someone else would have any way you look at it."

"Le Roy, I want you to meet Chin Lee. Don't let the Chinese look fool you none, he's hell-on-wheels in any kind of shindig. He don't speak much English though."

I nodded my head out of respect, though when I look back on it I don't know why. I didn't figure he'd understand me if I said something anyway. The Chinese man glared at me as we continued our conversation and I noted his bare feet once again. His glare was making me uncomfortable, but if he couldn't speak English, there was nothing I could say to him.

"Come on over to the fire. You might as well get down and stay for a while," I said. Turning my back to them I started for my makeshift lean-to. I plopped down and stirred the coals, then grabbed my coffee cup.

The two men walked their horses around the small knoll which kept me hidden from the roadway then began to unsaddle their mounts.

My friend pulled a blackened cup out of his blanket roll and the foreign fella did the same. We shared the coffee I'd prepared in my beat up old pot, because the Whipple's had taught me to share whatever I had, though my training had been a long time ago now. That Chinese fella started laughing when he got sight of my mule and wouldn't shut up.

"What's the matter with him," I said pointing more to the offensive nature of the man than anything. "He's going to get me sore if he keeps laughing at Regret. He might even hurt the mule's feelings." That Chinaman was walking around my mule in circles laughing like he'd never heard a joke before. "Tell him to sit down will you? He's going to make Regret mad and then I won't be able to ride him for a week."

"He doesn't understand English."

As if he did understand, the Chinaman sat down and filled his coffee cup then smiled across the fire at us.

"How's that? Better?" Darnell asked.

"Better," I said.

I still wasn't comfortable with the fellow. His grin was a goofy looking thing which would drive a fellow mad if he thought about it very much. He didn't say anything, just sat there staring at me with his stupid, funny white tooth grin wrinkling his face. His eyes didn't blink, they didn't shift back and forth, he just stared as if I were some sort of a freak for riding a mule.

I was nervous over someone who couldn't even speak the English language. Why didn't he wear boots? The fact he was barefoot didn't seem to bother him at all, but it bothered me. I had never been around a character like him before. He acted strange, weird almost, but then I had never met anyone from China, so maybe he was completely normal for a Chinaman.

He seemed older than us a good deal, but not like you would expect an old man to age. I couldn't quite put my finger on the difference. He was not dumb, not in my estimation, but he sure didn't try to hide the idea he might be. He rocked back and forth sipping his hot coffee as I watched him. For now, I was going to have to take Darnell's word. The Chinaman was supposedly hell-on-wheels in a fight, but as for me, I would have to see some proof because he didn't seem strong enough to stomp a stringy jackrabbit.

Chapter 3

We sat around the campfire talking and chatting some about old times. Every once in a while that Chinaman would throw out the silliest word at the most awful time, making no sense at all. It was as if he was trying to fit in, but the words he spoke were not part of our conversation at all.

I felt refreshed having met an old schoolmate right off. Maybe things weren't going to be as bad as I expected, yet I knew the others would be around. Their kind would never leave. It was their job to see to it that no one did any better than they did. They had to be in charge, had to run things and if someone suddenly became affluent, it was their job to see to it they paid their dues. Often times such people ran things into the ground and pinned the blame elsewhere, then they would start all over again someplace else.

The Chinaman finally seemed to relax and blew into his coffee cup. I wasn't sure about the man in the beginning, I mean he was strange, the strangest character I ever met. He had a long ponytail down his back, little beady eyes and didn't wear any shoes for crying out loud. He wore a black jumpsuit of some kind with a black belt tied around his hip and carried no gun that I could see.

"Isn't your friend a little bit under dressed for the times," I said.

"You mean reconstruction?"

"That's exactly what I mean."

"He's all right, he doesn't need a gun."

"I guess you're right. If he can't speak the language it's fairly easy to stay out of trouble."

"That's not it at all. You ought to see him fight. The Chinaman is a one man wrecking crew."

"That little ol' fella?" I said doubtfully.

"That little ol' fella could whip me and you both before we could even get our guns into action."

I knew Darnell Blankenship for a lot of things, but a liar wasn't one of them so I took another look at the Chinaman and he just grinned at me from across the fire.

"Fear of de Lord is de beginning of knowledge," he said with a white toothed smile.

"I thought you said he didn't speak English," I accused.

"That ain't English. That's some sort of Salvation Army gibberish he has memorized. He doesn't understand a word he's saying, he just belches out something he's heard before and usually it makes no sense at all. That time was an exception."

"I see. For a minute there I thought you'd become a liar."

"That'll be the day," Darnell said.

"Lean not unto thine own understanding," the Chinaman quipped.

Well, I looked over at him and he just smiled that funny smile and I wanted nothing more than to hit him. I wanted to knock the smile right off his face. That goofy Chinaman was getting under my skin, and what's more, I think he knew it. I sat there staring at him, wondering what he might look like with a couple of teeth missing and you know what? I think he knew exactly what I was fantasizing about.

"You were a hard lad Le Roy. When all that trouble began you believed we were all against you. I want to set the record straight, I wasn't. I was actually pulling for you. I didn't like Butch any more than you did. He had a habit of picking on those less fortunate and that's a good way to get killed in my book."

I was moved by what Darnell said, so much so that I got up to check my mule. I didn't want either of those boys to see me shed a tear. After patting him down good I went back to the fire under the lean-to.

Darnell Blankenship had become a gentleman. The War Between the States had ended just one year earlier and men were still returning home. It was a time to be wary of strangers, for a lot of men had not stopped fighting just because General Lee surrendered.

In the old days, when I was just a youngster I had taken nothing from the local community nor had I given them anything they could lay a hand on. Most of the local boys and their fathers disliked me from the start because I wouldn't buckle under and do as they said. I'd met their unforgiving nature with one of my own. I met anger with anger, fists with fists, malice with malice. I was like a mirror, whatever they showed me, that's what I showed them. If it was kindness, then kindness I gave in return, but I could count that type of behavior on one hand with fingers left over. So, I became what some folks referred to as a reactionary.

"With knowledge the just shall be delivered," Chin spouted out of the clear blue. I was almost asleep in my thoughts. He startled me so now I was suddenly wide awake again.

Darnell looked at me and said, "I've gotten used to him. I couldn't go anywhere without him if I wanted to. I've tried. He just follows me no matter how much I try to lose him. I figure one of these days he'll just up and take off of his own accord."

I poured myself more coffee and offered the last of it to the other fellas. They emptied the pot and we talked some more. Long ago Mr. Whipple taught me to share what I had, but few if any had offered me as much in return.

"These are harsh times Le Roy. There is evil upon the land. The Reconstruction people are moving in and taking whatever ain't nailed down. They're taking a few things which are. They're confiscating property and raising a ruckus with anyone who fought for the south in general. If they haven't already laid claim to the Whipple place, they will."

"Over my dead body," I responded.

"That's just what they want. For you to make a fight of things. They'll use any excuse available for killing a Johnny Reb."

"I'm no Johnny Reb, I fought for the north. I'll not give up the old place. I don't want any trouble, but I'll not roll over and play dead either."

"You fought for the north?" Darnell Blankenship was looking me over with a sudden caution.

"Calm down. A boy has to eat," I said.

After a moment of staring at me as if he hadn't seen me yet, he added, "Trouble is, that's just what they're looking for Le Roy. They have the army in here now and the Abernathy's are in sweet with them, showing them where everything is, telling them who's who and what's what. You go bucking the Abernathy's and you're bucking the Union Army."

"That bad is it?"

"Worse. Butch has taken over Belle Grove Plantation. How he come by the money I'll never know, but whether by hook or by crook, he seems to own it, lock, stock, and barrel."

"That doesn't give him claim to my place," I said.

"He thinks it does. And Le Roy, he's been talking it all over, if you come back he'll kill you. Not my words, those are his."

"The lips of a strange woman are sweet as honeycomb, but her end is bitter."

Well, I looked at that Chinaman what didn't know a lick of English and I paused. What the devil was he talking about? I had no woman, I didn't figure on having one anytime soon and here he was blurting out something about a woman.

"Don't look at me," Darnell advised. "I don't have a clue."

Those fella's were looking back at me, but what they were seeing didn't stack up as much. I had a worn maltreated hat I'd taken off a dead Yankee officer. I threw dirt over him the next day. I had an unkempt buckskin jacket which stopped at my middle, made by a jealous minded Arapahoe squaw out in the Rocky Mountains. I rode out there just to see the snow covered peaks after the war. My boots were black army issue and my shirt was green. My pants were old soldier blues with the stripe cut off.

"The belly of de wicked shall want," the Chinaman said.

"He doesn't do this all night, does he?'

"Only when he's awake," Darnell said.

I put down my cup and lay back against my saddle. It was time I got some sleep anyway. Closing my eyes I left the camp to my friends. I didn't hear the Chinaman anymore that night, but I can tell you he wasn't as dumb as I first figured. I didn't sleep right away, because I had some thinking to do.

Reconstruction was underway, and I personally wanted nothing to do with it, but listening to Darnell I got the idea I might not have a choice in the matter. If Butch Abernathy was rubbing shoulders with the army boys from up north, I had my work cut out for me. He would consider the Whipple's farm to be on Belle Grove land and Butch, having acquired Belle Grove, would cause me to prove my inheritance. My only proof of the inheritance as far as I knew was the letter in my pocket which left everything to me. It was not the actual will, but a letter explaining it all.

Where might the actual will be located, I wondered, and how could I get my own copy? I was feeling my lack of further education at the moment. I had no idea where to start. To ask was to embarrass myself. Cursing my luck I rolled over and pulled my blanket over me, damp though it was.

Chapter 4

I woke to the smell of fresh coffee and light in the sky to the east. I had overslept for the first time in years. I looked at the Chinaman to see the same white toothed smile plastered on his face as the day before. Glancing at Darnell I could tell they were waiting on me to get up.

"Fresh coffee on, might as well have some."

"I guess I was more tired than I knew," I said excusing my slumber.

"The slothful man roast's not that which he took in hunting, but the substance of a diligent man becomes more precious."

"I'm going to hit him," I said looking at the Chinaman.

"I wouldn't advise it," Darnell said. "That rabbit on the fire is his."

I looked then and saw the rabbit roasting over the flame.

"I didn't mention it yesterday, but another reason I let him travel with me is the fact he can fetch anything on short notice. I've not skipped a meal since the day he joined my outfit."

"You have an outfit?"

"I do. Of course it isn't much, but we get by," he said indicating himself and the Chinaman.

"The wrath of a king is the messenger of death, but a wise man shall pacify it."

"Are you sure he doesn't understand English?"

"I'm sure. He's kind of like the Bible. You know how you can open the Bible at any time to any page and get just the exact scripture you needed to read? Chin is like that. He spouts off the exact words we need to hear no matter what's happening.

"Don't you think that's a little bit frightening?"

"No, if I didn't believe in God and if his words didn't make any sense, then I would be frightened," Darnell corrected.

I shook my head and realized I was going to have to get used to Chin Lee if I had any intention of hanging around my old schoolmate Darnell Blankenship. Chin tore off a chunk of rabbit meat and extended it toward me as I lay beneath my blanket. I accepted the food he offered and tasted it. The taste was better than expected.

He tore off a piece for Darnell and then he took a piece for himself. To offer food to someone else before eating himself seemed odd to me. I would have dug in and not worried about my friends. Actually, I still wasn't sure if I was their friend or if they were mine, but we were sharing the same camp.

"I had enough fighting during the war, I don't want any more trouble," I managed between bites.

"James Le Roy, I don't know much, but I do know there are times a man can't dodge trouble, even when he sees it coming right at him. For you, this is one of these times."

"He that shutteth his lips is esteemed as a man of understanding."

"Well, you'll never have to worry about that," I said to Chin Lee.

The Chinaman wrinkled his forehead then as if trying to understand what I had just said. I believed he did understand some of what he was spouting off, otherwise, why the wrinkled forehead? He was silent then. I don't know how, but I think I got to him with my most recent reply.

"Le Roy," my friend Darnell said. "If your place is what they want, they'll have it. If you don't accept their rules with closed lips, you'll have all kinds of trouble. The only way we've been able to travel to and fro is because we don't say anything. When we're asked something we give an honest answer along with yes sir and no sir. That's the only way we've been able to get around in these parts lately."

Rain continued to fall among the leaves around us, and I had a sad feeling upon me. There was a deepening feeling that I had been offended, too. Not by my friend Darnell, but by the fact the Reconstruction effort seemed to be at my doorstep while there seemed to be nothing I could do to change my circumstance. Could a man not be left alone? Why was it every time I settled in somewhere I had more trouble on my doorstep than Napoleon fighting a war on four fronts? In the old days I'd met trouble head on. I didn't see any reason to change now.

There had been little chance in the old days of me becoming anything other than what I had become, an orphan with nothing but my pride. I had gone to New Orleans first, then to St. Louis by way of the *Natchez*, a steamboat operated by one Captain Blanch Leathers and she was a stern one at that. In St. Louis I had become one of The Gaslight Boys working the street by day, laying my head anywhere I could by night. The year had been 1858.

Although obviously one of the boys, I shied from running with the pack. There always seemed to be more trouble whenever a large group of the boys got together. On occasion I ran with a small group who called themselves the Wolf Pack. Most times though, I was a loner. Early on in the war I signed on with the Union and became a Powder Monkey what helped load the cannons on the ironclad *Carondelet*. I was just big enough so they took me, and then I ate regular meals for the first time in a few years.

Now it was the spring of 1866 and I was twenty one. I was a man grown now, with a man's hard judgment and some long days behind me. Since the war I had ridden with a gun for companionship. I had ridden west after the war and took up a riding job on the Bar J in the Texas Panhandle for a few months. Then I headed for the Rockies. When I returned to the Bar J there was a letter telling me that Ma Whipple had died leaving everything to me. The Whipple place was two hundred acres of good farm land and another hundred in the swamp. This all butted right up against Belle Grove Plantation.

There was deep within me a love for the land. The Whipple place had been my boyhood home for a few years, all I remembered. I knew there was rich soil a man could do something with. All the time I had been riding the dry land of the Texas panhandle I kept thinking of the green fertile land in Louisiana. Now I had me a piece.

Fresh back from Texas I wanted nothing but to settle in. I wanted to be left alone. If Butch Abernathy wanted trouble he could have it. I hadn't fought for the south; I had fought for the north. I didn't even know what the war was about when I signed up; I just wanted to eat regular. The way I figured, the north having won gave me some credibility when it came to my claim, and I was going to use my record. I didn't figure I had spent all of those nights standing guard on the *Carondelet* for nothing.

Chin Lee brought more fuel for the fire and dropped it at the lean-to I had made for shelter then stood there looking down at us. The shelter was large enough for the three of us to get in out of the rain. I figured right then I could put up with a man who could find dry fuel in a swamp where it had been raining for days on end, even if he did quote scripture.

"De light of de wicked shall be put out," Chin quoted and turned to make his horse more comfortable.

Their horses and my mule were tethered under a large cypress tree. There was room enough for a dozen more, but there were only the three animals. Little rain made its way through the Spanish moss and thick branches of the tree. The animals were sheltered even if the rain picked up, so were we. That left us with nothing to do but wait out the weather.

Chin Lee came back about noon with two more rabbits already skinned and I began to understand why Darnell set store by him. He wasn't even wet, not beyond his feet. If they had remained dry I would have saddled up right then and rode away without looking back except to make sure I wasn't being followed. I was to the point of being spooked by the man. The Chinaman had an uncanny way of putting the fear of God into me.

Good was the smell of coffee and the roasting rabbit. Our fire was not big, but served us well. The sound of the rain was a comfort upon the land. Sitting under those trees in the swamp I got to thinking how strange it was that Darnell Blankenship was any kind of a friend to me. Not that we had ever been close, because we hadn't, but from the beginning he had stood off and watched as things progressed between the school bully and me. Suddenly I realized maybe it was because I took his place under the guillotine. Had I not arrived when I did, Darnell would most likely have taken the punishment Butch had bestowed on me.

Darnell Blankenship had gotten an education. I could see that. In the last ten years I had gotten one too, but mine had been one of survival. His folks had acquired wealth. What he was doing out riding in the rain in the first place puzzled me. It was completely unnecessary for a young man of his stature. He had become a captain in the army during the war, though he had fought for the south. Now that he was home I could see that it would not be an easy thing where his pride was concerned. I was no better on that count.

"How many men do you figure died for no reason," I asked out of the blue.

"I figure all of them, but for one, Abe Lincoln. He was the reason the war was fought. He was to blame."

"Justice bears a high price then," I added.

"It most certainly does."

"What are your plans," I asked Darnell.

"I'm just returning home myself. I'll need to see how the wind blows, fair or ill."

"I thought you had been home for the last year."

"I have. I'm just returning from Texarkana where I made a deal for a sawmill. We'll be going back after it in a few months."

"I see. Well, if you need a hand I could use the job when the time comes. I've got a little money, but nobody has much right now, nobody but the boodlers."

"Folks will not have forgotten about the likes of James Le Roy Ware. The war was only a distraction, they won't have forgotten. There will be trouble enough for you without the Reconstruction and the Carpetbaggers moving in. Cowboy or not, you've got your work cut out for you," Darnell said.

"Darnell, you may not know it, but you just used three words which didn't even exist five years ago; Reconstruction, Carpetbagger and Cowboy. There's change for you."

"I never gave it a thought, but you're right. Good Lord, that's how language grows. A word is needed and someone coins it. Then it becomes part of everyday language."

Like I said, Darnell had an education and it was beginning to show. I would have never put two and two together. I did recognize the new words, but all else seemed unequal. I remembered then what the Declaration of Independence said about all men being created equal. But equality ends at birth. That particular statement in the Declaration of Independence was incomplete!

We are all born to a different family; we all grow with different experience and knowledge. Two children born on the same day at the same exact time could be eons apart by the time they are thirty years old, it all depends on how each deals with the circumstance he or she is dealt. At the moment I was years behind Darnell, but we had engaged life through different means, through different eyes.

I concluded then, any government who tries to equal the playing field by redistributing the wealth of its citizens is whizzing in the wind. It is not the government's job to see to it we all get equal pay for equal work. I understood then we were a land of individual responsibility. Man or woman you get to make your own choices in America. Your worth is your own responsibility. If you want to make more, it was up to you to make yourself worth more. America couldn't be any simpler. It is not the responsibility of successful people to bail out those who have been cursed, by their own actions, laziness or previous generations. There is such a thing as a generational curse, and I hoped right then I did not have one of those on me.

Chapter 5

With nothing to do while it rained we huddled over our small fire and fish storied the daylight hours away, with Darnell telling me of the war in the south and the State of Texas. He told me what happened and what he expected was going to happen. There was one anecdote I found especially intriguing.

"In the later part of 1862," Darnell began, "General Sherman left Memphis with 16,000 troops to join General Grant at Oxford Mississippi. Upon reaching the Coldwater River about half way between Oxford and Memphis he found the bridge over the river destroyed. I know, because I destroyed it. The water was very high; as a result the flood water was rushing by swiftly. This promulgated the necessity to build a new bridge before anyone could cross the now dangerous river.

"At this point I was witness to the Yankee ingenuity and genius of one man. Lieutenant Malmburg of the 55th Illinois was charged with rebuilding the bridge I had just blown up. There was quite a village on the west side of the stream, comprised predominantly of log homes largely forsaken. Malmburg went to work with his men using logs from the abandoned homes for cribbing and the stone chimney's for anchorage. In an incredibly short time he had two piers poised in the stream midway between the two river banks. Using more logs and the extra wood from the dismantled homes he built a magnificent new bridge by daylight the following morning.

"I watched in horror as the unit I was sent to stop crossed the river less than twenty four hours after I had blown the only bridge for many miles to smithereens," Darnell admitted.

None of what was about to happen shaped up as likely for the man known as James Le Roy Ware who was trapped fair in the middle of Reconstruction. I had no family waiting for me, nobody cared whether I lived or died, but here I had roots, and I owned property. It was here I aimed to stay, to try and grow a crop and make a name for myself. I carried a rabbit's foot in my pocket; the one Mr. Whipple gave me all those years ago. I felt for my lucky hare now with my left hand, if only to reassure myself the charm was still with me. It was.

I thought of how things were back then and realized I had been carrying my rabbit's foot for more than ten years now. For argument sake I was still alive and grown into the full measure of man, at least I thought so. Maybe there was something to the superstition. I knew one thing, if I was going to quit carrying my good luck charm in my left front pocket, now was not the time to test the waters, not with so much trouble lining my path.

I had a second chance at life this time around if I played my cards right, and I would do my best to make certain things turn out different, maybe better is a more appropriate word. In the old days nobody cared one ounce about my wellbeing but the Whipple's. Maybe I could have dodged my first bout with trouble, but after a few skirmishes with the local boys I was quick to defend myself, a stance which caused no end of trouble. Maybe it was my pride, but I understood now that a really tough man doesn't have to go around proving how tough he is. I had me a real good idea what I was capable of now and I didn't care one whit if anyone else knew of my abilities or not. When you're a young man things are different. When you're young, you think you have to show everybody you meet just how tough you are, lest someone think you're weak. I thought at that moment I really understood just how much grief I had caused by being on a short fuse all of the time.

When the Civil War busted wide open I was living in St. Louis just trying to get through another day with a meal or even a few crumbs. I didn't have much then. Come to think of it, I didn't have much now. I saw how everybody got so worked up about going to battle for one side or the other, but I was too small to be of much assistance any way I tried. I threatened to join right off, but the soldier boys told me to go away, they needed men.

A few months later, after getting their buckskins handed to them at Bull Run the Union was no longer so picky. They signed me up lickety-split and made me a Powder Monkey. Like I mentioned before I helped to load the canons on the *Carondelet*. It was a scary thing to have the enemy shells whizzing by your head landing in the water or bouncing off the iron side. I can also tell you it is a good deal more scary not knowing how to feed yourself.

Here I was one year after the hostilities of war and like a salmon I was returning to my home of origin. I was almost within shouting distance of the only home I could rightly remember, the place I spent most of my childhood and likely the only home I would ever know. I knew the Whipple place wasn't much, but there was land, plenty of land to make a living on.

In the old days I had been ready to quarrel. Life had delivered several knock out punches right to my head. Instead of folding and landing in a heap I fought back, shabbier than the rest of the children and too proud to beg forgiveness, I started spending inordinate amounts of time alone. In retrospect that was why I began going into the swamps. When a boy has no friends, he just naturally becomes a loner. Sometimes he's better off, sometimes he isn't. I had learned a lot in those days, many things which helped me to survive until I was all grown up. I knew of places in the swamps nearby which the Indians didn't know about.

Those days I wondered the swamp until nightfall. Then I would turn up home, eat a bite and go to bed. The Whipple's knew my whereabouts to a degree. They just told me to be careful and let me have my head. I became a pretty good hunter in the swamps. I could get turtle or alligator eggs. I brought home a baby lion cub one night and the Whipple's made me give it up the next day. Said the cat would never grow up tame. They were scared of it, but not me. It was a swamp leopard, a catamount they said, but the cub had to go back where it came from. I guess I was asking too much of them, now that I looked back on things. Any normal kid would have had enough sense to let such an animal alone. Lonesome like I was in those days I just wanted a companion. There's no explaining a young boy's feeling when he's lonesome in the world, he just has to grow up.

Now I was coming home. The farm would still be there, the fence around the house to keep the cattle out and the apple orchard would likely be all right, but the condition of the place was what worried me. There was the land to the south which stretched all the way down to the big grove. My thought was the land wouldn't be worth much, the home would be in disrepair and I would have my work cut out for me.

Staring at the flame of our small fire I felt a comfort I hadn't known for a long time. Listening to the rain drop from the tree limbs above, I had a good feeling upon me. I was home. There wasn't anybody who cared whether I showed up or left, but I knew the ground I'd inherited and I believed in what I could do if given a chance. I'd been a homeless drifter for several years now; there just wasn't any other way to say it. I was a hobo, the name given to soldiers returning home from the war which meant homeward bound.

My ideas for the old place were running through my head faster than I could have dreamed. First, I would clear the tall grass away from the house; clean the place of any rodents, spiders or snakes. Knowing it had been empty for nigh onto two years the place would be crawling with critters. My hope was that the white picket fence Mr.

Whipple had put up for his wife would not need too much repair. Those things done I would break ground and go to work putting in a crop. Those were the thoughts invading my head.

If the war hadn't changed everything I'd go into White Castle and do some horse trading. On Saturday they would rope off Main Street and bring in the horses to be traded, at least they did before the war. If they hadn't resumed the practice, I would remind them or handle the duties myself. A good horse trader was worth his weight in gold now the war had claimed so many good blood lines. I had learned a great deal about horses during the war by reading, so I was itching to practice some of what I'd learned.

One thing I knew; a whole lot of horse flesh died in the war, not just soldiers. It was going to take a good deal of work, time and breeding to restore the bloodlines that had been lost. I figured to get me a good stallion and start breeding him. I wouldn't get rid of ol' Regret because he'd seen me through some tough times lately, but I wanted me a horse ranch. One to die for!

Most of the breeders in the south saw their stock stolen, rounded up, or wasted on the war. My feeling was that a man with a good stallion, a good mare and plenty of grazing like I had inherited would do well for himself. I'd been told repeatedly that it mattered mighty little how much money a man had as long as he was content. Well, I didn't put much stock in that statement, mostly because I had never been content. I wanted to be somebody. I wanted a grand plantation of my own someday. I wanted to strut around with pockets full of money and help others whenever I saw a need. I wanted no constraints on me, not money, time or other folk's rules. I wanted the best I could get from this life and I was set to do just that.

Every man wants a woman, and I'd met a few here and there, but the ones I'd met weren't the marrying kind. I didn't see myself settling down with a saloon girl. I was still a virgin and I planned to remain one right up until I got married. It wasn't likely I'd find the kind of fair beauty I had in mind anywhere near this part of the country. For that I'd have to go a'wondering. Anyway, here locally the name of James Le Roy Ware would strike fear into the heart of any self-respecting girl. It wasn't likely anyone remaining in these parts would have anything to do with the likes of me, not now, not ever.

I had enough trouble on my plate so I figured to fight shy of the local folks at least until I had my feet securely upon a firm foundation. What I had in mind wasn't going to be easy and if Butch Abernathy was going to be my neighbor we were going to have to get an understanding around here real quick. I finally fell asleep with my thoughts and those fellows around my fire let me sleep.

Chapter 6

When I awoke Darnell Blankenship was feeding the fire with more dry wood the Chinaman had acquired during the night. I looked around and saw ol' Regret was doing fine so I sat up and Darnell handed me my cup of coffee.

"Boy when you sleep, you really sleep," he ventured.

"I hadn't had any for two days until I got here," I told him.

"I figure we can make your place today if you feel like traveling any at all. It would sure be a good deal warmer in the house, if you don't mind a few house guests," he said.

"You fella's want to ride along with me?"

I was surprised. I figured this close to home Darnell would likely want to invade his own place. He could see the consternation on my face so he spoke up.

"Our place was burned down during the war, Mom and Dad moved to California so I don't have anybody here anymore."

"You'll need a hand rebuilding it then," I said not thinking about how much work I'd have to do on my own place.

"Roy, if you were to lend a hand, that bunch at White Castle would likely burn the place down again out of spite.

Thanks for the offer my friend, but I'd better do for myself."

"When they see that Chinaman, they'll most surely burn you out," I said looking over the fire at him, "regardless of anything else."

The Chinaman got up and started gathering more firewood when I figured him for being asleep. He hadn't said anything or moved a muscle while we were talking. That fellow was a strange one. He didn't size up as much of a man, but I never knew Darnell to exaggerate or tell a lie. If Darnell Blankenship insisted the Chinaman was worth his salt in a fight, I had no reason to doubt him.

"Hands dat shed innocent blood are an abomination to de Lord," Chin said as he dropped more wood by the fire. Turning, he strolled off into the swamp once again.

I watched him as he walked and knew he was smarter than he let on. My guess was, if he couldn't speak our language, he was learning quickly as he spouted off those verses of his. He was getting some understanding. I learned from Darnell that he'd worked in a Chinese soup kitchen in New York. His kitchen had been right next door to the Salvation Army tent. This was how he had learned to quote scripture, hearing it repeated daily right next door.

Getting up I gathered my blanket roll and saddled up ol' Regret. Darnell followed suit and saddled his horse.

"What about Chin, don't we need to wait on him," I asked as Darnell stepped into the stirrup.

"No need to worry about him, he'll be along when you least expect him."

I stepped up onto Regret and we started for the home place. When we got back to the road there was no sign of our passing. The rain had mostly washed it away. We ambled down the swamp road a ways and pretty soon I began to recognize things I had forgotten. We passed through the thicket to the west of our place, then we waded through the swamp in knee high water for a while swinging wide around cypress trees and stumps. The stumps I figured were all that was left of a tree after a hurricane. There were many such landmarks in this part of the country. After a while we rode out of the swamp water onto dry land. When we did I knew exactly where I was. I was on the home place.

I looked around in all directions to see what had changed—nothing. I spun ol' Regret in the direction of the house and we took off down the old avenue now grown over with tall grass and weeds. I knew the trail, but no one had been here for quite a spell. By now the entire yard might be overrun with crabgrass. If so, I figured to have my work cut out for me. Turning the last corner up the back lane by which I'd come we came to a halt at the gate.

Before us lay my new and old home. The screen door was lying crooked against the door facing, the picket fence was broken in several places while the grass was tall. The flowering plants Ma Whipple had planted were overtaking much of the yard and needed to be trimmed back. The wisteria was overtaking much of the home structure and would need to be trimmed to get the bugs away from the house. I looked at the place and I knew I was home.

"Well Le Roy, there it is," Darnell said.

"It'll be no shortage of work, but I know whatever I do the land will bear up to it."

It seemed to me Ma Whipple would step into the doorway any moment and holler my name for supper, but I knew deep down she wasn't going to do so. No one at all was going to come through the front door which had been left ajar for nearly two years now.

I stepped down from my old Missouri mule which was bigger than Darnell's horse and opened the gate. I had to push and shove because of all the overgrown grass in the way, but once the gate was wide I left it open and walked over to the corral. Opening the corral gate I turned Regret loose and Darnell turned his horse in.

"Darnell, would you mind taking my saddle off ol' Regret while I look the place over?"

"Don't give it another thought. I'll take care of the animals," he said as he began to strip the saddles from them.

I pulled out my knife, slipped into my leather gloves then cut away a good bit of wisteria just to get on the front porch. If you don't know much about those beautiful wisteria shrubs, they'll choke out anything once they take root, especially in the fertile land offered in the deep down south. At the front door I had to cut away some more tentacles from the overreaching bush.

The door was still tight in its fit, but swung open at the touch. The door jamb had been the victim of someone kicking the door in. I looked around to Ma Whipple's busted spinning wheel but the rest of the furniture was gone altogether. There were a few holes in the walls, but I could fix them. I walked all through the house and witnessed the damage caused by vandals. I hated people right then. I thought to myself I would never have done something like this in my youth or as I now stood, but there were those human beings who just couldn't let things alone. Seems they couldn't get through a single day without busting something up.

Mrs. Whipple's bed was gone, the bureau where she used to get ready for church, the chest and dresser, all were gone. Dishes were broken and left all over the floor along with her glasses. The fry pans were gone as was the wood stove she had cooked on. The cabinet doors were broken off the hinges, but could be repaired with some work.

I heard Darnell's footsteps on the front porch and I wiped the tear from my eye hastily so that he wouldn't see me crying. I bent down and started pitching everything into a pile then, more to cover my emotions than to do any work. Darnell pitched in and soon we had the mess picked up.

"Well, we've got it all corralled, but what do we do with it?" my friend asked.

"That's a good question. We'll set the mess all to one side of the front porch for now."

The house was still in pretty good shape considering. Once we had the mess moved outside I repaired the door jamb so we could shut the front door. It wasn't a perfect repair, but it would have to do until I could acquire the necessary tools to make the repairs permanent.

We settled into cleaning the house and everything we touched that day. The hardwood floors were in good shape, but we were going to need some supplies from town. I needed a good straw broom, a hammer, nails and maybe a handsaw.

I decided then I would go into White Castle in the morning and get what I needed. I had a few Yankee greenbacks stashed for an emergency. I figured I could loosen my hold on a few of them. Darnell kept an eye on the house and I went shopping. I should have sent the Chinaman, he would have been treated better, but we had no idea of his whereabouts and I had no way of knowing my return home would start out so badly.

The first person I saw when I stepped down from my mule was Butch Abernathy. He hadn't changed none, still strutting it around town like he was the big he coon of the swamp. I knew better, I knew he wasn't as tough as he put on and what's more he knew I knew it. Right then I saw the fear in his eyes; fear I might tell others he wasn't so high and mighty. His nose was still laid over from where I had broken it years before. I gave him an evil stare and stepped into Thibodaux Mercantile.

The soldiers were in town, a blind man could see that. I picked up a broom and laid it on the counter, then a hammer and some nails. Looking around I found the saw I wanted and put it on the counter. I was just about to pull my wallet when Abernathy stepped up behind me and yanked my navy colt from my waistband.

"This is the trouble I told you about, Thibodaux. Sneaking around just like I suspected he would."

"Sorry son, but you'll have to buy your wares somewhere else," the storekeeper stated.

"Before you have even met me?" I asked.

"Butch said you'd be along and here you are. Sorry, but I can't sell to you."

"You've got no reason to draw down on me, or to take my weapon Butch," I said with my hands on the counter not turning to face him.

Suddenly I felt a blow to the back of my head and everything went black. I crumpled into a heap on the floor and that was the last thing I remembered.

Chapter 7

I awoke cold, wet, and trembling with fever. Looking around provided me with assurance Butch had dumped me deep in the swamp. I tried to move but the pain changed my mind. Reaching behind I felt the lump on the back of my head, the dried blood and matted hair did nothing to comfort me. Abernathy was getting smart. He figured to let the swamp kill me. He may well have succeeded, too.

I had to move. I had to get up and find my place. If I failed now he would win without my having a chance. I already had a fever so I had been here for at least a day, maybe longer. I stumbled to my feet but my head was swimming. Staggering forward I fell over a log hidden beneath the leaves and brush.

Pulling myself upright I continued on. The pain was unbearable. All that was left of my clothes was my pants. Both shoes and shirt were gone. I halted suddenly, stopping to check my pockets. Nothing. That no-good low- down varmint had taken my wallet, my rabbit's foot, buck-knife, everything. I didn't even have my belt anymore.

Each step was a struggle, but the deep-welling anger building within me kept me going. My thoughts were on Butch Abernathy and how I was going to teach him a lesson. He had ambushed me right in the middle of town.

He'd gotten away with it too which meant he had friends. He hadn't done this on his own.

I was headed north, picking each step carefully, keeping track of where I was as I moved forward. I kept stepping watching carefully as I went and then I came to the water. I had been headed north, but I wasn't in the swamp, I was on Marsh Island the best I could tell. Such a revelation did nothing to comfort me as it was better than a five mile swim back to shore. They must have brought me here in a boat. I dropped to the ground in despair.

The water around Marsh Island was black water. I concluded that I needed to reach the salt water out in the gulf, that would be to my south. If I had any remedy at all it was to soak my head in salt water until my wound was thoroughly cleansed. Only then would I have a chance of warding off the fever I'd contracted.

Struggling to my feet I turned south. I had to go to the south side of the island to reach the saltwater. More dead than alive, I made new tracks. As I struggled for each step I realized the sun wasn't going down, it was coming up! How long had I been unconscious? I kept walking, struggling to keep my feet under me.

Finally I reached the south side of Marsh Island and waded out into the water. Deeper and deeper I went until my head was the only thing above water. Carefully, I bathed my wound.

I wanted to scream the salt stung so bad, but knew I didn't need to attract any kind of attention to myself. I was wounded and I knew most wild animals would take a wounded animal first because it was easy prey. I didn't want any gators or anything else coming after me.

As the bigger chunks of dried blood came free I looked them over and knew I was hurt bad. I could feel my head was split open, but I had no way to sew it shut. All I could do was hope the salt water didn't cause me to bleed more or pass out in deep water where I might drown.

There in the water like I was with the drizzle of rain still coming down a fellow just couldn't get warm. I needed a fire, but had no way to start one. There was no dry wood and no matches. I was in trouble like never before and my unjust situation began to put the fear of God into me.

Finally I made my way back to shore once I believed I had done all I could do for my head. I was marooned on Marsh Island, a swamp some five miles south of the mainland. I was too tired to make a try just then, but I had to try and swim the bay. There was no other way. I could swim, but could I swim good enough to get across five or six miles of swamp water?

I walked back to the center of the island and settled down under a large cypress. It would keep the rain off of me and if I was lucky, shelter me from harm. My pants were wet so I shed them and laid them across a log to dry. With no fire I didn't have much chance unless the sun burned through the overcast.

I went to sleep, naked as a jay bird still nursing a fever. My wet pants would only hurt my situation. There wasn't anybody going to stumble on me out here, not even a guardian angel. Butch Abernathy had brought me here for a reason. Chances are I would die right here. Unless I could shake my fever and summon the courage to swim five miles or more to shore I was done for.

I closed my eyes, went to sleep and dreamed all sorts of crazy dreams. Thing is, there was an unknown girl in my dream. She was there with me at every turn, helping me overcome this or hugging and kissing me, telling me all would be okay, and she had a cat, one which never left her side. I had no girl and I had no cat, so why dream of that I'll never know.

In my dream I had the impression the girl was young and pretty, but all I saw was her back. She was standing over a large iron kettle hanging on a tripod stirring a brew of some sort. The cat was there also, by her side at all times. I watched as she sprinkled jimson weed into the pot, then added sulfur and finally pure honey.

She stirred the pot for a while, then dipped a cup into the brew and rubbed the cat. She took what was left in the cup and drank her fill. Surrounded by fog, it seemed demons were trying to get to her from every angle, but they couldn't get close to her brew. From time to time the cat would jump and grab one of the demons and drop it into the pot. There at the end, just before I awoke I saw the face of an angel.

When I came to my fever was still with me. It was dark and I could do nothing but listen to the noises of other creatures on the island.

My head still throbbed. I huddled beneath my two crossed arms and closed my eyes. I thought of Abernathy and what I would do if ever I got back to shore. Butch had gotten a good deal meaner if he was willing to break the law and do something like what he'd done to me. I had to consider the fact he was just plain evil.

I went back to sleep with thoughts of Butch and how I would get even. He had been a thorn in my side ever since meeting him. He would never change for the better that I could see. All I wanted was to be left alone, but I knew now that would never happen. I was going to have to make a fight of it just like in the old days.

The thought occurred to me that Darnell would be worried about me. Then again, how had Butch known I was coming? Had Darnell and the Chinaman been there to warn him? What if the little guy really could speak English? It would be an easy thing to pass the Chinaman off as illiterate.

As I thought of it, I dismissed the idea. There was no way Darnell Blankenship was that low down of a person. Of all the people in and around White Castle, he had been the one who stayed above the fray. He had a head on his shoulders and he could be anything he wanted to be. There was no need for him to turn ugly. Butch Abernathy on the other hand was just the opposite.

When I again woke it was daylight and my fever was gone. I had weathered the storm. I wasn't any warmer, but did feel warmer. My trousers were still damp and I didn't want to put them on yet, but knew I had to. I got up and took them off the downed log they had been laying across. They were still almost wet so I carried them in my hand for now. Naked as could be, I headed for the north shore and my uncertain destiny.

Still weak, I was running out of time. I had to get across the five to six miles of water just to reach the southern shoreline. I knew I had to take my chances now. I also knew there would be gators looking for an easy meal.

I stepped into my wet pants and pulled them tight then I waded out into the water. I went as far as I could before I kicked off the bottom and started swimming. I had been chin deep when I pushed off and began to stroke slowly. If I was going to make it I had to pace myself. If panic set in I would drown right here.

I focused on an extended peninsula which seemed the closest trees to me and kept swimming. For what seemed like an eternity I stroked and stroked making my way toward the big cypress trees. For a while there it seemed I was making no headway at all, but then I could tell I had gained some. My fear was the crossing would take too long. I would never make the shoreline like this.

I remembered floating as a boy so I rolled over onto my back and began to float, resting my arms. This tactic was slower going, but other than my head stinging from the water, my limbs were resting. I alternated then from floating to swimming and back.

When I did reach shore it was coming onto nightfall and it wasn't shore at all, just a bunch of cypress trees in the swamp. I was worn slap out and I could hardly feel my arms. I breathed a sigh of relief because I knew now I would live. Regardless of my condition, I was going to survive. I felt the hunger pains in my stomach for the first time.

I settled in under an old cypress I had focused on and waited. I would have to wait another day. The cypress trees I had landed in were still not on the shoreline, but well south of the beach. I had a ways to go, but I had managed to eliminate the longest stretch on this day.

Chapter 8

At sunup I was greeted by clear skies. Finally, it was going to be a clear and beautiful day. I was sore from sleeping on a log, but I was alive and took the sunshine as an omen. I was going to extract my full measure from the upcoming day.

Stepping down off my log, I waded the rest of the way to shore. I saw gators here and there, but they were far enough away I didn't worry about them. I did, however, keep my eyes focused on the water around me in all directions to make sure I didn't become their lunch. I had a few horror stories stored in my brain and I had no intention of becoming another one.

After nearly thirty minutes in the swamp water I found shore and began my long march home. While I walked I figured in my head just what it was I planned to do once I returned to the house.

First I was going to get my mule, my guns, and my rabbit's foot back. I might get another lump on the head, but I was going to get my personal belongings. Butch Abernathy didn't know this yet, but if he had done anything with my weapons he was going to buy me new guns also. Same went for my mule and clothes.

My head was sore and I kept reaching back to feel my wound and I knew it would have to heal some or I'd get myself killed, but it was a hard thing to wait. I wanted to take the fight to Butch right then and there. My better judgment told me to hold off. Butch Abernathy thought me dead. There was no need in tipping him off that I wasn't, not until I had a chance to heal.

Skirting the big thicket to the south of Lake Fausse Pointe, I kept walking. I had some more swimming to do, and got across the Atchafalaya the hard way then set out through the swamp. My feet were getting sore to add to my soreness around the back of my head. Along about dark I stumbled and decided to call it a night right where I was.

There was nothing I wanted to do right then but rest. The blow to my head made me weaker than I originally suspected. I had no way of overcoming my loss of strength, but to get some dearly needed rest. I made myself comfortable and settled into a good night sleep.

When I awoke in the morning I had been visited. Cat tracks were all around me and I shuddered. I had been a sitting duck. Why hadn't the cat attacked? When I was just a child I found a cub and brought it home, but the Whipple's refused to let me keep the animal. Said it was too dangerous. I didn't know I had a mountain lion, but they said I couldn't keep it. Surely this wasn't the same cat. Not after all these years. Was this the cat in my dreams?

Getting up I began to walk. I crossed several small ditches and walked around several lagoons. At nightfall I shuffled into the yard at my place in Iberville Parish to see no one about. I opened the door and went in.

I was cold, I was mad and I wanted rest. Where Darnell Blankenship was I had no idea, but he'd pulled out because none of his stuff was in the house. Of course I didn't have anything but an old blanket the Whipple's left behind. Seemed nobody wanted it, but I did. I needed to get warm tonight and I needed rest.

I curled up on the floor and put a makeshift pillow under my head. If I could get through the night unmolested I was going to pay Butch Abernathy a visit. He was mean as a skunk and I had in mind to put him in his place. I didn't care if his new friends were Union soldier boys or President Johnson. What he did to me was a crime. Just like the Romans of old feeding Christian's to the lions, he didn't want my blood on his hands, so he left me in the swamps of Marsh Island in hopes the gators would do the job for him. I had news for him; he *was* going to have to kill me with his own hands.

I fell asleep figuring just how I was going to handle Butch. When I awoke I felt much better, but I missed the entire day sleeping like a baby. Looking around I knew I was no longer alone. I had some new clothes. My guns and my saddle were resting in the room with me. I could hear someone shuffling about in the other room. I figured Darnell returned so I got up and looked to see.

I was greeted by the big sheepish grin of the Chinaman. He showed me his teeth then and I tried to smile, but my head hurt too much to do any good. I felt the back of my head and there was a bandage on it.

"Thanks," I said.

He just looked at me funny, then I remembered he couldn't speak a lick of English. I motioned toward my belongings in the other room and said, "Darnell?"

He just looked at me with that dumb look on his face so I gave up. Glancing out the window I saw Regret. Forgetting my pain I stumbled outside in the twilight to greet my old friend. Darnell must have brought him in while I was asleep. I gave him a big hug around the neck and began to pet him. I had no idea where Darnell was off to, but Butch Abernathy would have to wait. There was no doubt in my mind I needed more rest.

As I turned back to the house I saw those cat tracks once again. They were fresh. Going back to my blanket inside the house I settled into place once again, confident the company I had would at least keep watch. The Chinaman might not be able to speak English, but Darnell swore by him. I lay my head against my pillow and went to sleep.

I awoke to the smell of fresh bacon frying in a pan. That meant Darnell was back. My suspicion was the Chinaman wouldn't know a thing about frying up bacon. I got up and looked about to find Chin doing exactly what I thought he couldn't do. He was frying up some bacon in one, eggs in the other, so I sat down in the floor wrapped my blanket around me and waited. Coffee was on to brew and he also had bread. Then I remembered where he worked while in New York. Somehow, Chin managed to get food, which was a tall order considering the situation this far south. Darnell had to be somewhere close, but I really had no idea.

The wood stove had not been there at first so someone had become quite industrious. My guess was again Darnell. Chin, however, was the one using it to my satisfaction. He made his way around that stove like he'd been doing so for a hundred years. I knew he wasn't that old, but he was no doubt a good deal older than the two of us.

My mind drifted to the cat tracks then. That was no ordinary cat. The cat was, however, a very big one. Exactly what kind I had no idea, but the tracks indicated a panther of some sort. Out west such a cat would be considered a mountain lion.

I remembered the day I brought my cub home. All the little guy wanted to do was play and I thought I'd found me a new companion, but the reaction from the Whipple's had been one of horror.

"You can't keep a cat like that! It will have to go back to the swamp," Mr. Whipple said.

The next day he took the cat deep into the swamp south of Bayou Sorrel and returned home without it. I always suspected Mr. Whipple killed the animal instead of turning it loose. I could have been wrong which might explain the tracks I had been witnessing. The cat had been here when only little, was it back? In the far reaches of my mind I hoped the tracks were those of my little friend from all those years ago, though I had no way of really knowing. More than likely I'd have to shoot this cat if it became a nuisance.

Chin finished preparing a plate and handed me a portion. I was starving so I ate like a rabid animal. I was finished almost before Chin could step back to the stove. When he turned around I saw the look of astonishment on his face. He didn't say a word, but took my plate back and gave me a refill which I destroyed in like fashion.

Within a few minutes my stomach began rumbling from way down and deep inside doing all sorts of crazy dances. I never experienced such a catastrophic reaction just from eating before. I doubled over into my blanket then and I didn't come up for air for about thirty minutes. I made myself quite sick by eating so fast. Three hours later I was still experiencing the rejection as my stomach was set steadfast against accepting the invading food. For a while I was certain I was going to regurgitate, but I held on and never did.

Finally I got up and checked my gear. I dressed myself in the new clothes. Chin eyed me closely. He did a good job of getting me something to wear. Everything was missing including my lucky rabbit's foot, wallet and knife, items he wouldn't know about. Still I had not seen Darnell. Where was he? My weapons were what most concerned me. I'd have to get them back as quick as I could. I settled back in my blanket, still cold from my ordeal.

Usually I kept two or three rounds in each gun, but with trouble on me I decided I better change my procedure. Not that I would need that many bullets, but it never hurt a man to be ready. In any case, I didn't want to let Butch get the drop on me again. I fully intended to read him from the good book and put him in his place the moment I saw him. I didn't care who might be a witness.

There are times in a man's life when he needs friends. Up until now I prided myself on the fact I didn't need anyone. I didn't want anyone and I could care less what other folks thought about me. Now, as I sat huddled in the corner of my own home watching Chin handle the cooking chores I began to realize my error in judgment. A man needed friends, good ones if he was going to be set on with trouble in his life, and I was set to experience my own war, but at the time I didn't know it yet. If Darnell and Chin had not thrown in with me when they did back in the swamp, I would already be pushing up daisies somewhere, I had no doubt in my mind. The fact I was alive at all seemed a complete error in God's judgment.

Don't get me wrong, I was grateful for my fortune, because it seemed to me I could have my candle snuffed out at any moment the last few days and likely would have too if not for Chin being there to care for me. There was no way I could fix for myself so if he had not been there I'd have been in trouble.

I thought back to Darnell and wondered where he might be. I knew there was no use asking the sheepish permanent grin Chin wore on his Chinese mug. There would be no answer from the likes of him, not until he learned a bit of English, something besides Salvation Army stump preaching.

I fell asleep then. I needed the rest and there was not much I could do. That blow to my head did a job on me.

Any moving around at all seemed to aggravate the injury to my head and get the entire room spinning. I had no idea how long getting over my injury would take, but I wanted to get shut of my ill-timed wound as fast as humanly possible. My instinct told me I was going to need all of my faculties in order to deal with the likes of Butch Abernathy.

Chapter 9

When I awoke morning was again lifting light through the windows. I sat up to see Chin fixing bacon and eggs over the wood stove. I wrapped my blanket around me and huddled up to keep warm. He brought me a plate and I ate a bit more slowly this time. What amazed me was how good his cooking was. I had never been one to love bacon or eggs, but he did something to these things that I couldn't put my finger on and as a result they were better than your average fare.

When I finished, Chin took my plate from me and said something which made no sense to me at all. Obviously he was speaking in his native tongue and I hadn't a clue how to respond. I said thank you and he responded with another bunch of words in Chinese. I'll tell you this; I no longer possessed a desire to wipe that sheepish grin off his face. I was getting used to his permanent smile.

I finally heard a horse in the yard and figured Darnell was back. He made little noise as he put his horse in the barn and when he entered the house our undesignated cook handed him a plate of bacon and eggs.

"There you are. I've been looking all over Louisiana for you. What happened to you? One day you're here, the next day you're gone. I've been looking for you almost two weeks," Darnell said with a grimace.

"Two weeks? You mean it's been two weeks since I rode into town?"

"Two weeks. Now where have you been? We were fixing to pull out."

"I got hit over the head by Butch Abernathy and left for dead on Marsh Island. Thanks for getting my gear back," I told him.

"I didn't get your gear back. I've been riding all over tarnation looking for any sign of you, of which there was none I might add."

I stared at him for a moment then looked over at Chin who was scooping eggs and bacon onto a plate for himself. He smiled his white toothed grin at me and I knew instantly he was the culprit. He managed to retrieve my mule and belongings without using a gun.

At this point I considered just who Chin Lee was. He was like no man I ever saw. He moved different than most men and when he walked you couldn't hear his feet touching the floor. That was the major difference, I thought. He didn't stomp his feet to get anywhere nor did he drag them. He shuffled in silence.

The question in my mind was how he managed to round up my gear when he hadn't even been here at the cabin with me? What did he have to do in order to recover the stuff and how did he know where to find it?

"I told you he was good," Darnell said.

"Yeah, but how in the world?"

"I wouldn't ask. You'll not get a straight answer anyway."

There were things I wanted to know, but Chin was in a unique position to keep his dealings to himself. I, on the other hand, had no end of questions for the Chinaman.

"I was hit over the head by Butch and then left for dead. He even took all my clothes except for my pants. It seems that Chin got everything back for me," I added. "Everything except for my rabbit's foot, my wallet, knife, and these aren't exactly my guns."

"I never figured Butch would be that mean," Darnell said.

"I didn't either, but we'd better not underestimate him."

"Sometimes I wish that Chinaman could talk," Darnell stated.

"You and me both." I paused for a moment to study Chin, then continued. "I may need to rest for a few more days. That blow to my head like to have done me in."

"You rest or do whatever. Don't worry a bit about things around here, we'll keep any varmints out."

"Speaking of varmints, there are cat tracks in the yard, those of a panther. I don't want it shot."

"You're the boss, but why wouldn't you?"

"If it's the cat I'm thinking of, he's a friend of mine. I don't want him shot until I know one way or the other."

"You made friends with a panther?"

"When I was little," I said.

"Good Lord, we sure underestimated you Le Roy. I would have never believed a man or boy could do such a thing."

"Darnell, I figure a man can do just about what a man wants to do, he just has to believe in himself. That's something no one can do for you, you've got to do it yourself," I said, not knowing where my opinion came from. I surprised myself with the saying of it, for I had no answer as to how I acquired such a belief.

"You know how the devil can get after a man, especially in Louisiana. I was born here and I know a thing or two about Ol' Scratch," I added.

Darnell's mouth twisted in a grin, "You and everyone in Louisiana."

"What I can't figure out is why Butch didn't even give me a chance. I wouldn't have bothered him," I commented.

"Some folks don't need an excuse to do mean or evil things. I think Butch may be one of them," Darnell said.

"Well, when I get back on my feet, I'm going to make sure he knows what it feels like to be left for dead."

"You won't have to," Darnell replied.

"What do you mean?"

"He's laid up at Doc Webster's place. Somebody put three bullets in him the other day. He was found half dead outside of town lying on the road. Sheriff says it was those Reconstruction boys, but I'm not so sure. I do know they've taken over Belle Grove in his absence."

"That makes our neighbors a bunch of Yankee's," I said.

"Yep, it sure does."

"Darnell, what do you think those boys want?"

"I think they want everything. They're here to run our lives for a while, but if I had my druthers I'd just as soon run them off."

"You may get your druthers because I figure to run them off," I said.

"Now you know them blue bellies have reinforcements. You run one off and two and more show up in their place," Darnell said.

"Yes, I know, but if I can't live my life unmolested, I'll not live it. I'll make a fair game of getting myself killed running them out of the country."

"That sounds crazy."

"Yeah, well I've been called crazy before."

"I want to live here, Le Roy, but I don't want to get killed doing it."

"I don't either, but I have to fight to keep what's mine."

"I'll side you, because I've already lost what was mine, but let's at least try and stay alive," Darnell argued.

"All right, I'll be careful."

"A prudent man foreseeth evil and hideth himself," Chin spouted.

"Are you sure that Chinaman doesn't know English?"

"Positive."

"Sometimes he has a way of saying something that makes me want to hit him."

"I tried that once. I couldn't do it. After ten minutes I gave up."

"What do you mean, you couldn't hit him?"

"I mean he dodged every punch I threw. He's quicker to see a punch coming than you can swing at him."

"I don't believe you," I said.

"You don't have to take my word for it, try it sometime, but don't say I didn't warn you. Any time you want to look like a fool just take a swing."

"That doesn't make any sense."

"Not until you see him in action. When you see him fight you'll understand."

"How old is he?"

"I don't know," Darnell said looking over at him. "It's hard to tell about a Chinaman. He could be fifty or sixty, but I don't know."

"An old man like that, and he can dodge a punch?"

"Every punch you throw."

I thought about my situation. Never in my life did I see this coming. There were folks in this part of the country what didn't belong here. Mostly they wanted what was mine. While the war was over, I had the idea the only reason they were here was to take what was mine and leave me with nothing. I had no choice but to fight them. If Darnell was willing to side me, I at least had a chance.

I got out of my blanket wrap and stood up. I completed getting dressed for the first time in days. Like I mentioned, I had everything but my rabbit's foot, my knife and wallet. I was going to get those items back too. Of course it would be like looking for a needle in a haystack, but I had to have my good luck charm back. I felt naked without it. I needed my money and I wanted my knife, a knife given to me by a fellow soldier.

Chapter 10

Two days later Darnell rode into town with me to see which way the wind blew. Those Reconstruction fellows were acting like the whole country belonged to them and we, who grew up here, didn't have a say in matters. They were telling everybody they met what to do with their property and belongings. I took offence to such treatment and decided to let them know they weren't going to have a free hand anymore.

"You can't settle at the Whipple place," the captain said. "It belongs to the federal government now.

"No sir, it belongs to me, and I'm not moving."

"You'll move off or we'll come and move you," he threatened.

"You'd better bring your army, because I'm not leaving on your say so. I fought for the north on the ironclad *Carondelet*," I snapped.

"That makes no difference. The government has identified certain parcels of land which must be retained for federal use and your place is right in the middle of the map."

"They'll get it over my dead body," I promised.

"Your funeral," he said.

"You might think so, but I'll have the final say."

Turning on my boot heel I stepped out the door of his office and went back to where Darnell waited with ol' Regret and his horse.

"They told me to get off the place, it isn't mine anymore."

"You going to quit?"

"No, I'm going to fight."

"They'll make an outlaw out of you if you kill a Yankee soldier. Johnson's pardon won't do you a bit of good."

"I know it, but I'm not quitting my place, not when I just got home."

"Like I said, I'll side you. Just don't try too hard to get us killed," Darnell said sarcastically.

Stepping into my saddle I pulled myself into a comfortable position and we headed down Main Street. Main Street in White Castle was all of one hundred yards long and twenty yards wide. In the old days at horse auction time they would rope off the street all the way from the train depot down to the stables on the far end of town. To unload the horses they would run the stock out of the cars one at a time until the entire street was full then herd them down to the corral. I watched them many times when I was a young lad, but that was before the war had changed everything. Now there was a shortage of good horse flesh which is why I had ol' Regret. There just wasn't a horse to be had. The ones what didn't get killed in the war went home with a captain or some other officer when they mustered out. The ones that died on the battlefield got eaten.

I had eaten horse meat more than once, and it wasn't all that bad. In the war, horses went down as often as the men who were riding them. The troops needed to eat and there just wasn't any other way to feed an army. I was on the ironclad most of the time, so horse meat wasn't often on the menu. We mostly learned how to catch our food off the bottom of the river. Catfish seemed to be the only kind of fish we could bring in, so catfish is what we ate.

As we rode out of town we turned to the west. Two miles out we turned our mounts southwest and headed for the house. This would take us by Belle Grove Plantation. I wanted to see what was going on over there. If the Yankee's planned to run me off, I wanted to make sure I had a way of throwing a wrench into their plans. That would require looking the situation over.

We stopped at the edge of a grove of live oaks and looked at the plantation house. There were guards posted round about the place, too many for one or two men to take care of. The Yankee's were here in force. They were not going to leave any time soon, I feared.

I thought about Butch and wondered if he was doing all right. I didn't hate Butch, I just didn't understand him. I didn't know why he felt he had to pick on me all the time and I didn't see him as a friend or enemy, just someone who hadn't learned how to live with other people yet.

"You think Butch would talk to me now that he's been betrayed by these fellows?"

"There's a possibility."

"Darnell, I have an idea. Come on, let's go meet these fellows," I said.

We ambled toward the house. As we neared the front steps we were greeted by the posted guard who looked a lot like Darnell. I did a double take and then settled my eyes on him.

"You all going to call Belle Grove Plantation your home while you're down here?" I asked in my best southern drawl.

"Far as I know this is headquarters from now on."

"You do realize you fellows picked the most haunted house in all of Louisiana to settle in."

For a second a flicker of fear showed in his eyes, but he caught it. "It ain't nothing of the kind."

"Oh yes, it is. Why, there ain't a man in these parts crazy enough to set foot in that house except Butch Abernathy, and he's been shot from what I understand."

Darnell was eying me with suspicion and I didn't blame him none, for I was telling the tallest of tales, but it had been rumored at one time the house was haunted the day construction began in 1852. There was no proof in the matter, but what's proof when you're talking about ghosts to some Yankee soldiers a thousand miles from home?

I had the soldier's attention so I started to pile it on. "The owners who built the place wouldn't even live in it. You should have seen them when they scatted out, why you couldn't have caught their wagon with a good race horse." I paused for affect. "Well, you boys be careful. Hope you don't find any more dead bodies lying about."

"D—de—dead bodies," the fellow stuttered.

"You don't know about the dead bodies? Every two or three months a dead body appears right here on the grounds. Nobody knows where they come from, they just show up. How long have you fellows occupied the house?"

"Been here for three weeks now."

"And you haven't found a dead body yet? That's amazing," I said.

I nudged ol' Regret and we headed out of the yard the way we came in.

"I think you scared that fella," Darnell said.

"That was the idea. I can't fight them. If I do, I risk being shot or put in prison. This way we'll let the creatures of the night spook them. I don't think these northern boys are all that familiar with the sounds of our southern swamps. I figure to educate them."

"Roy, you are a dangerous man. Why, your idea is perfect in every way. I can see I'll be learning a great deal from you."

"Don't set me up so high. I'm just a poor boy who wants to keep his place."

"Maybe so, but I figure you might be smart enough to do it."

"Look, I'm no smarter than the next guy, I just get a clear picture in my head of what it is I want and I don't let go until I have it."

"I heard once, a genius is nothing more than a man who sees a target no one else sees, then he proceeds to hit the bulls eye dead center. That's you Roy, you are that man."

"I'm not exactly certain what you're referring to, but if you insist," I said.

"You'll get it, if I keep telling you," Darnell said.

When we rode into the yard I could see the big cat had been through again. I studied the tracks on the ground before me and then turned Regret into the corral. Chin met us at the door afterward and motioned for us to try his cooking. I never saw the like and wasn't sure I wanted to try such a recipe, but Darnell insisted it would be good.

"Are you sure it's all right," I asked.

"I thought just like you at first, but he's a real good cook, I promise."

We sat down and ate our supper which was slimy and wiggly looking, giving me the idea it came from the bowels of the earth, but once I saw Darnell dig in I braved a slight nibble. The food was good just like Darnell said it would be, but I still had no idea what I was eating. At first I thought it some kind of worms, but thank God it wasn't. Darnell figured we were eating some kind of root Chin dug out in the swamp. I didn't know one way or the other, but I admitted his explanation was much better than the one I was conjuring in my head.

"In God I will put my trust," Chin said.

We both looked over at him sitting there with his white toothed grin looking back at us. Right then we both suspected he knew more than he was letting on or he was learning fast. One way or the other he had to be getting a grip on the English language.

"And he doesn't speak English," I said.

"No, I don't figure he does, but I'm beginning to wonder."

I was beginning to wonder too. His quotes directly from scripture seemed to be delivered at exactly the right moment in time as if our conversation would remind him of something he heard years ago in New York City. Then, with nothing better to do he blurted out scripture which seemed to match our topic in one way or another.

Suddenly it came to me the problem America struggled with. If man didn't respect God's laws, what on earth possessed him to believe a man would be a respecter of man-made laws? There in lay the problem. If a person is no respecter of God, that same person is no respecter of man. That was why the founding fathers included God in the founding documents. Every state had its own constitution, and each one of the states to date included in their charter an understanding of man's relationship with the creator. Not one state in the Union was exempt. But then, the term Federal meant Contract with God, or Covenant.

This I remembered from my bygone school days.

Chapter 11

Later that evening, Darnell and I slipped back over to Belle Grove and gave those Yankee boys something to wonder about. We learned to duck for cover behind a tree after making a noise, because once scared those fellows would shoot at anything.

We stirred up all kinds of commotion for about three hours and finally got on our mounts and rode away. We left one of our friends with them, a skeleton from the local graveyard. They would never see the body in the dark, but come sunup they would sure enough find the dead body lying in the yard. I think Darnell was spooked more than those Yankee soldiers at first, but he finally calmed down and we did what we had to in order to leave the poor fellow with them.

Lord, forgive us for what we've done here tonight," I said as we rode away.

I didn't feel bad about what I'd done, except for the fact I'd disturbed the body of a dead man. In that part of Louisiana a concrete vault was placed above ground and the body placed inside in a coffin. This practice predated the Spanish invasion. A good hurricane would remove a coffin from its mooring and the coffin would eventually float away. We just opened one of the vaults and moved one of the permanent residents from his resting place, relocating him to the yard at Belle Grove Plantation.

"You figure those boys will scare?"

"Maybe not immediately, but they'll scare."

"I can see we're not going to get much sleep."

"Neither are they," I said.

We departed Belle Grove through the woods. Well after midnight we heard the screech of a panther. I knew instantly if we heard it, those Yankee's heard the same cat loud and clear, because we hadn't gone two hundred yards. Suddenly the swamp sounds died down to an eerie silence. That cat had everything in the forest frozen in mid-stride including our mounts. I had never seen ol' Regret so scared. He stood stock still, but he was trembling with fear. Darnell's horse wasn't moving any either.

"If that cat is a friend of yours, I sure would like to know it right about now," Darnell whispered.

"You and me both."

I nudged Regret forward and I thought he was going to jump out of his skin. The unexpected command startled him. He quickly recovered though, and we headed home through the woods. One thing was certain, those Yankee boys wouldn't be wondering off the plantation tonight. That screech was enough to curl the hair on the back of a dead man's neck. I thought about that and wondered, wishing I could go back and take a good gander at the skeleton we delivered to our friends from the north just to see if his hair had curled.

We continued to ride because if we stepped down there was a good chance our animals would bolt, leaving us to walk home. If Regret bolted, I wanted to be in the saddle, not hanging onto the reins with one hand.

Now, I hadn't mentioned it, but the night sky held a full moon whenever the clouds parted. We saw to it those boys at Belle Grove saw certain things, things a man isn't likely to see on a full moon or any other moonlit night. During a full moon you can see things up to a point, not completely like you would in the daylight, but better than full dark. Consequently, we could see things ourselves though we were riding in the swamp between my place and Belle Grove.

When we were about a mile from the plantation Regret faltered and came to a complete stop in belly deep water. I thought at first he was going to go belly up and plant me right there, but he got his feet under him and stood like a statue. Darnell stopped beside me to see what was wrong. I glanced up sensing some slight movement in the tree up above and froze. The cat we heard a few minutes before was lying across a fat tree limb with its paws dangling in what appeared to be a sleeping position, but he wasn't sleeping.

I pointed my finger in the direction of the panther and Darnell started to pull his pistol. I put my hand out to stop him. The cat's eyes reflected in the moonlight and the spots on his flanks appeared to come out of the dark at you, but the cat wasn't moving. He was about twenty feet up in the tree above us and we could see him breathing. That cat weighed two hundred pounds or my name wasn't James Le Roy Ware. I studied him for a moment and I knew or thought I knew.

"Hello Cajun, how you been ol' boy," I said.

There was no response, but he stared at me as if he were counting traits or physical attributes to make sure it was me. I tipped my hat and said, "I'd take it kindly if you'd keep an eye on our back trail."

This time Regret was ready to move. He took off at a much faster pace than I anticipated. Darnell and his mount were matching us step for step.

When we got clear, Darnell swept his hat off his head and said, "Roy, I don't suppose that cat understood a lick of what you said, but somehow I get the feeling he'll do just what you asked."

"Kind of like Chin, he doesn't appear to understand, but he does."

"If that's your cat, I want to know one thing. Are the horses safe?"

"I don't rightly know. I haven't seen him in ten years. I don't think he'll bother us, but then I don't have any real knowledge on the subject one way or another, just my gut feeling."

"I sure hope your gut feeling is right, because if you're wrong we're going to have to deal with that cat."

"His name is Cajun," I said. "If we call him by name when we see him, he might remember and not bother us, although I did only have one day with him."

"One day? Are you kidding me? You're banking our entire future on one day?"

"Seems to me we could do a lot worse than to befriend him," I said.

Just then Cajun let out another screech and our mounts took off through the swamp for home with no guidance from us. They wanted out of the woods and out of the swamp. I was of a mind to be out of them myself, because I wasn't one hundred percent certain that cat back there was Cajun.

We dragged back into the yard about midnight and unsaddled our mounts. Chin had some cold food for us, but it was good. The Chinaman could cook, even if I didn't know what it was I was eating. We settled in to sleep, for it had been a long day and night.

Chapter 12

The following morning, Darnell and I headed for town again, this time to see Butch Abernathy. When we got near Belle Grove we heard a commotion and all sorts of goings on so we rode wide around the plantation in order to stay out of gunfire range. No doubt our friends from up north had found the body we'd left for them.

At Doc Webster's office we had to wait a few minutes, but we eventually got in to see Butch. He wasn't any too happy to see us, maybe he didn't know what was going on all shot up like he was, but we extended a hand anyway.

"Them Yankee's have taken over Belle Grove," Darnell said.

"Them Yankee's shot me and left me for dead." The accusation was clear when he said it. Butch might be selfish, and he might be misled, but he was southern through and through. He was eyeing me as if he couldn't believe he was seeing what he was seeing. "What's he doing here?"

That was my signal so I stepped up beside the bed. "Butch, I got no hard feelings. I know we've had our disagreements, but I'm here to ask you to consider siding me and Darnell. We want to send those Yankee's packing."

"You fought for the north, you ain't even one of us anymore," he accused.

"I fought for the north so I could eat. Not for any other reason. You know good and well I was an orphan. When I left home I left because of the way I was treated by folks here in Iberville Parish. The hardest thing for me was finding a regular meal. That was a long time ago. We're in the same pickle now. Those Yankee's want what's our'n and I don't figure to let them have it without a fight."

"I won't be much help for a few weeks," he said.

"So, you'll join us?"

"If I'm going to be stupid, I might as well be completely stupid. There isn't a snowball's chance in Hell that we can win, but at least we're fighting for what's ours."

"Thanks Butch, you won't regret it," I said.

"Look in my pants over on the table. You'll find your rabbit's foot. It don't work for me. In my saddlebag laying over the chair you'll find your knife and wallet."

He didn't have to tell me twice. I dug into his pants pocket and pulled out my old rabbit's foot. Stuffing it into my own pocket I walked over to the saddlebag he pointed to and removed my personal belongings, then walked back to Butch. "Like I said Butch, I've no hard feelings. I just want to save what's ours."

"I got no call to like you, but our cause is now the same," Butch offered. "When I can get back on my feet I'll side you fellows."

"We're holed up out at the Whipple place," Darnell explained. "When you can ride just come on out. In the meantime me and James Le Roy will be scaring the wits out of those Yanks."

"Scaring them?"

"Yes sir. That was Le Roy's idea. He figures to scare them off."

Butch studied me and after a few moments he said, "I sure wish I could see it."

"You just get better and let us worry about the fun," I said.

I started to turn to go and Butch stopped me. "Le Roy, I been thinking. I owe you an apology. What I did to you was wrong. I got what I deserved. Folks say I'm lucky to be alive. Well, I know deep down you're lucky to be alive as well. I tried to kill you. I'm sorry."

"Don't worry about it. I'm not going to lose any sleep over it."

"There's one more thing. Your gun. You're going to have to figure a way to get that gun into action faster than the other guy. I never thought about it before, but I got three bullets in me because I didn't know how to get my gun out of the holster fast enough. Don't be a fool like me. You find a way to pluck it quick. It could mean the difference between life and death."

"Do you know where my guns are, Butch?"

"Old man Stevens has them down at the stable. I told him to hold them for me."

"You figure he'll let me have them?"

"If you tell him who you are, he'll hand them over. Tell him I sent you."

"All right, I'll do that. Be seeing you," I said and headed out the door. Once outside on the front porch I placed my hat on my head and stepped down to where ol' Regret stood waiting. I cinched my saddle tight and stepped into the leather. Darnell was already seated by the time I got aboard. When we turned into the street I couldn't help but notice all the bright shiny blue-bellies going to and fro.

We steered our mounts down to the stable and dismounted. Old man Stevens was near the back of the barn. I took the liberty of walking back where he was mucking out one of the stables.

"Mr. Stevens, I'm James Le Roy Ware, fresh home from the war. Butch Abernathy told me you were holding a couple of guns that belonged to me."

"Over there in my box," he said pointing to an old wooden box beside a roll top desk sitting in the corner.

I walked over to the box and opened it. They were there, looking just like I remembered them. I unbuckled my borrowed weapons, then picked up my pistol and gun-belt first, strapping them on my hip. I retrieved my rifle and closed the lid. I said thanks and we stepped back into the saddle.

"Town's busy today," I said.

"Yeah. Let's get out of here before we run into trouble."

Just then a soldier stepped up in front of ol' Regret. I didn't wait to see what it was he wanted. He put his hand up to grab the bridle and I spurred my mule forward. That soldier boy stepped aside like he was getting out of the way of the Old Number 9 headed into the rail yard in downtown St. Louis. I had seen that old steam engine move more than one casual pedestrian off the tracks.

When he let go of my bridle he made the mistake of stepping to the wrong side of Regret. The soldier was immediately sandwiched in between me and Darnell, both of us moving at a pacers clip. When he hit the ground we didn't stop to see if the soldier was all right, we put the spurs to our mounts and left a trail of dust General Lee or Grant would have been proud of.

A shot rang out as we turned the corner at the end of town, but the man who shot at us was not what I would call a marksman. The bullet ricocheted off the bell tower steeple and sounded the noontime bell. The bullet zinged off somewhere into the clear blue sky never to be heard from again. By the time the shooter could re-aim we were out of sight by plenty.

Now to be clear, neither Darnell nor I were afraid of those soldiers. We were boys who lost everything and what some soldier boy said to us didn't matter a lick. It didn't matter if it was a captain or a private, we wasn't about to listen, not when they were considered invaders on our own land.

When we were a few miles from town with no sign of pursuit we settled the animals down a mite and gave them a blow, all the time watching our back trail. I had a suspicion we just stirred up more trouble than we wanted, but that Yankee had no call to reach up and grab hold of my mule like that.

As we rode, I tried to get my pistol out like Butch advised and I found out immediately what he was talking about. If I had to defend myself against an already drawn weapon, I was a sitting duck. I fumbled with my revolver several times just trying to get my hand on the butt of the gun. I couldn't do it. My holster flap was in the way.

When we got home I put Regret in the corral and went in the house and got out my knife. I began to cut the flap which lay over my gun handle from my holster altogether.

"What's that you're doing?" Darnell asked.

"I can't get my gun out with this flap in the way. You better cut yours off while we're at it," I said.

When we were finished we had fairly destroyed two perfectly good holsters, but we removed the obstruction. I began to draw my weapon then, but I was almighty slow. I knew I was slow, but Darnell was even slower. He understood as well as me what Butch had been talking about. A man had to be able to defend himself against a mob, or an already drawn weapon. By all accounts we would need to get our weapons into action quickly.

We struggled for three days. We worked at getting our handgun out of the holster quickly. We emptied our pistols and practiced out in the yard with our rifles close at hand. Neither of us would have won any kind of contest in such a matter, but we were lucky that the first fast draw had not yet been invented. We were undertaking to do just that.

On the third afternoon Chin motioned for me to hand over my gun. I did so and he motioned for my belt. I handed it over and he buckled it on. He dropped the gun into the holster and then proceeded to draw it faster than I could have imagined. I watched as he repeatedly trained the gun on Darnell before Darnell could even get his gun out of the holster. I watched him, but I didn't understand. His movement was too fast, it didn't any make sense.

Finally he handed my hardware back to me and walked away shaking his head to shame me. I knew what he was thinking. We were a lost cause. The Chinaman, without any experience, could out draw us at will. That was not a good sign, but we didn't give up. We worked at getting our guns into action until our arms were numb. We felt we could get faster after witnessing what Chin did, but it was slow going.

When we were finished, Chin got us both up and stood in front of us within an arms length. He showed us how to hold our hands and then he began to slap us. In no time I was getting mad because that Chinaman was able to slap us and pull his hand back to his side before we could even react. I didn't understand this, but Darnell was just laughing.

"I told you, he's fast in any kind of fight."

"Yeah, but if he keeps slapping me, I'm going to pin his ears back."

I no sooner finished my statement than I was slapped again. I reached out to hit the Chinaman but he wasn't there. He ducked under my punch as if he knew it was coming. I tried again and missed. Then I stepped forward again and again swinging my fists as I went, but I connected with nothing but thin air. After about five minutes of this torture I leaned over to catch my breath and Chin slapped me again. I tried to tackle him like a raging bull, but missed. Straightening up I studied the man for a moment and tried once again. This time I fell flat on my face.

Before I could recover I again got slapped in the face. "Darnell, if you don't get him to lay off I'm going to shoot him."

"I tried to tell you. It's impossible to hit him."

"Where there is no council, the people fall," Chin said.

"Why you reprobate, you can speak English!"

"A tale bearer revealeth secrets," Chin offered.

"You are trying to teach us," Darnell interrupted.

"Yes, you are slower than turtle. Need much lesson."

Reaching down, Chin helped me up from the ground. Just for good measure I tried to blind side him. I missed and took a wicked punch to the stomach.

"Student must always respect teacher," he said.

Turning, he walked back into the house leaving me and Darnell to lick our wounds.

"Well, I guess he has learned English," Darnell said.

"He's learned a few other things too," I said extending my hand to Darnell.

"Shall we practice some more," Darnell asked.

"No, let's call it quits. My arms are about to fall off."

Chapter 13

The next morning we started to practice again and Chin stopped us.

"No, rest arms. Work no good."

He didn't get much argument from us. I don't think my arms had ever hurt so much. We rested as we were told. At noon we had visitors. They were blue-bellies.

"Captain Callahan say's you fellows have to vacate the premises."

The corporal spoke from the back of his horse. He was a dead ringer for Darnell Blankenship, only he wore a Yankee uniform. We stared at him and he stared back not sure what to think. The soldiers with him were just as astonished as we were.

"Corporal, this is my home. I inherited the house on the death of my adopted parents. I'm not going to move off just because you say so. I'm going to have to see documentation which says you have the legal right to take my property. I'm certain you don't have such a thing, and you'll never have it. We're not going anywhere," I said

Darnell was quicker than me to see what happened next, but those soldiers started to unlimber their weapons and we both had them covered before they could do so. They froze right where they were.

"You ride back and tell your captain what I said. I want to see the papers what say I have to give up my place."

"I'll tell him, but we'll be back and we'll be ready."

"What's your name, corporal?"

"Cook, my name is Corporal Cook," he said.

"You tell your captain we're staying," I said with my gun in hand and they rode away.

As they rode out of the yard I turned to Darnell and said, "I think tonight would be a good night for a haunting."

"I wonder what they did with the body we left for them the other night?" Darnell asked.

"If they haven't buried it already, there's something wrong with those fellows," I said.

"Something wrong with them?" Darnell shook his head. "We stole the body in the first place."

"Well yes, and we'll have to get another one tonight," I informed my partner.

I studied my friend then. What I couldn't figure was how any two people could look so much alike and not be related. Somewhere back down the line, they were. I was certain of it.

We looked around and Chin was gone. Where he got off to I had no idea, but Darnell insisted Chin could take care of himself. After going a few rounds with the character I figured Darnell was right. I had never been in a fight where I couldn't land a punch, not until the day I tried to hit Chin.

Near sundown we went to retrieve another body from the graveyard. Our first attempt was still floating around Belle Grove Plantation somewhere. There was no way we could use the same corpse, so we had to acquire a new one. I didn't figure the dead body, especially one that had been dead a long time, would care much one way or the other how it was used.

When we reached the graveyard we discovered the soldiers looking the sight over. They we're looking to see where the body we left them a few days ago might have come from. Having capped the grave perfectly there was no clue as to which grave the body belonged to.

Darnell and I were crouched in the edge of the trees watching those Yankee's when a noise like we'd never heard came loud and clear from one of the graves. I can't describe the sound other than it might be the noise a dead man would make if he were accidently wakened. Those soldier blues sat straight up in their saddles, their horses stood motionless and there was nothing but fear in the eyes of both man and beast. I contracted a little fear as well, because Darnell and I hadn't created the noise like we were known to have done in the past. I never heard such a sound and neither had my partner.

After a minute those soldiers started to leave and wasted no time about it. Suddenly that strange noise erupted once again. Those Yankee's put spurs to their mounts and lit a shuck so fast it would make your head spin. When they were out of sight we saw Chin come walking out of the woods on the other side of the cemetery straight toward us. I breathed a sigh of relief because I was fixing to shuck my pistol and do some shooting.

"A wise man clothes himself in strength and honor," Chin said as he came walking up. I wanted to hit him, but I also knew from recent experience that I couldn't. I needed much practice in the art of hand-to-hand fighting, but I had considered myself pretty good.

"You keep scaring those Yankee's just like you're doing and we'll be shut of them in no time," I told Chin.

"Wherefore the anger of the Lord is kindled against these people, their counsel shall come to naught," Chin added.

No man was more humble at that moment than I was. I wanted to build a home, a future and have a family, but not only did I have little to go on, I was undereducated, slow with my hands and unsure of every single aspect considering what was happening around me.

I had little to no faith in anyone, no faith in the good Lord or anything else. What I knew of men was not comforting. I knew deep down in my heart the only protection a man has in life is that which he can provide for himself, or enmasse. As I had shunned friends my entire life up till now there was no enmasse to consider. I had little to go on, but I did have two friends. My deduction was completely wrong at the time, but I didn't know then how God was caring for me.

"I'm going to the house," I said. Suddenly I was overwhelmed, tired and depressed. What was I fighting for? I hadn't even a girl. Any girl in these parts who remembered me would be long gone, and if they were still about they wouldn't be free. If they were free they wouldn't want anything to do with the likes of James Le Roy Ware.

I stepped into my saddle and turned towards home. I left Darnell and Chin standing beside the graveyard staring after me as I rode out. With no promise, no direction and no real plan, what could I hope to gain? A general didn't go into a battle without a plan. Soldiers had one. Other than claiming my inheritance, I hadn't one. This was a rude awakening for me. I had to prepare.

Up to now I had just been funning, yet how could I expect local folks to take me seriously if I didn't have direction? I couldn't. There was no chance I would stumble into a wonderful life of wealth and recognition; I don't care how lucky my rabbit's foot might be. I would never attain the things I wanted without a special plan.

Was that the secret to life? Was hard work and a plan all that a man needed? I knew in my gut I stumbled on the answer, but there was only one way to prove my theory. I had to develop a strategy and successfully implement the result. There simply was no other way.

Instead of going home I rode to an old hiding place I used as a child. It served me well in the old days when I wanted to be left alone, so I rode for the thicket. I got there a little before midnight and pitched my blanket roll. Regret was uneasy and I could guess why. The cat had been here, and we were now invading his home territory. Regret didn't like my picketing him none at all, but he stood still once I had him tied up.

Later in the evening we were visited by the panther and I knew it was Cajun. He sniffed the thicket a few times, circling. ol' Regret didn't let out a peep. Then the cat came into the circle in the thicket where he kept the place free of varmints while I was away.

He let out a few low rumbling growls and then lay down across from Regret. The mule must have figured if I wasn't scared he needn't be. Not one of the three of us seemed to want to sleep, so I sat up and talked the night away. I know they couldn't understand, but I did. At least I had company I could trust. I knew they weren't going to go blab everything I was saying to the Yankee's. I realized then, dogs and cats know their place in society, where many people don't. If people could be half as reliable as a cat or a dog.

Finally I fell asleep. When I awoke Cajun was gone. I saddled up ol' Regret who was looking at me like I was crazy and we headed for home.

As I rode into the yard I couldn't help but notice the girl standing near the corner of the property on the northeast end. Her blue and white dress was swaying in the breeze, which didn't blend in with her surroundings at all. She bent down to pick flowers from the wild flower grove Mrs. Whipple planted back in that corner many years ago. Her auburn hair blew slightly in the faint breeze and I brought Regret to a halt.

She continued to pick the flowers so I nudged Regret forward until I was within about twenty feet of her. When I stopped she heard my saddle leather creak and stood up straight, surprised anyone was around.

"Who are you," she challenged.

"Le Roy Ware," I said. "I own this place now."

"You're the little boy who never went to recess."

"I didn't see much use in it."

"Are you living here now?"

"I moved in a week or so back."

"I have a few things over to the house that belonged to the Whipple's. When people started to break in and destroy things I told Mother I was going to save what I could. Most of the furniture was saved, along with a lot of the Whipple's personal things. You can have them if you want."

"You've got everything?"

"I took everything that wasn't too badly damaged," she said looking at me all funny like.

I didn't have the faintest clue what was going through her mind at the time, but it didn't take me long to figure out what she was thinking.

"I don't know how to thank you," I said. "I thought all their personal things were lost."

"I knew you would come home someday, James Le Roy. I had a premonition about it."

"I don't even know what that means."

"I had a dream, and you were the man in it."

"Oh." I still didn't get her meaning.

"James Le Roy Ware, you don't even remember who I am, do you!"

"Well, I..."

"I've half a notion to not speak to you."

"I'm sorry ma'am, but..."

"Ma'am? Do I look like an old maid to you?"

"Well, no ma'am, I..."

"Ooooh! You sure know how to make a girl mad James Le Roy. Why, I'm no ma'am. I'm still a young girl, younger than you and you better figure out my name real quick or I'll never speak to you again."

I knew I was on the spot. I didn't have a clue as to who this girl was, but I did know how to add and deduct, so I started to study on it mighty quick. The only girl who lived nearby had been a six year old, so she would be about seventeen now at best. I was looking at a girl who fit the bill age wise, and I thought on it some more. There just wasn't anybody else.

"You're that little Townsend girl, the one who always tried to get me to carry your books home."

"Tried is right, you never did if my memory serves me, not even when I begged you."

"You're all grown up."

"Well, at least there's nothing wrong with your eyes."

"You sure get riled up easy."

"When the man of my dreams doesn't even recognize me, I have a right to get riled up!"

Well, I didn't know what to make of that statement, but I stepped down from ol' Regret thinking I might make her feel a little more at ease. That's when the meaning behind her words hit me. She set her cap for me all those years ago, and was still hanging onto her silly childhood dreams.

"You know, things may not be all hunky dory like they are in your dreams," I said and stepped closer.

"I know things might not be hunky dory all the time, but I know who I want to go through life with."

I took another step closer and said, "You certainly don't beat around the bush, do you."

"With you I can't afford to take a chance. I haven't seen you in nigh onto ten years." She paused, then added, "You are everything I remembered and then some."

I took a step closer to her then and noted she was breathing in an erratic fashion. I took her in my arms and kissed her hard on the lips. She melted into my arms so I pushed her back to look into her deep blue eyes.

"You've waited all of this time for me?" The question I raised made good sense.

"You and nobody else," she managed breathlessly.

"I'm not sure I believe you. That's quite a commitment."

"So is marriage."

"I'll come over and get my things in the morning. If you're going to be my woman, you need to get your things packed and be ready to move in with me."

"Don't we need to see a preacher first?"

"I'll be bringing the preacher with me."

"Le Roy Ware, you better be worth the last ten years of fussing and worrying. I took care of everything while you were gone. There wasn't anyone else to do it."

As she started to turn I pulled her back to me and kissed her again, only I kissed her harder, longer and deeper. As I pulled back from my kiss I looked down into her eyes and said, "I'm worth it. Now go home and get your things packed."

I swatted her on the rump as she turned away from me and I watched her sway back and forth brushing flower tips as she swept by. She was humming to herself and twice she looked back to make sure I was still watching her, then took off running through the woods.

I knew right where she lived, and come morning I was going to be at her door.

Chapter 14

At sunup I was in town at the livery renting a wagon and a team of horses so I could pick up my new wife and collect my inheritance. When I had the team and wagon I stopped by the chapel and told the minister he was performing a wedding today, so we rode out of town just as the sun was clearing the trees.

The preacher rode with me in the wagon, Chin and Darnell rode drag and we headed for the Townsend place. I was going to need some help to bring all that furniture back home, and the preacher, Mr. J. C. Givens volunteered to help us move, an unexpected benefit to be sure. "This sounds like a working wedding party," he said.

We rode into the yard about nine in the morning and she was ready, I'll give her that. She was in her wedding gown, a dress I didn't even know she had. Mr. Givens made us write out our wedding vows before he would consent to our wishes. Once we read them he delighted in performing the ceremony. When we were finished with the oratory he said I could kiss the bride so I did just that. I pulled her to me and kissed her hard like the day before, then I pulled back.

"We're not going to do this half way," I said, and I kissed her again.

"If we're going to get you moved, we better get busy," Darnell interrupted.

Now I know our love was sudden, but this girl waited for me to return to Louisiana for a long time. I couldn't even remember her first name until that Southern Baptist minister said her name when he asked me, "James Le Roy Ware, do you take Virginia Abigail Townsend to be your lawful wedded wife, to have and to hold, to cherish in sickness and in health until death do us part?"

I heard myself say "I do," and I burned the name Virginia Abigail Townsend into the back of my forehead where I could see it plain. I knew if she ever got wind of the fact I didn't know her name at the time of our wedding I was going to be in more trouble than a part-time Christian getting tossed into the lion's den.

I didn't know much about women. I'd never been around them much, but it seemed to me the older they got the more they wanted to be in control of things. I also heard horror stories about particular mistakes other men made with their wives. I didn't want to fall into that category, not now, not ever.

I kissed my bride long and hard, and we got a few whoops and hollers, but there was only five people among us. Now I really had no earthly idea what I had just done. A man does things sometimes because they feel right. Being with Virginia felt right, I couldn't give any other explanation for it, but I can tell you getting married is a life altering decision. You might think things will be pure and blissful until death do us part, but that isn't generally the case, and our marriage was no exception.

Our honeymoon was short-lived. No more than we finished saying our vow's we started loading the wagon.

We piled everything high, and eventually we learned it would require no less than two trips to get everything. I felt bad for Virginia's mother, because she was losing so much in the way of furniture, but I made certain she wasn't going to want for anything. Before we rode away I told her she could come and visit us anytime. It wasn't but three miles through the swamp on an old dirt road to our house.

We made two trips and I returned the wagon to town the following day. The rent cost me double because I didn't get the wagon back to old man Stevens in time for it to be rented again. I thought this was a made up excuse, but I was proven wrong almost immediately. Conrad Larimore, an old horse trader, showed up as I was leaving and wanted to know if the wagon was back yet. He was some put out because it wasn't there for him to use the day before.

I shook my head and turned Regret into the wind. I noticed of late that whenever traveling to the west, the wind always seemed to be blowing in my face. It was only natural for me to come up with such a saying after serving on the ironclad *Carondelet* like I done. Sailors on the high sea would put a ship into the wind in order to set the sail. Of late, every time I headed for home the wind was in my face. Today was the exception.

As I rode for the house I had a smile on my face. While Virginia and I were too tired to really consummate our marriage the night before, we fell asleep in our own bed while resting in one another's arms. This was the reason for my smile.

Darnell and Chin slept in the barn, up in the hay loft. I know it wasn't the best of accommodations for the two of them, but it was all we had at the moment.

I turned ol' Regret into the corral and my new wife met me at the door.

"I have a surprise for you," she said.

"What is it?"

"You have to close your eyes."

I closed my eyes and felt her hand slip into mine as she led me into the house. She told me where to stop, positioned me just so and then said, "Okay, you can open your eyes now."

I opened my eyes to see she had the house completely put back together, the curtains were hung, nothing was out of place save for the old spinning wheel Ma Whipple used many times over to create a wool yarn for making wool clothing. The spinning wheel was the one thing that had been destroyed.

I smiled and told her it looked great. She then led me over to the table where there was a bottle of wine resting between two wine glasses. I picked up the bottle and noted the wine maker was the Stone Hill Winery. The wine was Pink Catawba, whatever that meant.

"Don't open it yet, it's for after dinner."

"Where in all of the south did you ever find a bottle of wine?"

"Actually the Stone Hill Winery makes a world class wine, my dear. I have a good friend named Julia who sends me sample's all the time. She married the owner's son right out of school."

"Julia Givens?"

"Yes, you remember her?"

I just shook my head. I had been smitten with her as a young boy, but I daren't let go a hint to my new wife. I had no idea how she would react to such a revelation. It was best I didn't take a chance.

"You two are friends," I asked.

"We've been friends for a long time."

"I haven't seen her in ten years."

"You haven't seen anyone in years."

"I would have never thought your mother would allow you to drink a glass of wine."

"Mother takes a glass herself when the occasion is right. I'm certain to have more before we run out," she said.

"One bottle isn't going to last very long."

"I have several bottles, different types for all occasions."

"Now that's something I didn't know."

"There's a lot you don't know about me, Mr. Ware."

I grabbed her and pulled her to me. "I'll know everything about you in short order. There can't be any other way for us."

"Oh, I like your philosophy, Mr. Ware."

"Mrs. Ware, I want you to know I'm a little surprised. I never expected anyone cared one wit whether I lived or died."

"Surprise," she said and kissed me on the lips.

While she kissed me again I began to understand the full extent of what I'd done. Marrying Virginia was easy because I knew in my heart if I had a wife those Yankee's wouldn't be so quick to ride in here and burn me out. Maybe I was giving her too much credit for being able to change my circumstance, but I didn't think so. She might only be seventeen, but she was a girl who knew what she wanted and anybody who might tread on her property needed to be ready to deal with her.

Chin and Darnell helped her set everything up while I was gone to town to return the wagon. She had two new friends in those fellows because she was that likeable. They would do anything for her as would I, although I had no idea how much my pledge to her would be tested over time. I knew love would blossom easily for us, it's what I didn't know in my life that would test me, my resolve and my manhood.

You have to ask yourself, what makes a man? I didn't know it then, but I was about to find out the hard way. Life has a way of molding a young man into a particular individual based upon life's experiences with those who live around him, his neighbors and the community in which he chooses to live. I was no exception.

In retrospect I can tell you everyone has the opportunity to change his or her future, improve who they are and live a good life, but you have to make the right decisions for you and your family, because once you say, "I do," you have to consider the fact you are no longer alone in life. Any decision you make also affects your family, even if it is just a wife or a husband for the time being. There is no sense in making a wrong decision when you are already right. Too often I had seen someone do that very thing.

I noted my wife had some old fashioned dolls lying here and there, and there were a few small jars of different kind of spices she kept on the counter. She was only seventeen so I gave her a little leeway and didn't say anything about the dolls or anything else. If she wasn't ready to give them up just yet, I was all right with it, but I do have to say I was a little put out she held onto such childish notions.

Chapter 15

Late that evening as Chin distracted the soldiers at Union Headquarters, Darnell and I moved another body into place. We were sitting at the edge of the woods watching as they came back to Belle Grove and those boys almost had simultaneous heart attacks when they stumbled on the dead body lying against the front door. A holler went up and those Yankee's began to run. It was Corporal Cook who calmed them down and brought them back together.

Once he had them corralled he ordered the troops remove the body and put it in the barn with the other one they hadn't reburied yet. We decided to make ourselves scarce and headed for home. We hadn't gone two hundred yards when Cajun let out a screech and the animals side-stepped in fear. We eased them forward, mostly because we had to get home, and there just wasn't any other way unless we wanted to go miles out of our way.

"I sure hope that cat has eaten today," Darnell said.

I didn't reply, but inside I was hoping the same thing. I really didn't know where I stood with Cajun after all these years, but he did seem to remember me, otherwise we would have already been eaten. Chin met us a few minutes later and the three of us headed for home together.

Chin was an unusual sort, why I couldn't say. He didn't walk, talk or act like other men I knew. He was shorter, he was quicker and he was quieter. He knew when to make a noise and when not to. As for fighting, I still hadn't been able to hit him, but then I hadn't tried any since our first go around.

I felt for my gun and rested my hand on it for a moment. I needed to spend some time getting faster at drawing my weapon. I was certain I had to do better, if I didn't, I would likely have a short-lived marriage. I thought about Virginia then. She was quite a girl. We still hadn't been able to really show our passion to one another, but I knew when the time was right we would.

We were nearing the tree where we saw Cajun the first evening and I knew he was there tonight. Maybe not resting on the same limb, but he would be in that tree or close. As if on cue the cat screeched again and our animals brought up short.

"Well, I don't guess he minds us, otherwise he wouldn't have bothered to warn us," Darnell observed.

"Let's just hope you're correct," I said.

I nudged ol' Regret forward and fifty yards farther through the swamp we passed under the tree. The cat was there watching as if to see whether we were friendly or unfriendly. I spoke to him and kept Regret moving. I was certain of the cat now, but I wasn't certain what the last ten years might have done to him. It was best I didn't take a chance in the dark or with both of my friends along.

"We could circle back and get those bodies in the middle of the night," Darnell offered. "So far all we've done is concern them a little bit. If those bodies were to disappear in the middle of the night with no sign, we'd give them a real spook."

"I guess we should put them back where we got them," I said.

"We don't have to go under that cat again do we?" Darnell wanted to know.

"No, we'll ride around the long way and give those boys a chance to fall asleep."

"That's good, because that cat of yours is making me nervous, real nervous."

"Darnell, I don't believe Cajun is going to bother us at all, but he might just bother those Yanks."

We rode for three hours around through the swamp and back. When we reached Belle Grove again all was quiet. Carefully we snuck into the barn and retrieved the dead bodies. They were decomposing more rapidly now and we lost an arm. Once the body was draped over my mule we went back and got the arm. Then we loaded the second body which was staying together better. Carefully we rode off into the night. This time we took the short way home.

Cajun wasn't up in the tree this time, he had meandered off somewhere. I wish I knew, but I really had no idea. We returned to the house just before sunup and no one had to tell us to go to bed. We were in the hay before we could get a plan together for tomorrow. I had one though, it was called sleep.

When I awoke it was after noon and we had company. Virginia shook me awake because there was a menacing cat laying in the front yard. I laughed when I looked out the window.

"What's so funny," my wife of two days wanted to know.

"That's Cajun, he won't bother us."

"Cajun?" she asked.

"He was my pet cat. Now that I'm home it looks like he decided to come home too. My wife smiled a funny smile then, as if she knew a secret I didn't know. I looked her up and down, but she turned back to look out the window.

"He's awful big," she observed.

"I would agree, but for one thing. He makes a pretty good yard dog. If those Yankee's were to show up while he was here, they wouldn't set a foot in our yard. In fact they'd probably cut and run."

I went back to the bedroom and got dressed. When I walked outside Cajun turned his head to look at me and I could see in his eyes what he was thinking. Life played a trick on him. He had grown up and so had I. Stepping down off the front porch I walked over to where he was and kneeled down beside him. He remembered me and displayed some of the same playful moves he had used as a cub. I thanked my lucky stars it was him and lay down with my back against him. I looked back toward the house to see my wife standing on the front porch with a look of mischief on her face.

"I didn't realize I was marrying a cat crazy man," she smirked.

"I'm not crazy, we just get along."

"Do you really believe that cat can be your pet?"

"Yes," I started to say ma'am, but thought better of it. "Virginia, I may not know much, but Cajun is not like any normal wildcat. He understands me and I understand him."

"And he won't bother me?" she asked, as if she already knew.

"No, he won't. Why don't you come on out here with me," I said waving her on. "Now would be a good time to introduce the two of you."

I noticed Darnell and Chin out of the corner of my eye. They were at the barn door looking at me as if I were crazy, ready at any moment to duck inside and pull the door shut.

Virginia took a few steps toward us and Cajun turned sharply around to look at her which fairly halted her in her tracks. "Easy boy," I said as I reached up and rubbed his head. "She's part of the family."

"Are you sure he's all right?"

"He's fine, just come on out and see. Don't show any fear, just walk out here and join me," I said with my back to him.

She took another step and I lost my pillow. Before I could recover and before Virginia could turn to run, Cajun had her pinned on the ground and began to lick her face. Her screams were wild hair curling things, but Cajun was just funnin' with her. It took her a moment to realize she wasn't being attacked; at least that's what I thought. I learned later she had been taking care of my cat all these years.

"Get this dad blamed cat off of me!"

She was kicking and putting up a fuss which I'd personally never seen the likes of. I got to where they were and grabbed Cajun by the neck to pull him away and he tackled me leaving Virginia to stand up and brush her dress off. She looked at me funny then, smiled, turned for the house and left me to get reacquainted.

"Don't shoot him," I yelled at Darnell. "He's just playing."

"If he's just playing, I sure don't want to see what happens when he gets mad."

Darnell had a point, for Cajun was dragging me all over the yard as if I were a play toy. I couldn't stop him, couldn't bring myself to try. He was having too much fun and so was I. It had been a long time since I played at anything. Suddenly I felt like a kid again. I was relieved, I was happy while half the world seemed set on putting me in my grave.

I saw my wife doing something with one of her dolls through the front window, but I had no idea what she was up to. I just thought it was an awful strange time for her to be playing with her dolls.

I spent the next thirty minutes wrestling with my cat and we got to know one another all over again. No one dared interrupt us, but we had our fun and when the time came he let go of me and wondered off into the swamp. I was plumb tuckered out. He turned me every which way but loose.

Laying there in the yard I didn't move, I just relished the peace and the calm trying to catch my breath.

Darnell appeared above me and said, "You're no match for that two hundred pound cat. Are you all right?"

"I'm all right. Give me a hand up," I said extending my right hand.

He lifted me from the ground and I walked over to the house and entered. My new wife was just putting down a doll which looked like Cajun. There were a couple of notes pinned to him, but she folded them so tight they couldn't be read without unfolding them. I thought this to be strange, yet I said nothing.

Chapter 16

I asked her about the dolls that evening. I asked how long she'd had them, and why she seemed to always be rearranging them. I was prepared for any answer but the one I got.

"Those are my Voodoo dolls," she said.

I sat straight up in bed and looked at my wife as if I had never seen her before.

"Don't panic. I only use them for good."

Well, you better believe we had a conversation that night. I made sure she explained every aspect of what she was doing to me until I understood. I'll give her credit; she knew what she was doing with Voodoo. I always thought Voodoo was a black art practiced by witches or some other evil minded being, but she set me straight. Voodoo was mingled with Christianity in south Louisiana. When I was certain she was telling me the truth, and there was nothing she was hiding from me I went to sleep, but not one minute before.

As the sun began to gray the sky I awoke and got dressed. I stepped outside and took a look around. Every step I took seemed a memory to me, only now I was making new ones. This time I had friends, where before I had none. From time to time I'd stop in my stride and just stand there, reminiscing.

On some mornings, if the air was just right and the water was the correct temperature a mist would rise out of the nearby swamp and envelop the house. This morning was one of those mornings. I looked around me and each tree seemed suspended in a cloud as if there was no ground for anchor. I remembered back to my childhood and the sea of fog was the same. That at least had remained.

It was a cool and quiet morning, no wind, no breeze coming off the water and the sun was not yet high enough to burn off the fog.

I felt something tear at my arm and whatever it was spun me to the ground. As I was falling I heard the report of a rifle. I knew I had been shot. Before I could gather my thoughts I heard Cajun screech in the distant swamp. I heard a man scream and then all hell broke loose. The man was screaming and yelling and Cajun was squalling, then suddenly there was dead silence. I got up from the ground and walked back to the house.

Virginia met me at the front door. "You've been shot!"

"It's just a scratch," I said with my left hand cupping my wound in my right arm above the elbow.

"Sit down at the table and let me have a look at you."

Darnell and Chin busted through the front door and took a long hard look at me. "Are you all right?"

"I'll be fine. When this fog clears we'll go see what happened."

"If you don't mind we just as soon stay inside the house. We don't want to be outside with that cat on the prowl and we can tell you what happened. That cat of yours just killed whoever pulled the trigger."

"Are you certain?"

Chin was standing there shaking his head up and down, "I know. Cajun was stalking him from de moment he got near de property."

"That would sure be almighty comforting to know," I said.

"When this fog clears, we'll go out and find the body," Darnell repeated.

Virginia finished wrapping up my arm and said, "You boys might as well set down. I'll get breakfast going while we're waiting for the fog to clear."

I looked over at my wife then and I knew she'd do. She might only be seventeen, but she wasn't afraid of anything that I could see, except maybe that cat of mine. She threw a fry pan on the stove and tossed in some bacon, set some biscuits up to bake and went to the barn to get some eggs, sporting her basket as she left by way of the front door.

We had us some chickens from day one, courtesy of her mother. We had laying hens and two roosters. They were using the back corner of the barn to build their nests and she knew right where to go for our breakfast. Whenever Cajun was around they would hide in the barn and get real quiet, mirroring Regret and the horses.

We heard something thumping around outside and wondered at it. Suddenly the noise we had been hearing stopped and then we heard Cajun yawn. Well, I think it was a yawn. On cat's paws he slipped away. Just as I was about to get up and go check on my wife she stepped up onto the front porch and paused for a moment, then she opened the front door and stepped into the house.

She started cracking eggs into the fry pan and said, "There's a dead soldier on the front porch. He's your cat so it's your mess to clean up," she offered nonchalantly.

We jumped up from the table and staggered out the front door to witness what she was talking about. Sure enough there was a dead Yankee lying there all covered in blood. A strange revelation interrupted my thoughts at that moment; blood once spilled from its human vile could never be put back. It was Corporal Cook.

There wasn't much left to look at for he was bloody beyond any reasonable understanding, but his face was untouched. Then deep in the back of my childhood I remembered the unaccounted for wild game left on our front porch. When I was a boy often times the Whipple's found meat laying on the front porch right where Corporal Cook was now lying, but Mr. Whipple would never say how it got there. Now I understood. It had been Cajun all along. He had been looking out for us.

Suddenly I realized Cajun had been scouting for us all those years. I never even knew he was in the area, but now everything made sense. One day with a cub as a boy had produced for me a friend for life. I couldn't comprehend how such a thing was possible, but I knew in my heart it was. We were living proof the two of us.

"Darnell, we're going to have to take Cook back to Belle Grove." I broke the silence.

"In this fog, with that cat on the loose?" Darnell asked.

"No, when the fog clears. We'll ride on to White Castle and see how Butch is getting along. See if he's ready to raise a ruckus yet."

"I've got an eerie feeling on me, boss."

"What do you mean?"

"Look at that man. He ain't no different than me, only he's dead. What if that Cajun suddenly thinks I'm this here hombre."

"He won't. You're with me for one. Two, I've been told a cat can smell the difference in men. You don't smell the same."

"Lord I hope you're right. Cause if you're wrong I'm looking at the future me," Darnell offered.

"Relax, will you?" I said and headed back inside.

Virginia had breakfast placed on our small table, a fair setting for the likes of my friends. I took up residence against the back wall, my right arm hurting where I'd just been shot. It was only a flesh wound which had not penetrated to the bone, but man did it burn.

"You don't need to worry about Cajun," my wife promised Darnell. "He knows friend from foe."

"How does he know?"

"I'll show you sometime, when all this is over, but for now please trust me. He won't allow any harm to come to any of us."

"Now how could you possibly know that?" Darnell wanted to know.

"I can't tell you just now, but I do know you're safe as long as you're on our side."

The conversation sort of dried up then. We ate a hardy meal made up of eggs, toast and bacon with plenty of hot coffee to boot. While eating I thought about my cat. Nobody said much so it was a good time for me to make sure I didn't have a screw loose.

Cajun lived on his own all these years, or so I thought, yet he frequented the house since I first brought him here. I knew this now. He delivered meat to us on more than one occasion. Why? Mr. Whipple always said, "Look what the neighbors brought us." I now understood our neighbor was Cajun. Fetching meat and delivering it to humans was not a typical thing for a big cat to do.

I looked across the table at my wife and wondered what the extent of her intervention might entail. She did have a Voodoo doll to represent Cajun. She also spent all these years as his friend while I was away. Suddenly it dawned on me she knew him better than I did. Who was I kidding? She was doing things behind the scenes which nobody had the first inkling about including me.

Cajun sported a fine coat of fur which held a red tint in the sunlight. Darnell said that red coat of his was a rare thing for a catamount. I didn't know one way or another, but it was even more uncommon for one to befriend a human being, of this I was certain. In this case it seemed anyone I accepted, Cajun accepted or was that my wife's doing?

I'd heard of yard dogs, but I never heard of yard cats. A yard dog was very protective of his owners by nature.

What about Cajun? Was he suddenly my protector? I didn't quite know what to make of the situation. No one would be able to ride up to the house but us. My wife had no fear of the cat. My friends were another story.

"You better ride over to your mother's house and tell her not to come this way without an escort," I suggested.

"All right, I'll do that while you take care of the body."

"Chin, can my wife use your horse?" I asked.

He nodded his ponytailed head and kept eating. He ate such small bites it seemed he was never going to finish a plate. He did, it just took him much longer than I felt was necessary. I made a note to myself, one day I was going to ask him why he did this. Not that it mattered, but I was curious.

The fog cleared off a little after noon and we saddled up to deliver the corporal back to his command. I knew it was going to be a touchy thing, delivering a dead soldier back to his commanding officer, but it was obvious how the man had died. It had only been a few hours and his skin was turning pale yet blue at the same time.

Virginia mounted up and headed for her mother's house while Chin stayed behind to keep an eye on things. Getting the body loaded was a chore as he was much heavier than the two bodies we had pulled from the grave to deliver to Belle Grove. Cook was also messy with blood everywhere, so we wrapped his body with a blanket then secured him real good.

As we rode for Belle Grove I began to understand the extent to which my wife had been taking care of things for me while I was away at war. Only by sheer luck did I return home. If I had not inherited the Whipple place, I should never have married Virginia.

Chapter 17

When we rode up to the front steps at Belle Grove Plantation those Yankee's stood up and took notice. We had guns covering us from the moment we set foot on the property. This was more because we had a dead soldier in tow than for any other reason.

"Is the captain in," I asked.

"Moody, go get Captain Callahan. He'll want to see this."

We sat our mounts waiting on the captain who was in the house somewhere. After a few minutes he opened the front door and started down the steps. The captain descended the stairs slowly, studying the situation as he came. He looked me over good then he looked Darnell over. He didn't say anything at first, but eventually he looked up at me and said, "I am told you have one of my men. What happened?"

"He was killed by a large cat. We found him and figured you fellows would want to give him a proper burial."

"When did this happen?"

"It couldn't have been more than a couple of hours ago, while the ground was still covered with fog."

"Basil, Williams, get him down," the captain ordered.

"You gentlemen care to join me? I have a few questions for you before you go." Captain Callahan motioned toward the big mansion and the two of us stepped down. We ascended the stairs and entered the house which seemed to me was bigger than any barn. The rooms were covered with marble floors, the ballroom had pillars of marble and I knew right then I wanted a home like this one.

We entered the parlor and the captain took a seat at his desk. "Have a seat, gentlemen. I just need to clear a few things up. Tell me, where did you find the body of Corporal Cook?"

I spoke before Darnell could say the wrong thing which might get the two of us hung. "Sir, we heard the attack. It happened about two hundred yards from my home. It was foggy and too dangerous for us to respond until the fog lifted."

"I see. So you're saying the attack took place in the swamp?"

"Yes sir."

"What happened to your shoulder?"

"I was clipped by a stray bullet," I offered, not wanting to get entangled in what was happening any further.

"I guess this country is still dangerous a year after hostilities ended."

"Yes sir, I would agree."

"You haven't vacated the home?"

"No sir, I have no intention of leaving."

"You were ordered to leave."

"Orders don't count for much unless you're in the army sir." I could see right off when I said this Captain

Callahan determined in his mind I was nothing but civilian rabble. I was the scum of the earth and I needed to be removed for a thorough cleaning.

"Captain, I don't know if you know it or not, but this far south there is a religion called Voodoo. It is a long practiced religion which uses animals to get at people. Sometimes it uses people to get after folks, but it always works. It was brought over from Africa with the slaves when some African tribes were sold into slavery by their own people. Why don't you take your troops and get out while they still live."

"Are you telling me you practice Voodoo?"

"No sir, I surely don't. Mostly it's practiced by the colored folks. I'm just offering some friendly advice. It seems someone doesn't like you fellows, nor do they want you down here. If you're up against someone practicing Voodoo you're going to find things happening to your troops that you'll have no control over, things that will scare the daylights out of any normal human being. Things like what happened to Corporal Cook. I'm just giving you a heads up Captain Callahan, because you're dealing with things of which you have no idea."

"We can handle whatever comes our way, Mr. Ware."

"That's what Corporal Cook thought, sir." I turned to leave and the captain stopped me.

"I did not dismiss you yet."

"You forget, captain. While I once wore the Yankee blue, I don't anymore." We turned then and went through the door. We walked down the hallway with our boots clicking on marble floors then exited the front. Our mounts were standing free and we stepped into the saddles. Turing them, we didn't wait to see what order the captain might give his men, we high tailed it out of there.

"Is what you said back there true?" Darnell asked.

"You mean about the practice of Voodoo?"

"Yeah, that."

"Every word was true. Why?"

"I get the idea hanging around you, I'm learning things they don't teach in school. So Cajun can be used like that?"

"You're right Darnell. They don't teach a lot of things in school. One of them is how to be a man, but to answer your question about Cajun, I don't know for certain. I was just trying to scare the captain."

"You know what else they don't teach in school?" Darnell asked.

"What's that?"

"They don't teach you that it's okay to have a two hundred pound pet feline." After a minute he added, "Your story is working pretty good on me. I'm getting good and scared my own self."

"You don't have anything to worry about, you ride with me."

"You see, that's what I'm talking about. What exactly does that mean? There's a man killing catamount on the loose, and he's on the loose around your property, but you're telling me that I'm all right. Well, I don't feel all right, I feel like I'm next considering who it was he killed and drug up to the front porch this morning."

"Have a little faith, will you?"

"That's the second time you told me that."

"It probably won't be the last. Your faith is like weak coffee or tea, it isn't the strongest I ever saw."

"Well, what little faith I do have will have to suffice. I can't figure no way or no how we can win this here dispute, but I'll give you my shoulder and back just the same."

"Listen Darnell, them Yankee's don't know the first thing about southerners. I learned that serving on the *Carondelet*. If we feed them ghost stories, Voodoo and witchcraft, we'll have them itching to get out of here. I've seen it. They don't have the first clue about ghost's, haunted houses or creatures of the night what move around under cover of the devil's veil."

"You're scaring me, Le Roy."

"Look, I've got a plan what will send those boys running for the hills, but I need you along. I can't do it without you."

"Just what is this plan?"

"Simple. They'll be setting up with Corporal Cook's body tonight. I don't think those boys will be able to stay awake, they've been losing too much sleep. When the fellow who's watching him nods off, you slip into the coffin in his place. I'll make a racket which will surely wake him and when I do, you set up and say, "Let's trade places soldier!" I guarantee that soldier will sprint for the door."

"As funny as that sounds, I need to know he won't have a loaded gun, because he might come up out of his chair shooting."

"I'll make sure his gun isn't loaded."

"Le Roy Ware, you are a dangerous man."

"I've got more ideas, but let's worry about one thing at a time."

As we rode into White Castle we saw Butch sitting in a rocking chair on Doc's front porch. He was rocking back and forth just waiting on us to show.

"I've been wondering what was taking you fellows so long. I was fixing to come looking for you and would have too, but for some soldier riding in here a little after noon squalling about some cat what done killed his corporal."

"The fact is, it was my cat. It was Cajun what killed the man," I said without giving the first thought I might be endangering my cat's life.

"You have a cat that will kill a man?"

"He's my yard dog, I think."

"He's out at your place as we speak?" Butch wanted to know. I nodded. "I'm staying right here," Butch threatened.

"It's all right, as long as you don't attack me or my wife, you're fine," I added.

"Darnell, tell him what I said. I'm staying right here."

"He said he's staying right here," Darnell repeated.

"I heard him."

"I just got myself out of the Grim Reapers grip, now you want me right back in."

"He's right about the cat, Butch. As long as you're with us he won't bother you," Darnell peddled smoothly.

"We really need you tonight, Butch. We're figuring on scaring the daylights out of those Yank's," I said.

"You're on a ghoulish mission this evening?"

"We are," I confirmed.

"All right, I'll get my things, but if that cat sets to jump me he's getting a dose of lead," Butch promised.

"Get your things and let's get moving. I don't want to miss a perfect opportunity."

When we arrived back at the house supper was on the table and we told Virginia about our plans. The Chinaman was nowhere to be found, but Darnell assured me our Confucius wanna-be wouldn't pull out. As for our plans we went over every possible scenario to ensure our success. I didn't want anyone getting hurt, I just wanted the Yankee's to leave.

We talked of ghosts then and did a pretty fair job of rattling our own nerves. Butch Abernathy said that Mrs. Andrews had died in that house of unexplained causes during the war, that from time to time people stated they saw her ghost gliding down the hallway through the wall into the ballroom where she would dance with no one.

"I've seen her myself," my wife added.

That was a story which scared even me, because from what I could tell, my wife wasn't one to romance or exaggerate the afterlife, but she did confirm what the man said. Of course I hadn't been around her much yet, but the thought of an Andrews ghost parading up and down the hallway while we were trying to scare those Yankee's set me to thinking. What if we didn't have to do anything? What if the house really was haunted? What if the laugh was on us?

We needed to wait a while before leaving for Belle Grove Plantation so we planned our episode the best we knew how. I wanted both men to help me get the body out of the coffin, and once we stashed it in another room, Darnell could slip on the corporal's overcoat then step into the wooden coffin. We would have to be quick and quiet.

We heard Cajun prowling in the swamp nearby and it liked to have spoiled our plans, because Butch became frightened from head to toe. It was near impossible to get him out of the house once Cajun let out a growl. His growl was a high pitched thing which brought the swamp to an immediate silence. The silent aftermath was scarier than the growl.

About eight that evening we saddled up and headed for Belle Grove. Three lonely men headed into an uncertain future, trying for all we were worth to hang onto what little we had left.

The Civil War had been hell on this part of the country. Slaves rebelled, Union soldiers burned homes to the ground, stole all of the livestock so they could eat and generally tore things up good. What was left didn't amount to much. My little shack had been the exception to the rule. It had survived. Yankee carpetbaggers were claiming everything they could get their hands on. The soldiers at Belle Grove Plantation were part them. If we couldn't scare them out, it would come down to a shooting, maybe more than one. I wanted them out of the country clean and quick. Scaring them was our best opportunity.

Chapter 18

Once we reached Belle Grove all was quiet. There seemed to be one light in the hallway and no more.

"You know, you fellows are going about this the hard way," Butch insisted. "It's my house. We can walk right in. Once inside we can switch out the body. If anybody asks we'll say Darnell left."

"You're saying we don't have to hide?"

"Not in the least. Captain Callahan knows I'm coming home, he just doesn't know when."

We were whispering while keeping a trained eye on the house. A soldier opened the front door and started down the stairs with a lantern in his hand throwing the front yard into a shadowy relief. There, outlined by the light well away from the house stood Master Chin. I began calling him Master then for only a master of this life could have conceived such a plan.

"What in God's name?" Butch asked.

"Shhhhhhh, that's our Chinaman," Darnell whispered.

He had stripped down buck naked, painted himself white causing the glow of the lantern to make him appear as a ghost to anyone looking on. He moved slowly toward the soldier with the lantern who was now at the bottom of the stairs. The soldier apparently hadn't noticed him yet.

Sitting down his lantern he pulled out his tobacco pouch and began the makings. Suddenly Chin took off running and stopped just as he reached the bottom of the stairs. He leaned down and looked up at the same time. He was staring at the soldier. The Yankee stared back in astonished disbelief. Chin said something and jumped straight up in the air, twirling as he did so. He had me believing in ghosts he was so effective. What he did then was something I never believed a human being capable of. He spun three times in a circle and launched straight up into the air doing a backward summersault while landing on his feet.

The soldier was so spooked he dropped his cigarette and ran screaming up the front stairs. The lantern continued to glow right where the soldier left it, at the bottom of the stairs. Chin ran around the house and met another soldier coming around the corner. The Yankee went straight up in the air, and if I hadn't seen it with my own eyes I would never have believed it. He was running when he hit the ground. Chin did some kind of weird dance contorting his body in ways which defied explanation then suddenly he disappeared.

"Well gentlemen, shall we confirm their suspicions," I said as I nudged ol' Regret forward. The three of us rode out of the woods and arrived at the front steps just as a cavalcade of Yankee soldiers descended them.

"We don't know any more than you," I told Captain Callahan. "There was something out here a minute ago, we saw it, but I'll be a monkey's uncle if I can tell you what we saw."

"That was a ghost, captain, sure as I'm standing here. Nothing human could act like that," the soldier said. He looked to be the same soldier who had been rolling a cigarette only a moment before.

Suddenly Captain Callahan recognized Butch. "What are you doing here?"

"I asked my friends to escort me home. I am welcome in my own home, aren't I?"

"Well, uh, I hadn't thought you would be back this soon."

"I guess I should have sent word, but I wanted to see how you boys were getting along. If you don't mind, I think we'll just stay the night," Butch added.

"Well now, some of my men will have to sleep in the barn," the captain protested.

"Then some of your men will have to sleep in the barn." Stepping down Butch handed his reins to Darnell. "Would you see to the horses, Darnell?"

"My pleasure," Darnell said.

I dismounted and handed my reins to Darnell as well. I hadn't planned on staying the entire night as I had a wife at home who I felt would want me there with her, but with what we were planning on doing maybe it was the best thing. Darnell turned away with our horses and we two low-down, dirty rotten polecats started up the stairs of Belle Grove Plantation. I say that because there's no other description under the sun which was fitting for what we were about to do.

Just as we reached the top of the steps, that cat of mine let loose a squall which stopped everybody in their tracks. I suddenly realized what a grand opportunity this was, so I took it.

"Lord have mercy, that's the cat what done killed Corporal Cook. What's The Prince of Darkness doing in these parts?" I asked.

Captain Callahan stared at me as though I'd lost my mind. "The Prince of what?"

"The Prince of Darkness, Old Boggy, you know Satan. With him on the prowl no one is safe." I paused for a moment then added, "Captain, if he's the one stalking your men, somebody has conjured him here with Voodoo. You'd best get your men inside for the night and set them up for watching all of the doors and windows."

"I haven't said anything about my men being stalked," Captain Callahan objected.

"I'm sorry, I was just under the assumption they were being stalked." This I said so all the soldiers heard me. "That's why Old Boggy's circling the house."

"How is it that you're so certain the Devil is stalking my soldiers?" the captain wanted to know.

"Well sir, he don't ever come around these parts unless someone conjures his presence from that special dungeon in hell called The Dickens. In fact Old Boggy doesn't go anywhere unless he's first called for."

"If that damnable beast gets anywhere near the house, you men are under orders to shoot him on sight," Captain Callahan shouted to his men.

"Captain Callahan, I'm not certain a bullet will stop him. At least not unless it's silver." This I conjured from tales I heard about vampires or werewolves, something which I didn't believe in anyhow. "He's already dead."

"How is it you know so much about what's going on?"

"Sir, all I know about is the legend of Old Boggy. He doesn't kill like a regular animal. You've got to prepare for him, you've got to hunt him down in the middle of the night without mercy or make a blood sacrifice to him in order to get him to go away."

"That's the stupidest thing I have ever heard," Callahan said.

"It may sound stupid to a Yankee, but if you don't have a silver bullet, you can't buy your safety."

I noticed the captain's soldiers hanging on every word I said, so I figured, at the least, I had them hooked, and if I continued farther I might make a mistake. So far so good, but it was time to rein myself in.

"You don't have to believe anything I'm saying captain, but don't come running to me when things turn bad," I said. "Come on, Butch, let's get settled in for the night."

The two of us stepped into the house and took a look around. The coffin was set up in the ballroom off to our left plain as day. It was nothing more than a wooden affair, but it was all a soldier was likely to get. We walked into the ballroom and took a look at what we had to do. A private was sitting in the far corner where he appeared to be scared out of his wits.

"You fella's need s-something?" he asked, his voice shaking.

The captain and his men hadn't entered the house yet, so I fanned the flame a little without them noticing. "We just wanted to get one last look at Corporal Cook before Old Boggy drags him off."

"What do you mean? Who's Old Boggy?"

"The cat what killed him. He's Old Boggy. Didn't you hear him just now? He's coming to get the corporal tonight and drag his body to the depths of hell," I said, having too much fun. The worried look in Butch's eyes was all the confirmation that private needed.

"Where are we sleeping, Butch? I need to get some rest."

Butch pointed toward the spiral staircase and we started up the stairs. Darnell came in just then and joined us.

"You're going to sleep?" the private asked. He walked across the room in order he could witness our ascent.

"Got to. It's the only way to keep Old Boggy from taking you when he comes to get Corporal Cook," I said.

The Union private stared at us in disbelief. We turned and headed up the steps. At the top, Butch directed us to the room we were staying in, namely the captain's quarters. Butch did this just to get under the man's skin. It worked like a charm too.

When Captain Callahan opened the bedroom door, the three of us were sprawled around the room and not even Butch could have guessed how upset the man might get at being put out of his resting place. He started yelling at us like we were some kind of private fresh out of boot camp. When he stopped to catch his breath we all lay back down and ignored him. This infuriated him all the more and he really cut loose, but we didn't move. When he stopped a second time, he started for the bed where Butch was resting and suddenly the room filled with the sound of a hammer cocking on a gun.

Captain Callahan brought up short, and Butch leveled his gun on him. "You take another step, Captain Callahan and you'll beat Corporal Cook to St. Peters gate."

"This is an outrage," he yelled.

"The outrage is you, having me shot and left for dead in the middle of the road. That's an outrage. Now, if you want to see the sun come up tomorrow you better gather your things and sleep downstairs with your men tonight." There was no misunderstanding Butch at this juncture.

Captain Callahan picked up his carpetbag swiped in a few personal items lying about the room and left. I looked at Butch as if seeing him for the first time. In fact, I really didn't know him at all. I was proud of the way he handled the affair and I told him so.

Chapter 19

We didn't sleep at all. At approximately two-thirty in the morning we tiptoed down the staircase. The whole house was asleep but for the men guarding the entranceway outside on the front porch. If the private we encountered earlier wasn't asleep or a replacement, we were going to have a dilly of a time putting our plan into action.

The guard who was sitting up with Corporal Cook had fallen asleep, but not before moving the corporal over under the big window. We inched into the room to the coffin lying back along the front wall. A full moon hung high in the sky overhead casting an eerie shadow into the big room through the big plate glass window. The wooden coffin was opened which was the custom when setting up with the dead. The coffin was a pine box, but it did the job. We slipped the jacket off the corporal then onto Darnell who climbed into the coffin atop Corporal Cook and lay down.

"If I get shot, you boys are going to pay dearly," Darnell whispered.

There seemed to be snoring coming from every room in the house. I wondered suddenly if the private we spoke to earlier hadn't spread the word about making sure you were asleep when Old Boggy come calling.

Just as Butch and I turned the corner to get out of sight, Old Boggy made his calling. That cat of mine was so close it sent chills down our spine for he was just outside. It was so loud I thought for a minute he was inside the house. The soldier on watch jumped straight up from his chair and looked toward the front window.

Darnell slowly raised up from the coffin, turned his head to look at the soldier and spoke. "Shall we trade places?"

I saw someone get scared before, and we would have been scared ourselves, but we knew it was just Darnell Blankenship. That Yankee soldier boy, for he was little more than a boy, jumped straight up about five feet into the air. When he came down he didn't go left or right, he dove straight out the plate glass window.

Now in case you don't understand the significance of this act, the bottom level of the house was a good ten feet in the air, more like twelve. Belle Grove was up in the air due to the flooding swamp nearby. It was simply the largest antebellum home in all Louisiana, maybe all of the south. The front steps ascended for a good ten to twelve feet before you reached the front door. So, when that soldier crashed through the plate glass window, he had a long way to fall.

We ran to Darnell and helped him shed that jacket. Not having time to put it back on the Corporal we draped it over him and ducked into the back room. This was significant because like many houses of that day, you could do a complete circle downstairs on either side of the split stairway, something I did as a child right here in these very halls.

There was a terrible commotion outside and all the soldiers in Captain Callahan's command were suddenly gathered on the front porch. This gave us the opportunity to slip around come in behind them and sneak back up the stairs. Two thirds of the way up we stopped, turned around and hollered at the men.

"What's going on down there?" Butch shouted.

"That catamount done killed another soldier," one of the men yelled back.

"Who did he get," I asked.

"I think it was Riley," the soldier shouted back.

We bobbed back down the stairs and stuck our heads in amongst them as if we were part of the crowd. There was a gathering of no less than ten men huddled atop the front porch stairs. Captain Callahan had an ill-looking disposition for he had just lost another man.

"Ware, this is your doing," he accused. "I know it is. What happened here?"

"Sir, I don't know what you're talking about. I don't have any control over Old Boggy. I tried to warn you."

"Tell me everything you know about what's happening here."

"Sir, I'm sorry you lost another man, but it could have just as well been one of us. There is no rhyme or reason to where he strikes. I can't explain what's going on any better than you can."

"Earlier this evening you said someone conjured him here. Who's capable of doing such a thing?"

"Captain, Cajun's are known to engage in Voodoo. I don't know anybody who could do something like this," I lied thinking of my wife.

"Cajun's?" Callahan asked.

"Yes sir, and I don't know where they might be of late. I haven't been home in a very long time. They could be anywhere."

"I don't suppose I'll get a straight answer, will I?"

"Sir, we don't wish you or your men any harm, we did try to warn you. I can't help it if you're going to ignore matters when they're presented to you. Life in Louisiana isn't the same as in other parts of the country. You make the Cajun's mad down here and you're liable to wake up in an alligator's tummy." Turning to Darnell I added, "Go get our boots Darnell, I don't think we're safe here any longer."

"You plan on leaving with that cat on the loose?"

"Whoever conjured that cat, Captain Callahan, did so because you fellows offended them somehow, not because of us. Right now all I want is some separation. He's your problem, not ours." In my mind I was praying the Lord didn't strike me dead where I stood because I was telling some whoppers.

"So you're going to leave us to the mercy of that damnable creature?" Callahan wanted to know.

"Captain, at the risk of repeating myself, he's not our problem," I stated plainly.

At that moment Darnell came trotting down the staircase with our boots. I took mine and slipped into them. He was already wearing his. Butch stepped into his new pair and we pushed through the men and down the stairs. As an afterthought, I turned at the bottom of the steps and addressed Captain Callahan. "Captain, if we stumble across your man what the cat dragged off, we'll drop him by for you." I turned back to my friends and said, "Let's go."

We walked out to the barn, lit a lantern and started to saddle up. I never saw three animals who wanted to be somewhere else as bad as Regret and those two horses. They were jumpy and nervous as mounts could be and still be sporting their natural fur.

I looked over in the next stall to see Chin's horse and just about had a conniption. The Chinaman was still here! His horse had a bait of oats, been curried and seemed like he was at home, not a nervous bone in his body. I didn't say a word, because I didn't know if anyone might be listening. When we rode out of the barn I waited until we were well away and then I said something.

"Chin's horse was in the stall next to mine," I informed them.

"Now, for some reason that doesn't surprise me," Darnell said.

We came traipsing in about four in the morning and we were tired. I wanted to laugh at the thought of what Chin would do after we left, but I was just too tired to care. We put our horses away in the barn and while the other fellows climbed up into the loft, I headed for the house.

When I stepped up onto the porch I took a look to my left to make certain that we didn't have a fresh body lying there. I pushed open the door and my wife was there to greet me.

"Is everything all right?" she asked.

"I think so." I really wasn't sure, but I didn't want her to worry. "They lost another soldier tonight."

"What happened?"

"We scared him and he took off running into the woods. I think he ran straight into Cajun. There was an awful ruckus, but we don't know for sure."

"That's awful."

"We weren't trying to get anybody killed, we just wanted to scare them. Apparently Cajun follows me around like a lost pup. It may be that nobody is safe.

"I can assure you, the only danger is to those Yankee soldiers."

"He seems to have a mind of his own, but how does he know who is who?"

"Come on to bed. You need rest," my wife urged.

I did as she suggested and fell asleep within minutes. I don't know why, but I had a good woman here. I didn't feel like I deserved her. She was something out of the ordinary. Not once had she complained. She seemed to have a more balanced approach when it came to solving problems and issues between the two of us.

Chapter 20

Along about noon the following day I headed for the barn to check on my friends. They were still sleeping, but for Chin who was rubbing down his horse. I dearly wanted to ask him what he did last night, but I wasn't sure I would be able to understand him. His answer was likely to be a little on the strange side anyhow.

I shoveled hay to the horses, hay my wife saw fit to bring out from town while I was off gallivanting around the countryside. If not for her awareness, I would have nothing to offer the animals. Chin must have been reading my mind, because he offered his own sentiment.

"A virtuous woman is a crown unto her husband," he quoted.

Well, I just looked at him. How did he know the Bible so well when he had trouble speaking any English at all? I began to rub down ol' Regret and he was ready for it. He chewed on the hay I forked to him and let me do my bidding. Likely as not, this was the only pleasure or satisfaction my mule ever got.

Darnell and Butch climbed down from the loft just as I was finishing with my old Missouri mule.

"Darnell, I bet that's the most spoiled mule in all of Louisiana," Butch said.

"One of the reasons I can ride him with Cajun on the loose is because I do spoil him."

"Chin, what did you do last night?" Darnell asked.

"A better question would be; what was your cat up to last night?" Butch cut in.

"I wish I knew. I have a feeling I need to go south a ways and get Cajun to safety. He'll be hunted after what happened last night. I wouldn't put it past them to start setting traps to try and catch him. If they set traps, they'll likely succeed. I don't want that to happen."

"You did say some things to them Yankee's that will have them either hunting or running, I'm not sure which," Butch proclaimed.

"Their captain is a stubborn man. He'll hunt first. That mean's Cajun's in danger. I hope you boys will forgive me, but I'm heading into the swamps to the south for a while. I would appreciate it if you would keep an eye on the place and make sure nothing happens to Abigail."

"How long do you figure on being gone?" Butch asked.

"A couple of weeks for sure, maybe longer," I said.

"You do realize, you're trusting a trio of reprobates to guard your most valuable possession," Butch said.

"Meaning none of you live by faith," I confirmed.

"Exactly."

"Well, I would be willing to trust the three of you more than I would some folks who go to church every week. At least you are not hypocrites."

Butch looked at me then and shook his head. "We'll make sure nothing happens while you're gone. I do have one question though. Why are you calling your wife Abigail? Her name is Virginia."

"After we said our vows she told me she didn't like the name Virginia said she wanted to use her middle name from now on. So I call her Abigail."

"Good enough. I was just wondering."

Darnell interrupted, "Have you celebrated your marriage yet?"

"What do you mean," I asked not certain what he was getting at.

"A honeymoon. Have you spent any time with your wife uninterrupted?" He stared at me when he finished.

"You know I haven't. This is Yankee inspired mess is our honeymoon."

"Exactly, and you're running out on her already. Why don't you take her with you and we'll keep the home place intact."

"Well, I'm not sure she'd go. We'd have to camp out."

"Have you asked her?"

"No he hasn't," Abigail answered as she stepped into the barn. "Cajun is in the yard." She stared at me for a moment and then continued. "I think a honeymoon on the beach would be a wonderful undertaking. I'll get my things ready."

Without another word or waiting to see if I might object she started for the house. My thought was, she would never make it to the front porch before being tackled by you know who, but I was wrong. That silly cat was just waiting for me to exit the barn. When I did, he jumped me from behind and pinned me to the ground face down. I was hardly able to get my head turned enough to see what was about to happen when the full force of his body in motion tackled me. His two hundred plus pounds of weight nearly snapped my neck on the way to the ground.

I managed to flip myself over and grab him with both hands by the neck, but he was having none of it. He reached down and licked me in the face anyway. He slobbered me good and then stood there looking at my three friends who weren't about to come through the doorway.

"Well, get him off me," I yelled.

"You get him off," Darnell snapped. "We ain't moving."

"He's your cat," Butch added.

"What's sweeter than honey or stronger than a lion?" Chin asked.

"Will one of you get him off of me?" I pleaded.

Slowly the cowardice of my friends revealed itself. It was manifest fully when I saw the barn door pulled shut. "Why, you bunch of reprobates," I claimed. "If I ever..."

"When he gets tired, let us know," Darnell yelled from inside the barn.

I looked up into the eyes of my cat and said to myself, I'm going to be right here for a while. He wanted to play and I couldn't tell him we needed to go. Each time I tried to get up he re-secured his hold pinning me to the ground.

I realized as I lay there that sometimes as children we do things which will one day affect us in ways we can't possibly understand when we're young. All I wanted all those years ago was my little friend, but now I had a big friend, an uncontrollable friend, one who was going to get me into more trouble than I could handle if I didn't watch it.

This relationship was no bargain now that my lion had grown up. If I survived, if he survived, I knew we couldn't go on like this. I couldn't take it for one. For two, Abigail could easily be hurt and I didn't want that to happen either.

A moment later Abigail appeared above me and looked down into my pleading eyes. "Have you had enough," she asked.

"Yes, now will you get him off of me?" I pleaded.

To my amazement she patted the lion on the neck and said, "Come on, Cajun, let's go pick some flowers." He stepped off me then and walked beside her to the flower bed in the far corner of the yard. This was even more amazing to me, as the cat seemed completely tame in Abigail's presence.

"What have you done to my cat?" I said as she entered the garden.

"Our cat," she corrected. "And, I have done nothing." She bent over to pick flowers for the house. "He's been visiting me for years, or didn't you know?"

I sat there on my britches watching the two of them meander through the flowers like they were old time friends. This was a rude awakening for me. I suspected her association with Cajun, but to watch the two of them together now, I suddenly realized she was in complete control of my cat, which meant she was in complete control of me.

"Don't you figure on going anywhere without the two of us," she answered back. "You won't get far."

I sat on the ground looking at the two of them as if I didn't know them, and apparently I didn't. I heard the barn door squeak open behind me so I looked around. My three friends weren't budging, but they were willing to peek through the small opening they forced into the doorway.

"If ever a man needed new friends..." I said as I stood up to brush myself off.

"Why Le Roy Ware, you wouldn't know what to do without friends like us," Darnell reassured me while the three of them looked through the doorway ready to slam it shut at a moment's notice.

"I just bet," I said as I headed for the house to pack my things.

"What is this that thou hast done to us," Chin hollered from the barn door opening.

I started to turn around in my tracks, but I didn't want to hear any more of his Bible quoting madness at that moment and kept walking. If ever a man needed a good stiff punch in the mouth it was Chin Lee I thought to myself. The problem was I wasn't fast enough to land a punch. Suddenly I remembered what I needed to be doing. I needed to be practicing with my pistol.

Two more steps and I palmed my gun, spun around and took aim. My three friends all hit the dirt looking for cover, but I just holstered my gun and walked into the house. I had caught them unaware. Only because they hadn't expected me to do such a thing, I had surprised them. With a fair dose of luck, the gun fairly leapt into my hand. As I entered the house I thought to myself I was better off than I had a right to be at this moment in time.

Once inside I began to pack my things. I know I surprised my friends, but I also surprised myself. I learned something from practicing and it showed. I made a point to practice some more. Maybe I wasn't as slow as I thought I was.

I didn't know what they were thinking right at that moment, so I made a point to apologize to them before we left the house. Abigail came in and began to pack her things.

"So, you were just going to ride off without me?"

"Well, no I..."

"Yes you were, I was listening at the door," she said.

"Well, maybe, but I didn't. I came to my senses," I said in defense.

"I'm going to have to watch you real close, James Le Roy Ware. We make up a family now, and all those things you use to do on your own won't hold much water anymore. You have to consider me when you're making decisions or at least you better."

I just looked at her. I knew she was laying things out in lavender for me, but I still wasn't just real sure what she meant. I never worried about anybody but me before, and now I was being told things were different. I didn't quite know what to make of it. Seemed to me she thought she was running the show all of a sudden, but I was in no mood to let her do such a thing. I was the man of this house, and what was it Chin said, something about being a king.

"I think we need to get something straight," I said.

"What is that, dear?"

"I'm the man of the house. What I say goes," I told her.

"Why darling, what makes you think I want it any other way?" she said as she slithered up to me and put her arms around me. "I wasn't looking for a boy, I wanted a man, and you are a man," she said in no uncertain terms. "I will do whatever you say, and then some." She kissed me hard on the lips to prove her point and then stepped back to look into my eyes and said, "You do want the wine and blankets, don't you?"

"Well, uh, I guess so," I shrugged.

"I'll get them, you just keep packing," she said and she was off to gather what we were going to need. I stood there for a moment trying to figure out what just happened. Somehow, I don't think I won the argument. Suddenly it occurred to me, if we just had an argument, they were going to be short lived things.

I looked in the mirror which was hanging on the living room wall and thought to myself, I had no control over my own life! I had to make everyone else happy before I could even think about me. What had I done? I knew that in time love would grow, but did I really love her? I was hard pressed to answer yes at that moment.

"Are you just going to stand there, or are you going to help me pack a few things," she interrupted.

"I'll help you pack, but we have no wagon," I complained.

"Mother has a barouche, I'm sure she'll let us borrow it for a few days."

"I guess I ought to ride over and get it," I offered.

"No, no. I'll go get it. You pack what you think we'll need. I'll hop on Regret and make sure Mother knows how to handle him before I leave such a stubborn animal with her."

Well, I couldn't argue her summation of my mule, because the description was dead on. He would do anything I asked him to, but usually when he felt like it, unless of course if Cajun was nearby and then he dispatched my commands in a more timely fashion. I watched as she left the yard, but I was never more unsure of a relationship between a woman and a mule in my life. Abigail would be hard pressed to get Regret to do whatever she asked. At least that's what I thought at that moment in time.

Chapter 21

To make a long story short, we didn't leave out until the next day. Abigail took longer than expected with her mother, and I knew better than to hit the trail without her. Besides, she had taken Regret. I knew one thing after watching her with my old mule. She had an uncanny way with animals. It wasn't something I could explain or put my finger on at all, but she was good with them.

With the barouche loaded we set out at about ten in the morning headed south. Our cat was following along, but he hung back a ways until we were well south of the house. Then Cajun changed his behavior, as if he knew we were out of harm's way. He would come running through the woods, dart across the road in front of us like a coon hound on a chase and run off in the other direction. Suddenly I thought our horse should be jumpy, especially with a wild cat darting in and out of the woods all around us. I said as much to Abigail, but she set me straight immediately.

"Penny isn't frightened at all. She's used to Cajun or don't you understand what's been going on while you were away?"

"Apparently, I don't understand at all." I continued to steer the horse south then commented, "I guess you'll have to educate me. I seem to be at a disadvantage."

"The first time I came to the house after Mrs. Whipple died, I saw the place was going to be trashed or vandalized. Everything would be ruined. While I was there, Cajun, I didn't know his name then, attacked me, or so I thought. He wasn't attacking, he just wanted to play. It took me a few minutes to realize if he wanted to kill me, I would be dead. So we made friends and he's been my protector while you were away.

"For almost two years now I've been keeping your cat. Nobody comes near our place, and very few come near Mom's. I started a few rumors that kept folks at bay and for the most part they've worked. No one is going to bother us."

"You did all this assuming I would return after the war was over?"

"No, I did all this because I prayed for you to return, I believed you would, so I took what you might call a leap of faith. I acted on account the Lord told me you would be back."

"I've done some praying in my life, but it never really worked out that I can tell," I informed my wife.

"You probably did more wishing than praying, because I can tell you prayer works. Did you get down on your knees when you prayed?"

"Well, no I..."

"See what I mean? You don't even give God the respect He asks for. If you are not willing to bend a knee, what makes you think God is going to do anything? You have to show some respect. You have to do everything within your power to make things right."

"You make it sound as if I'm not even trying," I complained.

"Do you ever say a prayer at night before you go to sleep?"

"Not lately, no."

"James Le Roy Ware, you and I are going to have a good long talk with the Lord tonight, wherever we stop."

We rode on then, both of us lost in our thoughts. I could tell she was well read in Bible verse and I knew almost nothing, but for some scattered thoughts I had learned long ago. It dawned on me then; Chin probably knew more about the Bible than I did. I hadn't been keeping one to read, and reading wasn't my forte anyway. I found reading hard. My book learning ended in the sixth grade. That was as far as I got. I could read, I just didn't do it that much and the bigger words gave me no end of trouble.

The road south narrowed as we entered the pine tree forest. I noted there were many of these all over the south, but this one had been here a long time. As we guided the horse through the narrow lane I noticed Cajun sitting high up in one of the trees watching us from up above as we rode down the old trail.

It dawned on me then that Cajun would follow us home when we returned. All we were doing was buying some time. I had no way of making him stay this far south or farther. We could spend a week on the beach, but when we turned the barouche toward home, I knew he would be following right along.

This bothered me. How could I get him to realize he needed to stay away? I didn't know of any tricks or have any ideas in the matter.

I said as much to Abigail and she said, "I don't have any ideas either, but we'll be down here for a few days, maybe something will present itself."

Well, I didn't argue with her. I knew I couldn't come up with anything. Maybe, she could. The pine tree forest grew darker and taller as we went, then eventually the ground began to fall away and we suddenly found ourselves at an old rickety bridge I didn't think would hold a butterfly, let alone a horse drawn carriage.

I stepped down and got out in front of Penny. Taking her by the harness I began to walk across the decrepit structure. I knew if a board gave way under my foot, it sure wouldn't hold her so I hung on tight, not wanting to fall through to the swamp at any point.

The bridge was no less than fifty yards long, and it took ten minutes for me to lead horse and buggy across. Once on the other side I stepped back into the barouche and we continued on our way. The coast was still several miles off when we stopped about three in the afternoon to rest for a bit. The camp site was good so we decided to stay the night right there. We didn't figure to find a better one further south.

The country was familiar, but I had been gone a long time. I remembered this spot, and I remembered the old bridge, but it had nearly fallen down since I was here last. Bridge or no bridge, I knew things were going to get tougher as we moved south.

I picketed Penny so she had fine amounts of green grass to forage on then set about to build our campfire. Abigail lay out a couple of blankets and fixed something to eat. I busied myself with clearing the area so we could see if any type of wild varmint might be trying to sneak up on us. Mostly I was concerned about alligators this far south of the big thicket.

I should have been concerned about the Indians, but that wasn't something I thought about much lately. The Chawasha Indian's were a special tribe of Indians who made their living in the swamp. They didn't make things to trade. They gathered what was necessary for them to live by collecting alligator eggs, tails, turtle eggs, large birds and fish. They had many ways in which to eat and they were masters when it came to finding swamp food. They were also pretty good at cooking what they found, and that day they found us.

My first instinct was to warn Abigail, but any warning from me would be too late. They were on us already. I stood my ground not knowing what to expect. Abigail had her back to me fumbling with the fire and a fry pan, but there were seven warriors who stepped into view, and the clearing wasn't that wide, not by my estimation.

There were bows and arrows among them, at least three tomahawks, and two pistols. There was also a rifle. I had no chance to beat them. I might beat them to the draw, but I would never live to draw another breath. They stared at me then, each of them piercing me with their eyes, silently accusing me of things which I had not done, things like trespassing on their land. I was afraid to respond. I was about to die, I thought.

"Le Roy, what's the matter?" I heard from over my shoulder.

"We have company."

Suddenly Abigail was beside me holding my arm in her two little hands. It was my right arm she had hold of. How did she expect me to draw my weapon if she was going to hang onto me like that? Penny was tethered at the far end of our little meadow and suddenly their eyes turned from malice to fear. It was then I heard the usual breathing of Cajun as he stopped beside us. Once he got to where we were he sat down right next to me. I reached down my hand and petted him. Those Indian's started to take a step backward one at a time. Weapons were lowered and gradually the men began to back paddle until they were no longer visible in the thick growth of trees.

I reached down and petted my cat some more. "What do you make of that," I asked my new wife.

"The Chawasha tribe. Chief Eagle Feather and his men. I don't think we have anything to worry about as long as they perceive Cajun travels with us."

"Why does that matter?" I asked.

"An old legend was told by the Chawasha of long ago that said a man would one day come to the swamp and live with a catamount. It is said the man would be a peacemaker, he would rule from a large castle and direct many peoples in the region. This man would be a very powerful man, a fair man of great education."

"That leaves me out," I observed.

"I wouldn't exactly swear to that, James Le Roy. You've learned the ways of men. You're a man among men and yet you're young. I would not be so quick to impugn yourself. You do have a rather large catamount."

"You really believe that legend?"

"It doesn't matter what I believe, it only matters that they believe," Abigail informed me.

She was right. Even if I wasn't the man they thought I was, all that mattered is they believed I was him. As long as they believed I was the legend, I would be left alone. Abigail would be left alone. Maybe there was something to the old story, but I wasn't putting much stock in it. All I wanted was to be left alone.

We stayed the night right there, knowing we were being watched. For this reason we played with Cajun for a while to prove to the tribe we were in charge of the cat. We weren't, or at least I wasn't, but there was no reason why they shouldn't think so. About sundown Cajun wondered off into the woods and we heard him growl in the distance. Things were dead silent after that. If our Indian friends hung about to see what we were up to, they were making themselves scarce.

We went to sleep certain that we were safe. As it turned out we were. The next morning, Cajun caught up with us as we started to ride away, stayed with us for about half an hour then disappeared. For some reason, I wasn't worried about that cat. If anything, he seemed worried about us.

The area we were coming to now was called black water, and it was in the bayou. Our horse and barouche wasn't going to navigate much further, not without finding a new way to the gulf waters. I remembered suddenly how I came home from Marsh Island and I turned the horse in a different direction.

In no time we were in stumps up to our liver. There was no good way around them, but we managed to get through and then it was clear sailing. I remembered there was one small beachhead I saw and it was in a spot no one would ever find. I was headed there now. Cajun might find us, but no one else would care to come to such a God forsaken place this far from civilization. Of course, there are those who would argue this far south in Louisiana wasn't considered civilized anyway.

Just about dark we rode up to the spot. Abigail jumped down and took a look around in awe. "Why James Le Roy Ware, you sure outdid any thought I had in mind."

"If the weather turns bad we'll have to get out of here, but I don't think it's the season yet," I offered.

"Why it's positively beautiful."

"It is that."

With no one looking, Abigail walked to me and turned me around to face her. She kissed my lips and held me tight, then buried her head in my chest and just held me. I hadn't been expecting that, but there it was. She wanted to show her love for me. I wasn't all that thrilled about love yet, I just didn't want to be left alone. When a man gets married he can throw alone out the window.

Eventually she pulled back and looked up into my eyes. She studied me for a moment and then said, "Where is that man I married?"

I pulled her to me then, and kissed her hard on the lips. When I came up for air I noticed a slight breeze on the wind. We turned to face it and looked out over the water. It was beautiful blue water, and it was all ours at the moment.

We stood alone on the planet with no one else in the area. We held each other and we didn't let go for a long while. We walked then, from one end of the cove to the other. It was all sand, yet it was surrounded by inlets full of dark blue water. We didn't figure the water was fit to drink, but I could boil some then let it cool to make it fitting. A quarter of a mile up the beach the water began to turn black. After gathering wood for a fire I started it right there on the beach, but only after staking Penny near some grass. Once I had the fire going good I dipped our pot and set it on the flame. I knew we were going to have to boil water the entire time we enjoyed our honeymoon, but it was all we had.

Chapter 22

I understood one thing now that puzzled me from the moment I found Cajun again. How could the cat accept me so easily when I had been gone for so long? The answer was simple, he accepted me because Abigail accepted me. There was no other explanation. Cajun was Abigail's cat. Maybe he was mine too, but he'd been visiting with Abigail for the last two years or so, not me. This led me to one more conclusion. I had me a fairy-tale wife.

She was proving to be the perfect partner, a partner beyond planning, a partner beyond my understanding. She was simply the best I could have chosen. At least that was how things were shaping up for now. She was visibly smart for her seventeen years. I had my doubts as to whether I could match her pace when it came to intelligence. Little did I know; you become part of what you're around. You see, that's one of those secrets you don't generally learn until it's too late. You become part of what you're around!

When I was finished unhooking Penny from the barouche I secured her so she couldn't run off. I didn't want to have to go chasing her. Last night she had plenty of grass, but tonight there was little except back along the trail we used to get in here. I knew horse flesh well enough to know if she got the chance, she'd high tail it to the nearest good forage.

Abigail made herself busy with setting up our campsite just the way she wanted it. I didn't worry so much about her down here, but I did take care to see there were no stray alligators hanging around our camp site.

What she proceeded to do then I cannot say. There are some things which are meant to be between two people and no one else. It was like that. I couldn't go blabbing about the things we shared that evening, but I learned something. I was going to be a loyal man to my wife, especially if she was going to treat me so well. She deserved the best God could give her, and if I was the best in her eyes, so be it.

Later we talked the night away looking up at the stars, watching a few fall from the sky while sharing a glass of wine from the Stone Hill Winery. She brought all she had with us. There would be no shortage of wine on this trip. That first evening we shared a bottle of Steinberg White and followed it up the next evening with a bottle of Brut Rose.

We learned to swim together out in the prettiest water you ever did see, and we were skinny-dipping because neither of us had thought about what we might be doing with our days down on the coast. I hunted up some grub early the first morning in the way of turtle eggs. That afternoon we roasted a rabbit over an open flame on the beachhead.

Mostly we played like two juvenile children who couldn't figure out what our relationship was exactly, but it was time well spent, because it set the tone of our relationship for years to come. I never knew what to expect when I walked in the door them first few years, and that was an aspect of marriage I hadn't thought about. It was a good thing to be married to a woman like Abigail. If we weren't chasing each other around the yard, we were chasing each other around the bed. Of course, I always caught her, but she didn't always catch me.

Cajun couldn't resist jumping into our festivities from time to time, and he was welcome. But back to my immediate story, we were on the beach, what little there was of it. We lay out on the sand completely naked with no one to bother us but nature herself.

After five days at our little getaway we came to the conclusion we needed to be getting home. We popped the cork on our last bottle of wine from the Stone Hill Winery and it was Pink Catawba. It was a very good glass of wine, so we took one last look at our honeymoon spot then we stepped into the barouche to start home.

I guided Penny back the way we came or at least I thought I did. As it turned out, I discovered I should not try to drive a barouche when physically impaired. I got that buggy hung up so often I was beginning to think we were meant to stay on the beach. I lost count of the times we had to debark and lift it over a stump because of my driving skills or lack thereof.

We stopped about noon that first day and rested. I was tired, I had a headache from the wine and I was not in any shape to be driving. I learned that wine has a kick-back; it doesn't leave you like you think it does. It was going to be with me for a few days.

I told Abigail what I thought and she said, "I guess we're not meant to drink so much. I think it will be all right if we only drink it once in a while."

I didn't argue with her, but we spent the night right there because suddenly I knew what the term hangover meant. The following morning we made it to the bridge and once again I walked in front of the horse, because I didn't trust it one little bit. Not after all the work I already had to do just to keep our barouche rolling. I started out across the bridge one step at a time and suddenly Abigail stopped me.

"What are you doing?"

"I'm taking us across the bridge."

"No, I mean what are you thinking in your head?"

"I'm thinking we ain't ever going to make it without these boards giving out."

"Exactly my point. You're going to get exactly what you expect, don't you know that?"

"What?" I said while staring at her.

I studied her for a moment and with sober intent my wife stared back at me. She hopped down and walked up to me and took Penny by the harness. "I'll lead her across, because I believe we can make it just fine," she said and started walking.

Well, I didn't argue with her, because I still wasn't sure I understood what she meant when she said I was going to get what I expected. I pondered on certain aspects of what she was trying to get me to understand as we walked ahead of the horse and buggy.

"Are you saying, whatever I expect from life, that's what I'll get?"

"That is exactly what I'm saying. Le Roy, you're a good man, but you have a powerful lot of catch up learning to do where personal responsibility is concerned. You get what you ask for. Now, I don't know if you realize it or not, but I'm here because you asked for me a long, long time ago. I made myself wait for you because of something you told me one day ten years ago when we were walking home from school."

Well, I didn't have a clue what she was talking about as we walked across that black water bridge, but I was certain she was about to remind me, and in my little mind when she reminded me I realized she knew exactly what she was talking about.

"You told me if you ever got married, it would be to a girl like me."

I remembered now that she reminded me, but I would never have thought about it if she hadn't. She was right. I had told her that, and I remembered the day. She had been bugging me to carry her books for her and I wouldn't stoop to such a thing. She wanted a kiss from me, and I refused that. She was half my age back then.

When we parted company on the road she put the question to me.

"James Le Roy, will a girl like me ever have a chance with a boy like you?" That was when I told her if I ever got married it would be to a girl like her. I told her that because I wanted her to quit bugging me about such things and it worked, because she never said another word, but now I understood the full breadth of my statement. Oh, the power of the spoken word!

As we reached the end of the dilapidated structure, I turned to her and took her in my arms. "You do realize you had to grow up first."

"I know that, but look at all of the time we missed."

"Well, if you will let me beg-my-pardon, I plan on making up for lost time."

I kissed her then and we got back in the barouche and headed for home. It was late in the evening when we pulled into the yard. We hadn't seen hide or hair of Cajun all day, but we knew he'd be around. I thought it would be best if he would stay away for a few extra days, but I had no way of knowing whether or not he would.

Darnell came out of the house to greet us and carried a big grin on his face.

"What are you smiling about?" I asked while stepping down.

"We're just happy to see you folks home," Darnell said. "It was getting mighty lonesome around here without you two."

"Well, we're home now."

"I can see that. Chin Lee has been finding traps in the woods, traps set to catch a cat."

I looked at my wife and she said, "Don't worry, he won't step in one."

"How can you be so sure?" I asked.

"I have my ways," was all she said.

I watched her as she carried her things into the house and suddenly I remembered the fact she took her Voodoo dolls with her, and at times she did things with them, usually while I was distracted building a fire or some other chore.

Just how much did she depend on Voodoo anyway? Was she able to control Cajun with it? If so, what about me? Could she control me? Swiftly a sinking feeling came over me. I understood with no illusions I had a wife who could conjure any situation she wanted in life. If you have never experienced the feeling of helplessness, I did at that moment. If I ever made her mad, I was in trouble!

Chapter 23

Not much happened since we had left, but Chin managed to go over toward Belle Grove and scare those soldiers a few times. Otherwise, nothing of any consequence took place. I put the horse away in the barn and spoke with Butch for a few minutes. He was trying to urge me to kiss and tell, but I wasn't in the mood for telling. I told him he would have to marry his own girl to find out what happened.

"I don't have a girl," he complained.

"One of these days, if the good Lord's willing you will have one all your own. You've got the biggest house in Louisiana, seventy four rooms, slave quarters outside and a guest house for the doctor. You don't have a chance of escaping marriage with a place like that," I offered in rebuttal.

"When you say it like that, you scare me," Butch said.

"It's meant to scare you. I can't explain it, but I can tell you this much, when a girl sets her cap for you, it's all over but the singing unless you're a good runner and I wasn't."

"It can't be as bad as all that."

"You're right, Butch. But there are some things that should stay between a husband and a wife, a secret if you will."

"So it's secret as all that is it?"

"I'll tell you this," I said, "a man who doesn't keep certain secrets with his wife is a low down dirty troublemaker. I don't plan on becoming one of them."

"It's that important, huh?"

"It's that important."

"All right, I'll leave you alone about it," Butch promised.

"Good, we'll both live longer."

I finished putting the barouche away with the help of my friend and neighbor. Darnell and Chin went to the house to clear their stuff out of the living room. As I stepped out of the barn the sun was setting and we were greeted by five of the Yankee soldiers from Belle Grove Plantation, the ones who were occupying the home which belonged to Butch.

"You fellows look lost," Butch said.

"We're not lost, we came to deliver this," one of them said, and he handed me a piece of paper.

"What is this?" I asked.

"It's an eviction order from Colonel Green. You have ten days to get off the place or we'll move you off." He reached into his pocket and withdrew another one. "And this one is for you," he told Butch as he shoved the document into my friend's hand.

"You must have been promoted in Corporal Cook's place," I said as I eyed the man on horseback.

"I was. Now if you'll excuse us, we have to be getting back."

"Watch out for that cat what killed Corporal Cook, he's still on the loose," I told them, "and it's coming onto dark."

There was a sudden change in the look on their faces and the new corporal sank spur. He lit out of our yard like his tail was on fire, his army of privates clinging to his heels.

"Must have been something you said," Butch smiled. "Those fellows weren't very neighborly."

"No they weren't," I said looking at the notice in my hand. "Now we have a decision to make. Fight and stay put or pack up and go."

"Well, I plan to fight. They'll not steal Belle Grove Plantation this easy," Butch argued.

"Butch Abernathy, there's one thing you need to get through that thick skull of yours. You can't regulate the power of God. In other words, you can't regulate providence," I told him. "You can fight it if you want, but if I was you I'd take a look at the hand you're holding and cash in the chips while you still have some."

"You're telling me you'll not stay and fight?"

"There's been enough killing. I figure we can start over elsewhere, long as we're still breathing."

"We're going to end up in a sad state of affairs," Butch said.

I was thinking about the beach home where we'd just spent the last week. I could build a new home down that way. I know Butch wasn't about to side me in such matters, he was set to make a fight of things right where he stood.

"Fighting isn't the only option," I cautioned.

"It is if we're going to live as men."

I heard Cajun growl in the swamp somewhere between us and Belle Grove Plantation and I smiled at Butch. "That cat has got the best timing of any animal I ever did know of."

We both turned and headed for the house. My mind wasn't made up yet, but I sure didn't feel like fighting another war. All indications were I was going to have to fight, this time in my own yard on my own turf. I saw enough killing on the Mississippi to last me a lifetime, but what I didn't understand was the fact there are some things a man can't dodge. If he does, it only comes back to haunt him at a later date. I know this now, but back then I didn't.

We entered the house as Darnell and Chin were leaving. I looked over at Abigail and she had a strange look on her face. I didn't ask what for, I just sat down at the table and started reading the notice. It was direct and to the point, but was it legal? I didn't have any idea myself so I showed it to my wife.

"They can't do that," she yelled.

"They seem to think they can."

"I won't allow it. This is my home, our home. This is where we're going to build our family."

"We're going to have to go see someone who knows the law. I don't know if there's a lawyer left in this part of the country."

"Judge Rost at the Destreham Plantation of New Orleans. He'll know if it's legal or not. The Destrehan family negotiated the Louisiana Purchase."

"Then we head for New Orleans in the morning. We'd better get some rest," I added.

"I'm riding with you," Butch said.

"There is one other a little closer, but if we guess wrong there won't be time to ride to the next one. Zachary Taylor outside of Baton Rouge is also a legal mind, but Judge Rost will know about previous claims, current laws and things like that where land is concerned. He's our best chance to get this resolved in our favor."

"All right, we head for New Orleans at sunup. Butch, see if Darnell and Chin will stay behind and keep an eye on the place."

"They will, I'll see to it," he said as he stepped out the door. "They sure as dickens don't have any other plans."

I turned to my wife and spoke. "I'm going to need Regret on this trip. We'll leave the barouche with your mother. Do you have access to a horse or other mount?" I asked not thinking.

"I can ride Penny. She doesn't just haul that barouche around," she chided.

"That's a long time for your mother to be without a way to town."

"James Le Roy, this is Louisiana, not New York. Southern folks know and check on their neighbors. She won't go two days without a visit from somebody."

"Are you sure?"

"I've been living here all my life. I think I know my own mother's habits. I also know the habits of our neighbors."

"All right, we'll ride first thing in the morning. We'll leave from your mother's house."

We went through our things then, never more eager than to already be on the road. About midnight we hit the sack and tried to get some sleep. I had no trouble, but my wife didn't go to sleep right away. It was a sad state of affairs, but it couldn't be helped.

We had one hundred miles or more to cover and it wouldn't be easy, not with reconstruction underway. I knew we would get wet any way we rode, there was so much swamp between here and there, but I'd been to New Orleans a few times as a kid and if you navigated just right, you would miss the bulk of the swamp. There was a road which dipped in and out of the swamp if what I remembered of it was any good this many years after the fact. I just hadn't seen that particular trail in a long time.

Chapter 24

We were up before sunrise because Abigail hadn't slept a lick. She awoke me and I went to the barn to hook up the barouche. While in the barn I woke Butch and he got ready. Suddenly, I thought it was nice to have him as somewhat of a friend and neighbor rather than my enemy.

Once Penny was harnessed to the barouche I walked her outside and looked around in the fog. It was a thick heavy fog and would not clear off early. I helped Abigail load a few things she wanted her mother to care for in our absence and we were off into the darkness.

Once at her mother's house I was pointed to the barn, unhooked the barouche and saddled the mare for my wife. Penny was a good horse, and I learned quickly even better when she was being ridden with a saddle. It pained me that we had to ride three miles in the wrong direction in order to get ready, but it had to be done.

We took off then with fog hanging thick and heavy in the early morning hours, two stout horses and an old Missouri mule, two men and a girl barely seventeen. We galloped back to the house and rode right on by. We waved at Darnell and Chin as we went through, but we never slowed our pace. We barely saw them in the fog.

At noon we were nearing St. James and Abigail insisted we stop to give the animals a breather. She said there was an old school mate who married a land owner down this way, but I couldn't remember her no matter how much Abigail and Butch tried to explain her to me. It was when I saw her standing on the front porch of her home that I remembered the girl. She too had grown up.

She married a fellow named Lafitte, Conrad Lafitte. He was the grandson to the pirate who used to have his way with shipments of cargo coming in and out of New Orleans. He survived the war, but now limped as his left leg had been wounded and he never quite recovered. He made his living as a gunsmith, buying repairing and selling all types of guns, at least this is what I thought on meeting him. He also liked to make handcrafted swords. The hand-held weapons he made were one-of-a kind pieces of art. I never saw the like, but I knew I wanted one someday.

"Come on in, Abigail, we'll fetch some lunch for the men," Lizzie told my wife.

The two girls disappeared into the house leaving Butch and I to introduce ourselves to Mr. Lafitte. He didn't move at first, just stared as if he didn't trust us. Slowly he began to grumble under his breath and I felt unwelcome. With no warning he stated clearly and plain, "Yankee's ain't welcome in these parts."

I looked to my right and stared at Butch knowing full well I couldn't open my mouth without feeling as if I were lying to the man.

"That's good, because we're southern raised and we're being evicted by those Yankee's. That's why we're riding to New Orleans," my partner explained.

"They can't do that," Lafitte growled.

"That's what you say, but they are doing it," Butch said.

"I'm Conrad Lafitte," he introduced himself. "Get down and welcome. Tell be about this land grab."

We stepped down from our horses then up onto the porch to join the man. Now I was intimidated, and there wasn't much in this life that intimidated me anymore. I lost both of my parents at a young age, and now at a young age I was without the folks who raised me. I knew if I lost Abigail I wouldn't give a hoot about nothing for the rest of my life, but Conrad Lafitte was a man to be afraid of.

He wore a colorful shirt with a wide three inch cartridge belt wrapped around his belly. In his belt was a pistol, a knife and a sword. He was a man who went armed. He wore a nine inch beard which hid the lower part of his face. I learned several days later it was to cover a scar from a fight when he was much younger. By my estimation he was an old man now, but he was only forty four. His boots were a strange thing to me because I never saw a boot that folded down at the top in the shape of a cuff. He was not a heavyset man although at first glance you'd think it. There was a strength about him which did not go unnoticed. Like I said, he walked with a limp and used a cane, but that was a deceiving thing I later learned.

"Never show all your cards," he stated.

We sat down on the front porch at his beckoning, for we were afraid to assume anything, especially his hospitality. If I wasn't so certain he would have been offended, I would have gotten back on my mule and rode away. How in the world Lizzie Seymour ever met and married such a man was beyond anything I could fathom. She was half his age. Of course I had seen such before, but she wasn't going to build much of a family and if she did, she would be left to raise them on her own sooner or later.

"Let me see one of those eviction orders."

I reached into my pocket and produced mine, handing it over. He studied it for a long moment and then said, "Why they're crazy. Them colored's won't have a clue how to hold on to the land if they are given it."

I hadn't taken the time to read mine, but I was going to get an education. "What colored's?" I asked.

"They plan to give forty acres of plow-share to anyone who claims to have been a slave under southern rule. That's what they intend to do with your land. They say you haven't paid your taxes in seven years, the last year being 1860. They're taking your land for back taxes."

I sat there with my jaw agape. I didn't understand all of this, but we had been fighting a war up until last year.

"Mister Whipple died in the spring of 1860. His wife must not have been able to pay her taxes during the war."

"Well, there you have it my boy, pay your taxes and you're in the clear."

"Does it say how much they are?"

"One hundred and fifty-seven dollars including penalties."

"What penalties?"

"That's the way Yankee's like to wipe folks out. I hate 'em!"

"What do they mean by penalties?" I repeated.

"Cause you didn't pay your taxes on time they're sticking you up."

Well, the man did have a unique way of presenting the facts. I had to admit, my plight suddenly didn't seem as bad as I thought. I looked over at Butch and he was reading his own notice.

"Mine says the same thing, only I have to pay seventeen hundred thirty-five dollars and eighty-five cents. Good Lord Almighty, where do they expect me to come up with that kind of money? Half the money in circulation right now is counterfeit," he exclaimed.

"Gold is better, if you know where to find it," Conrad winked.

"And where does a man find gold in Louisiana?"

"My grandfather was the pirate Jean Lafitte. I have gold, buried treasure me lad. I only have one problem, I can't dive anymore. I would require your services if we're to recover the treasure as it rests on the bottom of the sea. I know where it is. You are young and capable."

"How are we supposed to do that? We don't have a boat. I can swim, but you're talking about straight down. We have to swim straight down to it, then what, we'll be out of breath on the bottom of the ocean floor," I rested my case.

"You're a Doubting Thomas I see. I have a plan, and the shipwreck is in shallow water just off the shoreline. It will be an easy recovery, if I can keep the bloody mongrels what infest the bay from swiping it once we bring her aboard."

"What bloody mongrels?" I wanted to know.

"Pirates my boy, there be pirate ships in the sea."

"Do you have a boat?" I asked.

"Do I have a boat? You ask the grandson of Jean Lafitte if he has a boat?" The man started laughing as if he were going to bust a gut. He continued to laugh, right in our faces. Finally the girls stepped out onto the front porch with lunch and Lizzie asked her husband what was so funny.

"They want to know if I have a boat," he shouted pointing at us between laughs.

"He has an entire fleet of boats," Lizzie answered, and suddenly I understood why she married the man. He was her protector, her knight in shining armor. He was her defender and bread winner for the family, although there were no little ones running around yet. The man would be able to do anything he wanted just by intimidation, but he had resources we didn't have.

Chapter 25

The five of us rode to New Orleans where Lafitte's fleet was in the harbor working here and there to make improvements on the town waterfront. He commandeered one of the craft and we set sail early the following morning headed south toward Barataria Bay. The ship was called the *Regiment* and we listened like little children to the man as he told us of this ship or that marooned in the waterway as we passed by. He was able to name them all, because his grandfather Jean Lafitte had sank them.

"The boat we're after is off Grand Terre Island farther south. If we don't get the gold now, the hurricanes that blow through here will have the ship so far from where it originally sank we'll never find it," he said and then barked more orders to his shipmates. He was the captain of his ship when aboard. The regular captain yielded to him and Conrad had his hands on the ship's wheel. No longer was he a cripple when aboard a seafaring vessel, he was captain, and he was in charge. It was amazing to hear and witness the crew working like a team of veterans who knew the orders before they were even barked.

Grand Island was a long piece of sand sticking out of the water as if blocking the entrance to the bay. It didn't quite do the job though and both ends were open around her. We took to the east end of the island to come around and then Conrad took her out into the gulf a ways. He brought her around one hundred and eighty degrees and sailed strait north for Grand Terre Island. He ordered the mast brought down and coasted her to a point about two hundred yards shy of the beachhead.

"Drop anchor," he yelled and the anchor was cut loose. It hit the water and a moment later when it hit bottom the first mate set the lever. The boat brought up hard fore and started to swing to the port side, then without warning settled in the water right where she was.

"It's a Spanish Galleon I look for," he said and he stretched out his spyglass for a look see. I watched as he seemed to set his mark on the island, then he dropped the glass and said, "There, in the water just off the bow, you'll find the ship lying on the bottom. There is a chest of gold in her cargo hold. If you don't delay, we can set sail for home by nightfall."

I looked over at my friend and swallowed hard. I could swim, but I didn't know if I could hold my breath long enough to reach bottom. Butch was looking a little pale himself, so we stared at one another for a minute before we were interrupted.

"Are you young'uns going to go after the gold or do I have to plug you with my pistol?" To validate his statement he pulled his pistol from his cartridge belt and pointed the muzzle straight at yours truly. Lizzie gasped and so did Abigail, but that old hoot owl couldn't hold his composure any longer and started laughing at us like he'd just witnessed the funniest episode of his entire life.

He shoved his gun back in his belt in between laughs, then ordered certain men to turn to. I thought I was about to die aboard ship and he was playing games with us. I was fixing to try my fast draw, because the last thing I wanted was a ball of lead in my gut, but he already had his gun out so I had hesitated. This alone averted tragedy because I thought the man was serious and I was fixing to shoot him full of holes.

Relieved from duty I took a look around at our surroundings to see the beautiful blue water, the green trees growing on the island, the birds in the air and on the beach, and I saw a couple of dolphins swimming by the boat. It was heaven on earth, as long as I didn't have to dive.

Then I looked down and saw the shadow in the water below us. There, like a ghost, a ship from long ago lay directly below the *Regiment*. The name of the boat below us turned out to be the *Santa Margarita*. She had sailed in here trying to get a shipment of supplies into the docks in New Orleans during the Civil War and was blown apart by cannonade from Yankee ironclads. She never made her delivery of war supplies, and she never offered up her treasure chest.

The first man dove off the bow and swam straight down. I watched in amazement as he spent nearly three minutes under water. Everyone on board waited for him to surface, before the next man dove. When he popped up out of the water he yelled at the captain, "The chest is there, locked like she should be."

"Can we bring her up?"

"If you drop a line, I'll get it around the belly," the man yelled.

"Drop the line," Lafitte ordered.

Three men set about dropping the line, which to me, was a rope. I marveled at their ability to work together and as they continued to prep for the drop of the line, the man from the water appeared on deck. He took the line into his teeth, surveyed the length of rope pulled and dove once again headlong into the water. The rope unfolded as if it were a ballerina in a choreographed dance. The precision with which the men worked was long practiced.

The four of us not involved in actually doing anything looked on in awe. The girls had never seen the like, although I had witnessed some of the art form when stationed on the *Carondelet*. I had to admit though, those navy boys had a lot to learn, but then they were just beginning to get their noses wet. It was clear Conrad Lafitte had spent the majority of his life at sea. He was not just the captain of a ship, but a captain of captain's.

I became a little jealous of the fact a woman could marry a man and suddenly she was wealthy, yet a man couldn't do this in reverse. For instance I would have never been able to get a rich woman to take a second look at me, but Abigail could have found someone with money like Lizzie and I would have been left out in the cold.

I checked my negative self-talk right then. Suddenly I realized what I was doing. I was convincing myself that I wasn't good enough for the likes of Abigail. That was not true and I would not let it become true. I was a better man than my original estimation, and besides, Abigail said you get exactly what you expect. I had no reason to doubt her on such important matters, especially when they made so much sense.

Was it possible for a man to change his life by changing his expectations? For instance, could I change my outcome in life by expecting better than what I had experienced so far? It was worth a try, but how was a man supposed to do such a thing, especially one who didn't know any more than I did? I had no experience which would allow me to do such a thing easily.

I watched as the diver popped up out of the water again and gave a yell, "Bring her up!"

He'd done it. How? It dawned on me then a man couldn't operate outside of what he believed of himself. You couldn't be any more than you thought you could be. You couldn't act outside of the picture you painted in your mind, not for very long you couldn't. I just witnessed another man do something I didn't believe myself capable of. He didn't possess any more skills than me, yet he latched onto the chest full of gold and tied a rope around it in some very deep water. Was it because he believed he could and I didn't?

Men pulled on the rope as Captain Lafitte continued to bark orders, "Pull, set, pull," and the chest started to rise. If the chest was loaded with gold as he suspected, it would be much heavier once it cleared the water.

"Lower the skiff," Lafitte yelled at a couple of his other men.

The skiff started downward yet I did not understand its meaning. Did the man intend to go out in the skiff? What for? I could not deduct any reasonable explanation. Suddenly the boat splashed down into the water and the captain ordered his men down the rope ladder on the side of the ship.

Once in the boat they rowed to the rope where the chest was coming to the surface. They held still waiting for the treasure. When it cleared water the men really began to grunt. I motioned to Butch and we grabbed onto the line to help out. The chest was at the surface, but we had to get it up out of the water then onto the ship.

We tugged and pulled when suddenly Lafitte yelled, "Hold it. Don't let it drop an inch."

We stopped like all of the other men on the rope, but I had no clue why. Then he ordered us to let it down easy. We did as he said and the rope relaxed.

"All right men, get her open," he shouted over the side of the boat. I realized then the men in the skiff had the chest so I ran to look over the side.

"There we be, sonny boy, enough gold to beat those Yank's all the way back to Washington."

"You've done this before," I accused.

"And I'll do it again, sonny. If you're a friend of Lizzie, you're friend of mine," he said. "That goes for all of you," he added swinging his cane in a wide arch. It was not by accident I realized his cane was a weapon. Any man who could wield a sword like he was able to do was a man who could handle a cane as well. I noted this fact and came to the conclusion that anyone who attacked Conrad Lafitte would surely be dispensed in rather unique fashion. The man was a pirate, a chip off the old block. I wondered then just what kind of man his grandfather Jean must have been.

I learned firsthand that evening as we sat around the captain's table on the *Regiment* eating supper. Gold coin was lying across the table in front of us, from one end to the other. Lafitte ordered the coin spread so we might count it. I didn't know how much we had because I didn't know a dollar from twenty and all of these coins were Spanish minted. I could, however, count them out, and that's what we did.

According to Lafitte's tally, there was just over five hundred and fifty thousand in gold and one hundred twenty thousand in silver. It sat on the table stacked in front of us like the treasure it represented. This money was going to change people's lives. It was going to save our places from the Federal Government, but why should we get any of it? This was all Lafitte's doing.

Conrad Lafitte was a sight to see then. He was a man of action, a man of legend just like his grandfather, but instead of robbing people, he was acting like a saint. He didn't want anything from us.

"There's more where that come from, but only I know the location," he shouted as he hoisted his chalet of wine. We were huddled around the table and he had our attention, so it was he began to tell us of his grandfather.

"No greater pirate than Jean Lafitte ever lived. He was known from the Isle of Falkland to the Spanish Main.

He smuggled more goods around the globe than any man before or since, and he was my grandfather.

"Governor William Claiborne of Louisiana once offered a price of five hundred dollars for Lafitte's capture. My grandfather, not being one to be outdone immediately offered fifteen hundred dollars for the governor's head. All efforts by the United States to apprehend and prosecute my grandfather as a pirate failed, which leaves me in a unique position because I know where all of his treasure is resting, whether at the bottom of the ocean or under a palm tree on a sandy beach.

"My father died young, God rest his soul, which is why Jean left all of this knowledge to me. He's retired long since, but the old man still breathes," he cautioned us with his evil eye. "He is young at heart, a true sea captain and he's happy."

"Jean Lafitte is still alive?" I couldn't believe what I was hearing.

"That he is, sonny that he is. He's still a resident of New Orleans, although his identity is kept a secret on account he doesn't want to be bothered. He will entertain me upon my visits though."

"How old is he?" Butch wanted to know.

"Ah, that's something he does not talk about, but I know this, he is past eighty. He would be about eighty seven or so, if what I know about my grandfather is correct, and he has enjoyed his life at all stages, something I should like to duplicate. He doesn't let his age bother him, and he looks to spend every day writing in a journal. I have those journals, and only I have the means to uncover the gold he eludes' to in them."

"That's fascinating," I said, "but I don't understand. The gold belongs to you and your grandfather. How is that going to help us?"

"Young Le Roy, you present a worthy cause. You want to save your home. I, on the other hand, have more money than I could possibly spend in two lifetimes. I don't have many friends, either I am too gruff and mean to people, or my size scares the daylights out of them. Folks don't friend me easily. I'm not getting any younger, and you present a certain satisfaction for me if you will allow me to help you in your plight. I'm not trying to buy your friendship, but I would like to have it, for Lizzie's sake," he said toasting his wife.

I sat there staring at the man as if I hadn't seen him before. The situation was nothing like I expected. This was the same man who scared me just to look at him. I thought he was going to offer us a way to earn the money, a loan and some way to pay it back, but the man seemed set on giving us what we needed. I honestly didn't know what to say or where to begin. He took mercy on us then and told us some more stories about his grandfather.

"In 1814 the British were at war with the United States. They offered my grandfather thirty thousand dollars, a king's ransom at that time, a pardon and a captaincy in the Royal Fleet if he would aid them in attacking New Orleans. This he would not do. He refused the offer, told the United States government of the British plans and offered the aid of his men in order to help fight the British at the battle of New Orleans. He fought under General Andrew Jackson, and consequently received a pardon from President James Madison for his efforts. Upon receiving his pardon he swore off pirating and settled down with my grandmother a very wealthy man."

I felt as if I were sitting amongst royalty myself. If Conrad Lafitte was anything like his granddad, the man had to be special. We ate our supper then and talked the evening away. We talked of pirates, ghost ships and treasures as the gaslight burned dim.

Chapter 26

The following morning our boat was slicing through the darkness before sunup. Having felt its movement I knew we were underway and went topside to stand beside the man I could not put my finger on.

He glanced at me and then said, "Take the wheel young man. Every man should know the feel of a ship's wheel in his hand."

I took it and held on. It was pulling me over and suddenly Lafitte put his hand on the wheel to steady it. "You weren't ready, now take it again and this time set your feet so you can hold onto it."

I did as he said. I set my feet but the wheel still wanted to lift me from the deck. I suddenly had new respect for all ship captains. If someone had to hang onto such a wheel at all times, it was no wonder a ship captain's arms got so big.

"Keep the boat pointed in the same direction up river, and I'll be back in a few minutes," he said.

I started to object, because I couldn't see anything, fog was everywhere. But, I didn't let go of the wheel either. I kept the boat pointed in the same direction. We were moving slowly, so if I was lucky I wouldn't hit anything. I was scared to death at that point. What if I did hit something? What would Captain Lafitte do to me?

It seemed like forever, but I'm certain it was only a couple of minutes when Lafitte returned to the wheel. "You did fine, Le Roy, you did fine," he said and took the wheel from me.

I breathed a sigh of relief and thanked my lucky stars I hadn't run aground. We were sailing blind as a bat. You couldn't see anything but fog, then I listened; Captain Lafitte was sailing by sound. There was an echo in the fog which bounced off the nearby shores and he could tell where he was in the river by making certain sounds.

I marveled at his skill and thought to myself, no wonder captains were respected with such high esteem. I learned things I never knew.

We were docking the boat in New Orleans before the sun burned through the fog. We went immediately to the stable to retrieve our horses and then procured a wagon for the gold. We rode from the waterfront straight downtown to the Old Dix bank. The Old Dix name was still on the front of the building, but above the door it said Bank of New Orleans. I didn't know it then, but that bank was the reason folks called the old south Dixie.

Lafitte could see my concern and comforted me. "The war changed a lot of things in the south, but money is still money. Gold is the best money of all. This is where we get the ball rolling."

Stepping down from our horses we men walked over to the bank door and Lafitte entered with me on his heels. Butch stayed with the wagon to keep an eye on things out front.

"How can we help you today, Mr. Lafitte?" the teller asked through his iron bar countertop.

"I have a deposit to make, and we shall be opening two additional accounts today."

"Is this deposit similar to the last one," the teller asked.

"Very similar," Lafitte confirmed.

Closing his station the teller came out of his booth and looked at us. He then walked over and took a peek out the front window.

"Lord of mercy, I'd better get some help," the man said and he was off to another room. Presently he returned with three other men and they all went out the front door to retrieve the chest sitting in the middle of our wagon. They were not able to lift it, so they were back inside in short order to get some money bags. Once outside again I watched as they began to fill their bags with treasure from the chest.

It took several hours for them to account for the money, and while they were doing so Lafitte gave us a tour of the town. I wondered if he could really trust the bank man, but Conrad set me at ease.

"Those boys know full well that I have already counted what's there, it will be right," he said and kept going.

We were riding down Canal Street headed south when he stopped his horse and got down. "If you care to meet Old Pappy hop down. I need to say hi while I'm in town."

"Old Pappy?" I said.

"Grandpa. He actually likes meeting people," Lafitte explained.

The building was a two story brick affair with an iron gate with an iron rail balcony upstairs. I saw someone part the curtain in one of the upper rooms while we entered through the gate and walked up the brick sidewalk to a front porch. The porch contained seven steps, about ten feet wide. At the top there was a front door made of solid wood with brass hardware. I later learned it was not brass at all, but gold. There was one window high up which was oval shaped. On the other side of it was a curtain with tiny ships on it.

Lafitte rang the doorbell, and it was a doorbell, one which hung beside the front door. It sounded much like the dinner bell which was aboard ship, the one on the captain's table. A moment later a servant opened the door and took us all in. The five of us were a strange mix, when you thought about it. The younger Lafitte was old enough to be the father of everyone he was traveling with, yet he was married to one of the girls, I to the other.

The servant was a short man of maybe five four and walked with caution at each step. His suit was that of a butler. He led us down the long hallway to a room in the back of the house. He ushered us in and closed the door behind him.

"Conrad, my boy, what brings you to New Orleans?"

I knew the old fellow in the wheelchair must be Jean Lafitte, the feared pirate, but he was old and frail now. His face lit up at the sight of his grandson, and he held a smile on it for the entire time we were present to interrupt his day.

"Have a seat my boy, have a seat."

"I will, Pappy, but first I must introduce everyone. This is Le Roy Ware and his wife Abigail," he said pointing to us. "And this fellow is Butch Abernathy." He paused for a moment and then said, "This is my wife Lizzie," and he ushered her forward.

"She's been my wife almost a year now," he added.

The old fellow studied Lizzie as if there were no one else in the room. His eyes became dark and foreboding as his forehead wrinkled in disapproval.

"You bear the name Lafitte," he challenged.

"I do," Elizabeth confirmed, though she was shaking where she stood. I could see she was scared and ready to run.

"So, you're the one who will inherit the Lafitte fortune," he accused her.

He never took his eyes off the girl. It was as if he had complete control of everyone in the room. No one moved for fear of retribution. Even Conrad was at his grandfather's mercy as we waited for the pin to drop. Of course there was no pin, just dead silence.

The old sailor looked on with piercing eyes, then leaned back in his chair and said, "You done good my boy, you done good," he smiled.

Suddenly everyone in the room relaxed except for Elizabeth. She was still scared half to death. Conrad sat down, so did we all, but Lizzie was left standing, still trying to figure out what just transpired.

"Sit down honey, it's all right," Conrad instructed.

"It's not all right. You almost gave me a heart attack."

Jean Lafitte let out a hardy laugh and said, "Welcome to the family. Elizabeth. That grandson of mine is spoiled rotten. I hope you can get the better of him, I sure wasn't able to."

"Is it like this all the time?" she asked incredulously.

"Yes it is. I wouldn't live life any other way. It would be quite a bore," the old pirate said.

Conrad was smiling so we all smiled at that point for the ruse was an effective one. Elizabeth sat down and I could see her visibly taking notes in her mind. She was jotting things down as the two men spoke of the goings on around New Orleans and farther west. The wheels in Elizabeth's head were marking every spot she might ambush her husband or even Jean Lafitte himself. I knew in my heart she was about to get even with them, the sun would not set without her doing so.

Chapter 27

About an hour into their critique of the situation in Louisiana and nearby states the butler interrupted and said lunch was served. I had been smelling food, but I was not sure where the aroma was coming from. He entered the room just in time, because the smell was making me hungrier than I could bear.

The butler escorted everyone to the dining room. We sat down and the old man continued to talk. This was perplexing to me, because I didn't see any food. Presently, a beautiful lady in a long black gown entered the room and walked to the far end of the table. She bent low and kissed Conrad on the cheek then sat down. The butler pulled her chair for her and I knew this had to be Mrs. Jean Lafitte. She was as beautiful as any lady twenty years her junior. I marveled at the grace with which a pirate's wife would walk, how she sat straight, and her manner.

"I don't think you've ever done that before," he said.

"My dear Conrad, it is so nice to see you and you brought guests."

"Grandmother, this is my wife, Elizabeth," Conrad offered.

"You're married? This is how you introduce me to your wife? I should be surprised, but I am not. Good manners," she chided, "is one thing I never was able to teach you."

"My dear, how old are you," the lady inquired.

"I was nineteen last month," Elizabeth said.

"Well, I am surprised. Conrad, you're going to have to let me spend some time with her."

"I agree, Grandmother, but now is not the time. We're on urgent business and it cannot wait."

"Very well, we will visit later young lady. Who are the others," she inquired of her grandson.

"This is Butch Abernathy. He owns Belle Grove Plantation and these are his neighbors, Le Roy Ware and his wife, Abigail."

"And what is this urgent business if I may ask?"

"Some Yankee carpetbaggers from the north are trying to steal their land, we intend to put a stop to it," Conrad advised her.

"Well, that is urgent business. I will not discuss such matters at the dinner table. Only after we're finished eating will we talk about such things," she said.

The conversation around the table continued while I dropped off into a thought stream of my own. A young colored lady entered the room at that point carrying a big covered tray. It was made of silver. It was then I noticed the plates and the silverware placed on the table. I never saw such fancy dishes. They were full of designs with flowers and petals. Taking a closer look I began to see a few birds, blue birds, red birds and yellow canary birds all hand painted into every dish and plate.

Where did a man buy such fare? I would never own the like myself; at least I didn't believe such at the time.

That's the thing about being young; you never know what lies ahead in the future. A man can live his entire life in poverty and suddenly become famous, living in the rich lap of luxury. That's why I never understood people who commit suicide. Put politely, it is the most selfish act on planet earth. When a boy or girl does such a thing, they are engaged in being selfish, thinking of no one but themselves. A foolish tragedy to be sure, but a man doesn't have any idea where he will end up, so to kill one's self made no sense to me. I could never imagine a situation where I would consider doing such a thing.

I looked at my wife and smiled as the paid servant served us. Two years ago the young lady would have been a slave, but now she was free. The hired cook.

"Le Roy, Mrs. Lafitte is talking to you," my wife interrupted my thoughts.

"Ma'am," I said, not having a clue what she had just asked me.

"How do you fit into all of this?"

"Abigail and I are Butch's neighbors and the Yankee's are trying to take our land as well."

"I see. We'll discuss that later, for now I want to know about you and your wife. You are newlyweds you said? What are your plans for the future? Have you made any yet?"

"Not really. We want to raise a family, I know that, but otherwise we haven't had a chance to talk too much about it."

"Big family or little," she wanted to know.

"I don't know, I..."

"Big. I think a big one. Otherwise why bother," Abigail interrupted. She was smiling at me as she said it.

"We wanted a big family, but after Conrad's father I wasn't able to bear any more children. I will pray you do better."

Pray? The wife of the most notorious pirate in a lifetime and she is given to prayer? Mentally I was dislodged from my comfortable surroundings. I sat mesmerized looking on at her, but I could no longer understand who she might be. She was married to the biggest pirate to ever land in this country and she was mentioning prayer. I couldn't grasp this. I struggled to come to grip with my feelings, but my attempt was fleeting. I looked to Lizzie and she calmed me with her ever-present smile.

"May I ask Lady Lafitte, where you attend church?" My wife was curious.

"St. Louis Cathedral across from the square, why?"

"I was only curious in that I might attend someday as your guest," my wife answered.

"That would be a wonderful idea. A lady can never have enough prayer partners."

I noticed Old Lafitte was beginning to squirm in his wheelchair so I leaned forward and asked him to please pass me a biscuit as we at least had that much on the table. I received it post-haste and changed the subject.

"We have a cat named Cajun, and he lives nearby in the swamp."

"You'll lose him one day," the elder Lafitte assured me. "The gators will get him."

"Not Cajun, he's a full grown catamount," I answered.

I suddenly had everyone's attention. "Why don't you tell them about our cat honey, you're more familiar with him than I am. I've been gone for several years, but you have been right here, all along."

I felt her kick me under the table, but she took the lead and began to tell them about our cat. "Cajun isn't your normal cat. He protects us. He's killed two of the Yankee soldiers in recent weeks and he will not tolerate other folks bothering us at home."

"You have a cat which knows the difference between a Yankee and a southerner?" Conrad wanted to know.

"I think so. He doesn't really distinguish them as Yankee's, just someone who wants to do us harm. If it was a southerner who wanted to harm us, I believe Cajun would yield the same result. Something in our senses tells him we are afraid, or we don't approve of someone, and he does the rest."

"What I would have given for a companion like that," the old man stated. "Why I could have been master of..." He looked at his wife and tapered off. "Makes no difference now, but I could have ruled the world."

"You rule enough of the world, my dear."

"A wife is a wonderful thing gentlemen; a man should know where his bread is buttered. She takes wonderful care of me, and with enough of her praying, I might just make it to Heaven." He slapped his hand down on the table and said, "Let's eat, the food is getting cold."

We ate a good meal, half a ham disappeared along with all the trimmings. I hadn't eaten that well before or since.

Ultimately Lady Lafitte, (I never did hear her first name), excused herself from the dining room table in order to let us men get back to our knitting. She was as graceful as a queen I thought, a monarch would envy her. I looked across the table at my young wife and knew she had the makings of such a woman, but how did one become like Mrs. Lafitte?

It's like young folks to fret over that which they can't control, just as I was doing at that moment. I had more than just the makings, and time would provide the necessary ingredients, but these are things you don't know when you are young and I was young.

Chapter 28

We left the home of Lafitte the pirate and rode straight to the ferry. We crossed the river and rode for the Destrehan Plantation several miles out of town. The plantation lay just to the west of Kenner Grove and then south to the Mississippi River. I was saddened in my heart at all of the destroyed buildings so soon after the war and I wondered how long it would take to rebuild. A long time, I thought to myself. Well-to-do folks no longer had slaves to order around, and if the colored folk could get by on little to no money, they would not work. Rich southerners had gambled their fortunes and lost.

As we rode into the yard at the Destrehan house I wondered at the flowers which defined the grounds. We had not a flower on our place which matched the majesty of these. The house appeared to be a two story affair but on further deduction I figured it had to be three and I counted no less than eight pillars across the front. We were greeted by a fellow named Shemp who took our horses and one mule then placed them in the barn out back. While he was doing this chore another fellow came to us and took our party around to the back entrance where we could clean up to make ourselves ready to meet the judge.

This was a beautiful home; as beautiful or maybe more so than Belle Grove Plantation. They were on opposite sides of the river and Belle grove was just south of Baton Rouge, but both of them might as well have been castles as far as I was concerned. The pirate Jean Lafitte had nothing on these folks, I thought. Of course, I had not the concept of a man being rich and not showing it. I thought if you were rich you would flaunt the fact, but I soon learned this was an insecure behavior. Men who flaunted what they had were not confident men, they were weak-natured.

I didn't realize just how much I was learning in those days. I had no clue I was being molded by life's circumstance, and while I understand all of this now, I didn't see it coming. My wife was a big part of molding the correct response for life's challenges, but so were the folks we were visiting now.

The Destrehan house was full of children, all of them adopted. I learned this was because Lady Destrehan lost her children several years before to yellow fever. This I learned was a government experiment gone awry. Afterward, in the middle of the Civil War she took a steamer upriver to St. Louis and recovered many orphaned girls and boys. She hand-picked each one of them to return to the plantation with no less than twenty-one unfortunate or fortunate little souls if you counted the fact they now were cared for.

We waited three days for Judge Pierre Rost to get the necessary documents in order, to pay the back taxes and to clear up our affairs. As it turned out, Butch didn't really own Belle Grove at all, he was just caretaker for the place in John Andrew's absence. That didn't matter to Lafitte and who paid the taxes anyway.

Conrad and his wife stayed with his grandfather while Butch, Abigail and I stayed on as house guests of Louise Drestrehan Rost while the judge rode into New Orleans to handle our legal affairs. I was impressed with the letter from Thomas Jefferson which was framed in the judge's study and a few letters I saw from other folks.

I didn't go through Judge Rost's things. I only looked at what he had hanging on his walls. I was impressed with the magnitude of the Destrehan family. It seemed they were involved heavily in arranging the Louisiana Purchase via Louise Destrehan's grandfather, one Jean Noel Destrehan who had been assigned to the Territorial Council at the onset of the purchase by Thomas Jefferson. I felt at times as if I was walking on hallowed ground, but the bustle and chatter of children put me at ease.

I knew nothing about legalities, deeds, tax liens or much else when it came to the law of the land, especially now that we were under Yankee rule, but Judge Rost took care to prepare everything.

Conrad and his wife returned with the judge on the third day where he handed us the completed documents and assured us we were in no danger of losing our homes. so we were ready to head for home. I didn't want Captain Callahan to think he was going to have a free hand in matters, and if we stayed away any longer that's exactly what he would think. So, even though it was late in the afternoon we headed for home, this time by a different route which kept us on the north side of the river until we could reach the ferry at Boudreaux Landing. The landing was about seven miles shy of White Castle and it was the only ferry on this end of the river operating since the end of the war. Prior to the war there had been a dozen of them servicing the plantations along this section of the river.

We covered thirteen miles that first evening then found a likely spot to camp and built a fire. It was time to be getting home. I had a feeling our destiny would not wait, but we couldn't cross the Mississippi in the dark of night, not with the girls along. If it were just us men, we would no doubt have tried, but the ferry wouldn't go in the dark so we were left to wait until morning. As the crow flies we weren't that far from home, but the mile wide Mississippi River stood in our way.

At sunrise we saddled up and started out again. At noon we came to Boudreaux Landing and spotted the ferry on the other side of the river. Conrad unlimbered his pistol and put a shot in the air to get the attention of the operator. He acknowledged our presence with the wave of his arms and started stoking his boiler. I looked at the contraption and wondered how it could even float. It was the most disagreeable looking ferry a man could imagine.

First, it was too small. I thought the insignificant craft should be a good deal bigger, but what did I know? What I saw coming toward us was going to have a hard time boarding five horses with riders. As we waited I could see the roofline of Belle Grove Plantation in the far off distance. Belle Grove stood majestically on the other side of the river awaiting her reprieve from an uncertain destiny. I knew Butch was about to send some Yankee soldiers packing and I was looking forward to the sight. He had the updated documents in his pocket just like me, and there was no way we were going to vacate our homes.

When the ferry docked on our side of the river I shuddered at the sight. It was a patchwork of broken shattered wood reassembled into a working boat of sorts. The boiler was in open view, the coal pile in front. There were rails along both sides, and a rope at each end to secure the paying passengers. The board planks seemed as if they would give away under our feet as we stepped onto the decking, but they proved deceptive and held solid. The paddlewheel was centered to the rear of the boat and spun slowly as we loaded ourselves onto the contraption.

"This is a rough looking old ferry. You think it'll make it back across the river loaded," I asked Conrad.

Overhearing me, the operator answered my question. "I know she looks rough, young man, but she's all that's left of the *Delta Star*. She was sank three years ago right over there. I salvaged what I could to build a working ferry. You're on it."

"I wasn't intending any disrespect, I was only..."

"It's all right. I'm getting use to such comments. She may not be the most beautiful boat on the river, but she gets the job done."

He pulled the lever and the wheel started churning faster, but in reverse. Then when we were about thirty yards out the boatman pulled the lever again, pulled another one to reverse the wheel and shoved the lever forward. The wheel started spinning in the other direction and we started upstream.

"She gets upstream easier than a regular steamboat because she weighs so much less. That allows her to overcome the current easier," he said as he took control of the rudder and guided the boat into the main channel. Our animals were tied to the side rails so they couldn't move around much. My guess was too much weight on one side of the boat would likely sink the contraption.

We had quite a ride, as the boatman took us up river a ways to get the ferry in position to dock on the other side. The way back was longer because he couldn't put the boat between the two sandbars from the east side without the risk of running aground. This, he explained, had been learned the hard way.

After nearly an hour on the river we led the animals off the boat and paid the man for crossing us. It was a dollar a head for the mounts, but folks crossed for free. When Conrad handed him a ten dollar note the man held it up to the sunlight and studied it, "A lot of folks have tried to pay me with counterfeit bills of late. Lincoln's Secret Service is falling down on the job."

"No offence," Conrad offered. "If he had assigned them to protect the President instead of going after the counterfeiters', he might still be alive."

"Yes sir, that's a sad shame, but when it comes right down to it the Bible predicted his outcome many years ago," the boatman said as he stuffed the bill in his pocket.

"How so?" I wondered.

"He who lives by the sword shall die by the sword! It doesn't take a genius to figure a man who lives by the gun will die by the gun," he told us.

I reached down and touched the gun on my hip and looked at the rifle in my scabbard. Suddenly I wished the man hadn't said that. We were living by the gun. Every person among us went armed, it was a sign of the times. If you didn't go armed, it was likely you would be robbed and killed for whatever you had in your possession.

The only thing that would stem the tide of violence was if there were more good guns, guns ready to dispense justice. I thought back to the Destrehan Plantation where we'd just been, and I knew many of those young men would one day be lawmen. They were studying law now. It was only natural some of them would want to get their hands dirty. Some of them would no doubt become lawyers, but others would become lawmen on the front lines. These things I thought about as the boatman counted out five dollars in change.

Chapter 29

When we entered the site known as Belle Grove Plantation my heart sank into despair. The carcass of a big cat hung from one of the big live oaks, stripped of its pelt. It was being carved up by the corporal who replaced Cook. The head was lying at the base of the tree covered in blood and the pelt was at the barn being stretched by a couple of privates. I cringed inside for I knew my friend Cajun had been unjustly killed. I swallowed hard and my stomach felt queasy, ready to give up my morning breakfast, but I gritted my teeth and held on so no one would know my torment.

We rode up to the front steps and Captain Callahan greeted us at the bottom of the massive stone staircase. "I see you've returned. There's no place for you here, so ride on," he instructed.

Butch pulled his documents from his pocket and handed them down to the captain. "I think you're the one who needs to go. The back taxes are paid in full and this proves clear deed to the property of John Andrews."

Captain Callahan was a stern, unwavering soldier. Once his mind was made up on a particular subject, it would take an act of Congress to move him. He studied the document for a moment and then pulled his cigar from his mouth and lit the papers on fire. "Corporal, arrest these traitors!"

His yell was a signal and he dove from the front steps while pulling his pistol. We pulled ours and started shooting while turning our animals to get out of the yard as fast as possible. The entire event had been a set-up, an ambush. Bullets whizzed by us in all directions and I thought I heard a couple of them hit flesh, but the ensuing melee was too crazy to take time out to see what happened. We had to get away from the house or we were all going to die. I knew I was all right, and Abigail who rode in front of me was fine, I could see that, but I was afraid to look back.

My wife and I cleared the tree line and descended deep into the woods well out of sight of the house. I took the chance to look back and everyone was there. Lizzie was in the saddle, but she seemed a little pale. It didn't register at first, but I took another look and pulled up.

"Abby, hold up," I yelled at my wife.

She brought Penny around hard and rode back to me. The others pulled up and I hopped down just in time to catch Lizzie as she slipped from the saddle. She was covered in blood. Her eyes had the wild look of terror in them, her breathing was raspy and she was losing blood nobody could put back. I knew immediately she was dying right here and now. She was never going to take another step.

Conrad lifted her from my grasp and held her tight. "It's all right honey, you're going to be all right," he said as he rocked her. But she wasn't, she died in his arms.

Butch stepped up and said, "Those Yankee's are coming."

I looked up then and I could see he had taken a bullet too, but his was in the leg. He wasn't letting on. He tied his bandana around it to stop the bleeding. "We've got to move or they'll kill us all."

Conrad understood what I said and he lifted Lizzie into the saddle in front of him, then turned his horse into the woods and we followed. Butch took up the reins of Lizzie's horse and led it along. We went this way and that into the swamp and then zigzagged some more. Eventually I took the lead and headed for home. We would need Darnell and Chin if we were going to have any chance at all.

I smelled the burning embers long before we rode into the clearing which surrounded our house. When we did get clear of the trees I pulled up short. The house and barn were dying embers, everything we owned was gone. Even the flower garden had been trampled beyond any recognition. Little tendrils of smoke lifted from the burned rubble which was our home and faded into the clear blue sky up above. The corral had been pulled down with a rope and the poles tossed onto what remained of the barn, these were burning afresh.

Abruptly any chance for diplomacy had ended. This was war. The Yankee's from up north violated me. They violated my family and my friends. They killed Cajun and now Lizzie. A swift death was too good for them. Right then, I wanted to kill them all.

"Le Roy, we have to check on Mama," my wife reminded me.

I was scared then. I was scared what we would find when we got to her mother's place. Butch rode up beside me and handed me the reins to Lizzie's horse, "I'll lay back and keep them off you. I'll also see if I can figure what happened to Darnell and the Chinaman."

I took those reins and we headed down the road to the Townsend place. I wasn't holding out much hope, not for a woman living alone with such despicable characters hanging around. She knew how to take care of herself, but this here was an entirely new kind of species, a special kind of low down dirty varmint new to the area. I could only hope I was wrong.

We started down the road and Conrad sat quiet. He held his wife in front of him with a look of doomsday on his face. You couldn't blame him. All he'd done was try to help, and for that; he lost his love. I couldn't even imagine what he was thinking. I had my own special sort of thoughts running through my head. James Le Roy Ware was about to become a killer. I'd had enough. I knew now no one cared what happened down here this far south of the Mason Dixon. A man's only defense was what he could provide for himself or with sufficient numbers to send the Yankee's packing.

I had no intention of sending them packing. I was going to plant them right where they were. They were wrong to ambush us, to kill Lizzie and I was mad about the killing of my cat. There was no way out for them now. At that moment I had but one purpose left in life; that was to make them Yankee's pay. I knew as soon as we buried

Lizzie, we would have another partner in Conrad for he was a man who would want to even the score.

I wasn't thinking of getting even, I was thinking of getting way ahead in the game. If we eliminated the Yankee detachment and left no trace as to their whereabouts it would be months before anyone came looking for them. By then we could have a story all made up and ready for the replacements, and if they didn't leave we could do it again. I no longer had feelings for them, and I had fought for the north during the war. I fought so that all men could be equal, but now I understood something I didn't know back then. All men are created equal ends at birth!

We now had a government that wasn't committed to equality, but to the destruction of anyone who didn't agree with the powers that be. I felt then it was only a matter of time before everyone would be slaves to the Federal Government. I don't know how I concluded that, but it was my prevailing gut feeling. They would be working to see to it we were all slaves eventually.

I know this now; evil remakes itself after every war so that the next generation will no longer recognize it. In this way another generation is tricked into another war, and another, and the next and so on. It was happening even now before my very eyes. How would the government lead us into slavery? I thought about that as we rode and I knew it would be through debt. If they could spend enough tax payer money, point their finger at us and say pay up by use of the tax system we were doomed. At some point, we wouldn't be able to pay up and the only option left would be slavery.

How long would such a thing take, five years, ten or a hundred? I had no way of knowing, but the scenario was clear in my brain. If the politicians in Washington ever saw the bottom of the barrel where Americans were concerned, we would all be turned into slaves.

Chapter 30

Abigail rode beside me as we neared the clearing where her home stood these many years. The house was still standing, but something was wrong. As we rode into the yard I could see the front door ajar. Abigail hopped down and ran inside calling her mother's name. Something arrested my attention so I rode around behind the house. It was Mrs. Townsend. She had been raped and left for dead. The two bullets in her chest were there no doubt to make certain she never told her story to anyone. I took down my blanket from behind my saddle and covered her up.

I dropped to my knees right then and started my prayer. "Lord, I am not a praying man, but today I am. I pray that the men who did this may receive seven fold the torment they have caused this day. An easy death will be too good for them." I felt a hand on my shoulder. "Lord, you know their deeds. You know who did this. I pray that those men never see the light of another day. Exact your revenge that I might be spared the duty. In Jesus name I pray, Amen."

I looked up to see my wife beside me weeping. I stood and we embraced. She cried then, she cried for a while until my shirt was soaked with her tears. When she pulled back she said, "Thank you. I don't think I could have survived finding her first."

"Go on back in the house. This is going to be our home now. Conrad and me, we'll dig the graves."

"Daddy's buried down by the old sawmill. Ma wants to be with him," she said.

"All right, I'll see to it."

She turned and went back into to the house. I headed for the barn, took out the shovel and dropped it in the wagon. I unsaddled Regret and hooked him to the harness, then went and got Penny, hooking her to the other side. I steered the wagon over to the front porch where Conrad was still holding his dead wife, but now he was sitting in Mrs. Townsend's rocker.

"We're going to have to dig a couple of graves, Conrad. I could sure use a hand," I said.

Getting up, he carefully placed his wife in the rocker. He never said a word, never acknowledged the fact I spoke other than his actions. He walked to where I awaited, stepped up into the wagon, glanced over his shoulder at the shovel and then looked straight ahead.

I slapped the reins and we headed toward the old sawmill. It was about a quarter of a mile from the house toward town. I did remember seeing it when I rode out here to marry Abigail. It wasn't much as some sawmills went, but it got the job done. Off to one side I found the grave of Mr. Townsend and started digging. When I got tired Conrad spelled me, but still he never said a word.

I tried to relieve him once, but he jerked the shovel back into his possession. Right then I decided to stay out of Conrad Lafitte's way. I realized with alarming revelation that he was more upset than me. He had a right to be. He had done nothing to offend the Yankee's, but he had paid the heaviest price. I sat back under a big oak tree and waited for him to tire, but he never did. He dug those graves without my help once I turned the digging over to him.

When he finished I tossed him my canteen. He took a swallow and capped it. He was still standing in the second hole he'd opened up. We heard some shooting then, and it was off in the distance. Late afternoon like it was now, I had a feeling it was one of my friends either shooting or running. Conrad never said a word. He shucked his pistol, checked his loads and shoved the gun back in his belt.

He got up out of the grave all by himself, walked over to the buckboard and got in. I figured this was the signal to leave so I got in and we headed for the house.

Back at the house he still didn't talk, but he did walk over to his wife and pick her up to lay her in the wagon. I drove the team around back and he helped me pick up my mother-in law. We got her loaded in the wagon and when we came back around to the front Abigail and Butch were sitting their horses waiting on us.

"What was that shooting we heard earlier?" I asked Butch.

"I don't know. I was in the house with Abigail getting my leg tended to."

"Well, let's hope we don't have to dig anymore graves," I said as I slapped the reins to the animals.

I thought Abigail should be on the wagon riding with me, but then I looked over at Conrad I decided she was giving him a wide birth just like I was doing. My feeling was, we were fixing to see just what Conrad Lafitte was capable of. He had not been the pirate his father and grandfather had been, but he had their blood.

There was no time for formalities, no time to wait on a pine box. We buried them as they were, wrapped in a blanket. When we were finished covering the bodies, Conrad finally spoke.

"Goodbye, my dear Elizabeth. I shall see you soon," he said and he turned to the horse my wife had been riding. "Let's go, we have some planning to do," he ordered. He stepped up onto Lizzie's horse and my wife and I piled into the wagon. Butch hopped on the tailgate and pulled his horse along behind. In this way he was able to watch our back.

"I'm going to be spending a lot of time down here now that Mama is here too," Abigail whispered in my ear.

She leaned her head on my shoulder as the two of us rode in sorrow. Actually, there were more than just two riding in sorrow, but we two were together forever, for better or worse. Our wagon was hitched to the same team of horses, never-mind one of them was a mule. Our paths did not cross, but had been running in the same direction step by step ever since we had said our vows.

As we pulled into the yard we could see Yankee soldiers coming down the road from the old house. They were still a good distance off and we scattered for cover. Just as I got settled behind the rain barrel at the front corner of the house I heard a screech in the woods nearby.

It was Cajun! My cat was not the one which was hanging from the tree at Belle Grove earlier that day.

Them Yankee's pulled up short just then. They were figuring to have an easy time of it, and to be honest, I didn't figure things would be much different. We were outnumbered, outgunned and probably outsmarted. Cajun had his own distinct squall when he was on the prowl. He used it now. Again the screech came howling through the swamp and those Yankee's turned tail right there a half mile shy of the house. They lit out like their tails was a'fire.

There were five of them, so it would have been a good fight, but when they heard that catamount they tucked tail and headed for home, in this case Belle Grove Plantation. I watched as Cajun came onto the road right where they had been assembled. When he saw me he started a long stride which startled Conrad. He lifted his rifle to take aim and I said, "Hold on Conrad, that's my cat. You might want to step into the house until he gets use to smelling you here."

Conrad, a man I didn't figure was afraid of anything at that moment in his life, ran for the front door. He closed it and locked both locks behind him. Butch sat down in the rocking chair on the front porch while Abigail and I walked out into the yard to greet our friend. When he got to the yard he stopped and rolled over a couple of times, then jumped up put his paws on my wife's shoulders and licked her in the face. A moment later he was slobbering all over me.

At that moment I saw Darnell and Chin come out of the woods on the road in the same place Cajun entered the scene. They waved and headed our way. Suddenly I was happy. I was happy that somebody was alive. After losing Lizzie and Abigail's mother I figured the worst. Now we had something to fight with.

When the two of them walked their horses into the yard I asked them, "What happened?"

"Those soldiers lit the house and barn on fire before we even knew they were there. We were lucky to get the horses and sneak them out the back way. If we tried to make a fight then, we'd be dead," Darnell said.

"Well, we've got them right where we want them now," I said.

Darnell looked me up and down like I was crazy. "You reckon they know how much trouble they're in?"

"Come on, you two, let's get the horses put up before Cajun has them all spooked," my wife advised.

We turned to then and put the animals in the barn along with the wagon. When we were finished Cajun was laying on the front porch beside Butch who hadn't gotten out of the chair. I noted he had been petting Cajun and was making friends with him.

"He'll grow on you," I said as I knocked on the front door.

Conrad pulled the curtain back and looked to see us standing there. He looked as far as he could to either side of the window to make sure the cat was not going to enter the house with us then he opened the door. Once inside

Abigail closed the door behind us and I introduced my friends.

"Conrad Lafitte, this is Darnell Blankenship and Chin Lee. They're friends of mine and good men in a fight," I added.

"That's good to know, because we're sure enough fixing to have us one," he answered.

We all found a place to sit natural like in the front room. We looked at one another for a minute and then Conrad opened the ball. "You fellows sure the horses are all right with that cat on the loose?"

"He won't bother our horses. I can't say what he'll do with the horses what belong to the Yankee's," Abigail offered.

"I thought the cat they hung from the tree this morning was Cajun," I admitted. "Sure was nice to hear him in the woods a while ago."

"I thought the same thing," Abigail added. "Conrad, I'm sorry about Elizabeth, she was a good friend and she would have been a great wife, if only she had the time."

"Who was the other lady we buried?" Conrad injected. "I presume she lived here?"

"She was my mother," Abigail told him. "She did live here, but it's our place now."

As she finished a tear fell from her cheek and the conversation sort of dried up. We lost two good women today. Two good women who were better than any two or three Yankee women I ever saw. I have to admit, I hadn't seen but a few, so my exposure to northern women was limited. It was a time of sorrow, but we had to decide what to do. I didn't want to start the conversation, but it seemed as if we were all flailing in the depths of despair.

"Trust in the Lord with all thine heart, lean not unto thine own understanding," Chin quoted out of the Bible.

Conrad studied him for a moment and Darnell explained, "He quotes scripture, but I don't think he understands what it is he says."

"I think we best get a good night's rest and in the morning we'll know better what to do. Right now we're still suffering from the shock of what happened today," Conrad said.

"Vengeance is mine sayeth the Lord," Chin added.

"Does he do this all the time?" Conrad asked.

"Mostly," I offered.

"Well, let's get some rest," Conrad repeated.

"That's a good idea, but we'll eat first. They didn't take all of the food," Abigail said.

Chapter 31

There are times in a man's life when he doesn't know which end is up. That was me the following morning. I didn't know what to do. I said my prayer over Abigail's mother and she overheard me. When we went to bed she reminded me what I prayed, so when she said, "Let God handle this." I didn't understand her at all. I was ready to kill some Yankee's and my wife was telling me no.

"If you have even one ounce of faith, let God handle this," she repeated. "His justice will be more appropriate than anything we might do."

Well, I didn't understand her one bit. I understood an eye for an eye. What she was proposing made no sense to a man who just fought a war. If God was so almighty powerful, why hadn't he stopped the killings in the first place? I wasn't going to go against her wishes, but she was not making things easy for me.

At sunrise there was a dead Yankee soldier lying on the front porch and I realized with a sudden premonition my wife was correct. Those Yankee's were no match for Cajun, let alone God. He would whittle their numbers down one by one. I felt somewhat vindicated as I looked down on a private whom I knew not. We checked him over to learn his name was Parker, Bartram Parker. He had no money on his person, but we were able to identify him by the name stamped on the inside of his belt.

I was set to bury our carpetbagger friend, but before I could get started Conrad told us what his grandfather used to do in order to scare his pursuers. He took the body up the road a ways and hung it from an overhanging tree so that the fellow was dangling in the middle of the roadway. The body was bloody, torn to shreds, a hideous looking thing, but it was the best way to put the fear of God into the minds of those Yankee soldiers according to Conrad. I didn't know if Cajun would let the body alone, but he did. He sniffed at it once or twice while we watched and then he trucked off into the woods toward Belle Grove.

The next morning at sunup another dead Yankee was on the front porch. This was another private, but in this case we were unable to identify him. His face was literally torn off and he carried no identification. Conrad and me loaded the body into the wagon and took it down the road toward the old sawmill and strung it upside down about three feet off the ground. He tagged a note to the man's chest which read; "Met his maker!" He then prepared another note for Parker to wear proudly and this one said, "Yankee gone home." We studied it for a few minutes and then went up the road and pinned it on.

"We start a small fire to burning near each one of the bodies, but in the middle of the roadway so the light reflects off the note. It will help to cast a shadow upon everything, and no man will ride directly into a camp wondering if he is next to be killed," Conrad explained.

"I think Chin can do an excellent job of keeping out of sight and still keep the fire going," I suggested. "I'll take care of the other one for tonight."

"That isn't exactly what I had in mind. I want to watch the other one. If those Yankee's come hither, I'm going to add to their list of dearly departed. They killed my wife," Conrad's voice was flat, no emotion evident and that scared me more than if he'd ranted and raved.

He didn't wait for a reply, he said what he said and it was final. I respected the man. He was an experienced hand when it came to battle. So were most of us, but his kind of experience was advanced. He had a leadership quality I did not yet possess. He turned on his heel and headed for the house. His walk was distinct, purposeful and he didn't hesitate or waste any movement.

I struggled to keep up with him. He wasn't what I considered mean, and he wasn't a pushover, he just didn't like to waste movement. At least that was my thoughts. That was what I supposed before I saw him in actual hand to hand combat. I soon learned the man was the last human being on the planet I wanted to get into a fight with. And it didn't take me long to learn.

Later in the evening as we sat together back in the woods away from the fire we heard the horses coming up the road before we saw them. Conrad eased out of his restful position and stepped behind a large oak. I mirrored what he was doing and settled in out of sight. As the horses drew near Conrad shouted, "That's far enough.

My name is Conrad Lafitte, grandson of Jean Lafitte and you're trespassing."

"This is Federal land now." It was the new corporal and there were three men with him.

"It is not Federal land, it's James Le Roy Ware's land, and you should know you can't come south, kill innocent women and ever expect to go home."

Conrad's argument fell on the darkness corner in the minds of men who recognized their companion hanging from a large tree limb. The firelight danced to and fro casting a moving shadow on the silhouette. The new corporal reached for his pistol and Conrad blew a hole in him you could ride a horse through. I don't know what he used to load the shotgun, but it was an extra special charge which disemboweled the soldier who slipped from his horse to lay dead on the ground.

Stepping out into the roadway he swung his sword in the direction of another who folded over his saddle in no better shape. Another soldier started to swing his gun into action and Conrad pulled him to the ground relieving him of his pistol as he did so. He ran the soldier through with his blood red sword and turned to the last man who was down from his horse coming at him with his own sword. The firelight set the scene as if it was a choreographed dance.

The firelight flickered and the soldier lunged at Lafitte who drew aside and sliced the man's coat open. They circled and parried looking for one another to make the first mistake. Suddenly the man lunged forward again and once again Lafitte sidestepped him. I stepped into the roadway to make sure the first three men were dead and to gather the horses.

I heard gunfire from the other camp, the one on the road which lead to our old place. Chin was under attack as well. Confirming the three soldiers were dead I straddled one of the horses and rode for the other camp. Lafitte was in no danger that I could see. He was about to lay another Yankee in his grave.

I rounded the bin near the house and spurred the horse to a faster pace. Two men were fighting in the roadway up ahead and I could tell one of them was the Chinaman. Two others lay dead near the campfire. As I came up, I realized I was too late. Chin was letting the last one fall as I rode up. He turned to me and said, "Too late boss man."

"I see you're figuring this English out?"

"I figure, not all de way."

"That's good enough," I said.

"What do now?"

"Stable the horses and hang these men right here. If them Yankee's think they're going to even the score, they have another think coming. Are you okay?"

"I fine," Chin replied. "No worry 'bout me."

"What kind of fighting was that?"

"Kung Fu, ancient Chinese boxing."

"Chinese boxing. You'll have to teach me sometime."

"Chinese boxing need all time."

"All of my time?"

"All time, no more."

I understood his meaning; it wasn't no more, but no less. He was acquiring English, but it wasn't anything like his refined scripture quotes. These he had no doubt memorized while working in New York City next to the Salvation Army. I thought about the Salvation Army in St. Louis and realized what it must have been like.

When I was a boy living on the streets I would hang around the Salvation Army tent in order to get fed. It was, for the most part, all of the Christian upbringing I could remember. I knew there was more, but it was farther back in my memory, many years hence. I tried to remember, but for some reason what I went looking for just wasn't there anymore.

We struggled to hang the bodies of seven men then. Mostly we hung them on the road, but a few were hung in the swamp. They had become hideous and grotesque things, and I wondered if I wasn't becoming such a thing myself; guilt by association as they say.

By the time we finished I realized we just strung up half the Yankee detachment. Captain Callahan wasn't going to like what happened and my guess was he would eventually come looking. When he did he was going to get a barrel load of shotgun right in his face. That's not my words, but Conrad's. He insisted he would see the captain dead for what he'd done to Lizzie and you know what? I wasn't about to disappoint him or stand in the man's way. The Yankee's did a bad thing to Conrad Lafitte. He would never know the joy of raising his family with Lizzie. He had done nothing to anger them nor did he act outside the law, yet he had been unjustly harmed. The Yankee's down here surely made Conrad mad. I knew if something happened to Abigail, I would not be stopped from killing the men who did it.

I felt for my friend, though we hadn't known each other very long. He was a good man in his own way, but he would never be one to disrespect a woman, nor shoot her in the back. He would, however, fight to his dying breath to rid the area of Yankee's. I knew it without saying.

Chapter 32

Abigail fixed something for all of us to eat when we finished hanging our trophies. Again, that was Conrad's wording for the dead Yankee soldiers. I noted with relief, I myself had yet to kill one, but there was that other factor lingering in my brain; guilt by association.

The six of us sat down to a good breakfast, yet it was slim fixings. The Yankee's took all the livestock to Belle Grove when they raided the place so we were going to have to get some of it back. I said as much and Chin promised he would get some of it later that evening. I didn't pretend to know what he had in mind, but after watching him butcher those three men the night before I knew he could take care of himself. I wasn't going to worry much about Chin. As for me, I was worried.

My deed was in my pocket, a deed which was free and clear, but my home had been burned by the Yankee's. The war was supposed to be over, but if they were going to come down south and move people out of their homes or burn them out just because they wanted all the land they could grab for themselves they were fixing to meet with plenty of opposition.

I had my wife, we had a home, but I was not at all happy with how we got it. This was the home Abigail grew up in so I guess I ought to have been thankful there was a roof over my head. I could have been sleeping out in the woods without one if not for the Lord watching over me.

No one was saying much, but as we ate breakfast we heard rustling on the front porch. That's the thing about homes in America, they seemed to all have a front porch. Some had porches that wrapped all the way around the house. I knew it was Cajun dropping off another poor soul.

"Sounds like Cajun has been at it again," I commented.

"You mean he's brought us another one?" Conrad asked.

"That would be my guess."

"Them Yankee's must be cursed," he said.

"I can assure you they are," Abigail nodded in agreement.

"Well, at least it isn't us," Butch said.

I looked across the table at my Abigail and thought about what she just said. She could assure us that those men were cursed. How? Had she done the cursing? I realized then that I knew little to nothing about my new wife. What was she doing behind the scenes? What kind of deviltry was she engaged in? Maybe deviltry was the wrong word, because she did believe in God, but doesn't the devil himself believe in the existence of God? I stared at my wife and tried to detect the depth of her meaning, but I was unable to grasp anything.

"How do you know they're cursed men," I asked her.

"You can't go around killing innocent people without bringing the wrath of God down upon your own head," she said.

I breathed a sigh of relief, because I was conjuring up in my mind the idea she placed a curse on each and every one of them. I could see her standing over a large black kettle dropping herbs and spices into it, then maybe a touch of rattlesnake venom while whispering a curse into the wind. I was relieved my imagination got the better of me.

"There are things we need to do here," I said to my friends.

"Give thanks unto de Lord," Chin said.

We all looked at him then, and he smiled his white toothed smile. "Buy the truth and sell it not," he added.

What he said didn't make any sense at all, but yet it did. His words were not part of our conversation, yet they spoke the truth. I wondered if the man was really as challenged in the English language as he first let on. I had my suspicions.

We talked the morning away around the table sipping hot coffee as there was plenty of that. Chin spoke up one more time and I began to appreciate his presence.

"There is no man who has power over the spirit, to retain his spirit in the day of death. A man hath no better thing under the sun than to eat, drink and be merry," he said.

"I'm going to hit him," Conrad said.

"I wanted to do that when I first met him," I explained. "Now he actually makes a bit of sense."

"Well, if I hit him, he's going to know it."

"If you hit him, we'll be surprised. None of us have been able to land a punch," Darnell said.

"Whatsoever thy hand findeth to do, do it with all thy might; for there is no work, nor device, nor knowledge, nor wisdom in the grave, whether thou goest," Chin said looking right at Conrad.

A sword swung free and everyone ducked away from the blade. It swung down hard and dented the tabletop coming to a rest with the point only a few inches from Chin Lee.

"You have offended me for the last time, Chinaman!"

We all drew back farther from the action, but the Chinaman didn't flinch. He locked eyes with Conrad and began to measure the man. They stared at each other while the rest of us were either too surprised by the situation or too scared to intercede. I took Abigail's hand in mine as we watched. Suddenly Chin pulled back from the table and smiled.

"Consider the work of God, for who can make straight that which he has made crooked," he said. "God also set one end over against the other to infinity so that man would find nothing after him." With cautious footsteps Chin backed away from the sword and made his way around the table out the door. He never turned to look over his shoulder, he never flinched, he just walked out closing the door behind him.

"Them Yankee's are starting to smell. Why don't we cut them down and take them to town. We can at the least let the undertaker deal with them," I suggested.

"Only the first two, the others can hang where they be." Conrad was specific in his statement. I didn't want to cross him so we only took down the first two which were the one's starting to smell.

Butch and I drove the wagon into town. There was no sign of Chin. Where he got off to I had no idea.

When we arrived in White Castle we explained things to Sheriff Jessup Cobb. He said he wouldn't ride out to see what was going on at Belle Grove. He also said if he rode out there with an arrest warrant the soldiers would just kill him, so we were on our own, but he wouldn't interfere if we were defending ourselves.

"Them Yankee's ain't welcome here no way," he insisted.

Dresden Holliday was the undertaker and he took the dead bodies off our hands. He had all the help he needed so we didn't even have to unload them. Captain Callahan no longer maintained an office in town, he moved everything to Belle Grove, said it was more to his liking.

"If he thinks he's going to keep my home he's got another think coming," Butch stated as we rode away.

"Give it time, he'll quit."

"How many men do you figure he has left?" Butch asked.

"No more than a dozen, maybe less."

"Well I'm not going to wait all year for him to decide to pick up and leave, I'll have the place back in short order. John Andrews would expect nothing less."

"John still owns Belle Grove?"

"He does, but the place was entrusted to my care and I have to get it back."

"Well, what happened to John?"

"He went to Italy, turned his slave's loose and left town. He asked me to keep an eye on the place for him."

"So everything you're doing you've been doing for him?"

"For the most part, he and my dad were once partners."

"Is he coming back now that the war is over?"

"His last letter said there was nothing to come back to. Without the slave labor he could never produce the sugar necessary to make a profit. He's buying goods from India and shipping them around the world now."

"So the house is yours?"

"It seems that way."

"Well, before we go off half-cocked, let's give Cajun his head."

"You mean let him whittle them down?"

"Don't you think that we should? Half of them are gone already. If we let Cajun continue, they'll be gone in two weeks or less."

"You don't think we should help?"

"I don't like guns going off around me," I said.

We continued toward the homestead and watched for ambush. Those Yankee's weren't exactly going to kiss us if we ran into them. It crossed our minds that they might lay in wait for us along the road somewhere. A few miles from town I heard Cajun in the swamp to the south of us. He was near Belle Grove Plantation. Butch and I looked at one another and smiled. That cat was more terrifying than a firing squad, I thought. Yankee's sent out on their own or posted to guard duty were disappearing. By now they knew they killed the wrong cat. Those men were not coming home.

We rode to the ready, but nothing bothered us and we arrived home a little after noon. Butch put the horses away while I unhitched the wagon. My wife was not smiling when I entered the house. She was starting to get a mean look on her face. This we had to change. I didn't want a mean wife, I wanted a happy one.

"What's the matter, darling?"

"Those men hanging from the trees. I don't want to live like this."

"Such a thing is only temporary," I assured her. "In a few days they'll come down and we'll take them to town like the others."

"I hope you're right, because I'm starting to get spooked in my own home."

"Well, we can't have that now, can we?"

"No, we can't."

"Where are Darnell and Conrad?"

"They're outside in the swamp somewhere, said they would keep an eye on the house from the woods."

"I know having those men hanging out there is a tremendous paradox for us. I know it isn't right, but neither was the killing of Lizzie. She did nothing to those men, yet they shot her. If they didn't want to hang from a tree, they should have acted more civilized or neighborly. It's too late to turn back now."

"I know you're right, but those bodies hanging there like that, it just bothers me to no end."

"If it didn't bother you, I wouldn't give two cents for you. Now relax. They'll be gone soon. They can't hang there forever."

"I want you to know something," Abigail said as a light illuminated in her eyes. "I love you."

Well, I could have gone through my entire day without hearing those words, but her saying of them, fairly halted me in my tracks. I don't know what I was fretting about, I was married to the girl, but still, those three words were not something I was used to hearing. I stood there staring at her for a moment and she leaned up on her tiptoes to kiss me on the lips.

I returned the favor and then stepped back. She wouldn't let go of me, so I pulled her close and she wrapped her arms around me again.

"Just hold me for a minute," she said.

"All right." I pulled her to me even tighter.

We were standing there like that when Butch walked into the house.

"The Yankee's are coming," he warned.

Chapter 33

I grabbed my rifle from the barrel sitting just inside the door. Conrad suggested we do that to easily retrieve our weapons in an emergency. That was the first thing we did. I checked to make sure my rifle was fully loaded and then I pulled a shotgun from the barrel. I handed this gun to my wife and said, "Stay out of sight, but let them see the barrel of the gun through the front window. Crack it just enough to point the gun at them. If shooting starts, unload both barrels."

I stepped outside onto the front porch and waited. Butch stood to the other side of the porch with his rifle cocked and ready. The soldiers were led by Captain Callahan. He was in a foul mood that day and he didn't like what he saw; his men hanging everywhere. Those with him had their guns at the ready, so he came on to the house, one step at a time.

He halted his horse soldiers in the yard about ten paces from the front porch. I saw him glance at the front window where I knew what he noticed. There would be a shotgun pointed right at them, and at this distance, it wouldn't miss no matter who pulled the trigger.

"Captain, what can we do for you?"

"You hung my men."

"You shot and killed an innocent woman," I said. "Your men were dead when we put them up there."

239

"You didn't kill them?"

"No sir. I haven't killed my first man. My wife has been holding me at bay."

"You don't expect me to believe that lie, do you?"

"I'm not lying. I haven't killed my first man, but I won't hesitate to do so if I'm pushed."

"Then who killed them?"

"They died in combat, sir."

"Young man, the war has been over for a year now. There are no combat operations."

"That's what I thought, but they sure were set on killing folks, just like they were on orders from their captain," I said.

"Who's mule is that over there?" the captain asked. He sat the back of his roan as if was born to it. There was a certain authority to his voice, but I had the idea he was not necessarily a man who spoke with the backbone necessary for the authority he was claiming. The sound was there, but his voice seemed empty. "This place is supposed to be deserted."

Looked to me like this was my moment for talking, so I dug deep for the courage I would need to face these men and I started. "Captain Callahan, my mother-in-law owned this place until your men burned my place to the ground then came over here raping and killing. My wife and I now live here. This is our home. I will fight you to the death in order to keep it. We'll not be burned out again."

Captain Callahan eyes turned cold as steel. The accusations stung him and he didn't like what I had to say. There was no retreat in his expression, no pleasant soul hidden there, his face lost all expression and his eyes resembled those of a rattlesnake set to strike. He was an unforgiving man, yet an empty man. He didn't like losing, but then who did?

I won the argument because the cold black eyes of my gun barrel were pointed in his direction and he didn't relish the thought he might be the first one to die if it came down to shooting. I don't know why such leverage works so well and convincingly, but it seems to work every time.

While it was Captain Callahan to whom I spoke, my attention was on one of his men. I hadn't seen this man before and he stacked up as quite different than the men he rode with. Sure, I kept my gun trained on the captain, but this other man was a whole new fish to fry. He was a full-fledged trained mercenary who didn't care who he killed, as long as he got paid. I don't know how I knew all that just by looking at the man, but a man stays alive by practicing discrimination. This was one man to whom I was giving a very discriminating eye. He would not die easy. He was a fighting man from way back, a man for whom war must have been created, the only problem was, the war was supposed to be over.

"Captain, the mule is mine," I said. "I set store by that mule and if anything happens to him, anything at all, I'll cut loose on you six ways from Sunday. You and your men will never live to see home." I turned my attention to the man I'd been eyeing. "Seems to me I should know you." I looked at him directly for the first time.

"Tope Holloman is my name. I came into this part of the country since you left."

"Tope, I see you don't wear a uniform. If you ride with these men I don't care if you're in uniform or not, you're liable to get shot just the same. I hope I never have to line you up in my sights."

"I'll heed the advice carefully," he said.

"Were you ever in Piute country?" I asked.

Tope's eyes suddenly became alert, "Maybe. A man gets around."

"Ware, you're known in these parts as a troublemaker. I don't want any more trouble with you. I've lost too many good men already. I will consider this meeting a treaty between us. The slightest sign of worry from you, or any evidence of interference with the Federal Reconstruction Program and I'll have you in irons. Also, I intend to confiscate this land because those living here were an enemy of the Federal Union.

"I fought on the decks of the *Carondelet*, Captain Callahan. You know it well. The fact I now own land in the south should be a relief to you, but if you insist on carrying out your charade, so be it."

"You intend to go on fighting then?"

"Captain, I don't know if you realize it or not, but I never stopped fighting. I fought in the war, and now I fight for myself against the very government I swore allegiance to."

"Then you are a traitor."

"I'd look at my whole card, captain. I'm only fighting you because you've set out to destroy me. I'm not fighting the Union, I'm fighting to save my land and my home, nothing more and nothing less. The men who fight with me don't object to the Union, they are also fighting to save their land. I have sworn such a statement to Judge Destrehan in New Orleans just in case you do manage to put me behind bars."

"I would like to gather my dead and take them home, but I need your word that you won't attack us while we are retrieving the bodies."

"We won't bother you, captain, but I can't speak for my cat."

"So, the truth comes out. The cat belongs to you."

"The cat doesn't belong to anyone. He does as he pleases. We've just gotten used to having him around," I explained.

"You specifically said he was your cat," Captain Callahan said.

"We think of him as family, but he's his own spirit. I can't control him any more than you can."

"He doesn't seem to bother you and yours."

"No, and we thank God for that," I said.

"Do I have your permission to gather my dead?"

"I won't stop you. There's two more in the swamp, one over there and one over there," I pointed using my rifle.

"We won't be long," he said and jerked his horse around. His men turned their horses in like manner and followed behind moving in a slow predetermined manner toward those who were hanging over the road to the south. A snapping turtle crossed the road in front of them, not bothered by the oncoming men.

Conrad came from around the back of the house and stood watching them. "We heard them coming through the swamp. If they figured to start a fight we were fixing to let them have it." Only with his use of the word "we" did I realize Chin was there also. He was so quiet I never even noticed him. Chin still didn't carry a gun, but I was fast learning he didn't need one.

"Let them take their dead," I told them. "I don't want to smell the bodies anymore and I think we made our point."

"Darnell came out of the barn and walked over to us. "You know, now would be a good time to move into Belle Grove. I don't think there's a Yankee left who isn't riding with the captain at this very moment."

"I count eleven men," I said. "Why don't they leave? They know what's going to happen if they stay."

"Maybe stubbornness, maybe pride, I don't know, but they're all going to die if they don't leave while the gettin' is good," Conrad stated.

"We can't take Belle Grove back by force, we'll lose it for sure if we do that," Butch told Darnell.

"It was just an idea."

"It will have to wait. When they leave on their own accord, that's when we move in," Butch said.

We watched as the soldiers cut down the first man and laid him over a saddle. Then they repeated the process on the second and third. Two men went into the swamp to retrieve the ones we hung there. Once they returned the entire group came back into the yard and Captain Callahan addressed me.

"Can we borrow your wagon? We're going to need a wagon to get them home."

"It's in the barn. You're welcome to it, but you'll have to use your own horses. Throw the saddles in the back and the harness is hanging on the wall next to the wagon."

"Thank you, I'll leave the wagon in town for you."

"That will be fine."

Callahan instructed two of his men to dismount, unsaddle and hook up to the wagon while the other worked to get the dead bodies into it. Ten minutes later they rode out and stopped down the road by the sawmill to gather the rest of their dead. We kept a keen eye on them as they made off with our wagon.

Tope Holloman was the man I kept my eyes on. He was a mercenary, a killer for hire. I couldn't think of any reason why the Yankee's would need him except one. He was sent for so he could kill. Today wasn't the time or the hour, he only rode along to size us up, I was certain of that much. Once the soldiers rode away I called everyone into the house.

"Tope is only here for one reason. He was hired to kill," I said. "That's all he does, so watch your backs."

Chapter 34

The following morning we woke to a heavy fog. Again a steady rain fell. I sat down outside in the rocker and listened to the sounds of the swamp. A heron cried in the distance, frogs chirped at the water's edge and for the first time in several days things felt peaceful. Abigail brought me a cup of coffee and sat in the corner chair.

"What do we do now?" she asked.

"We go to town and get our wagon back. While I'm gone, you be ready. If them Yankee's try to pull something that would be when they do it."

"I'm afraid James, please take me with you to town."

"All right, you go with me. We'll leave the house to our friends."

Three hours later Abigail and I rode into town. The wagon was at the stable just like Callahan promised. The undertaker was busy building coffins, otherwise the street was empty.

We started to enter the mercantile because there were a few things we needed. Callahan was there waiting for me. He was three to four inches taller than me, rugged, brutal and some heavier. He had been drinking. He was dressed in his uniform, but it seemed dirty and un-kept now. He stripped out of his blouse and turned back to me pulling the door shut behind him so Abigail and I could not enter the building.

"Strip off that gun mister, and I'll thrash you," he said.

A half-dozen men appeared out of nowhere, men who were there to watch the show. I'd seen this set up before, witnessing such tactics on the streets of St. Louis when I was younger and homeless. I would fight my best fight, but if I won, the others would beat me in retaliation.

Suddenly it seemed like old times! I threw caution to the wind and unbuckled my .44. Callahan rushed while I was still working to unbuckle my weapon, so I stepped aside and he landed face first in the muddy street of White Castle. I finished unbuckling my weapon and handed the pistol to my wife butt first.

"If anyone interferes, shoot them," I said.

A dozen men were watching now, and none of them were apt to be my friend so when I turned around to face Callahan he rushed me again. I sidestepped him and landed a right into his solar plexus. The captain folded and dropped to his knees where he suddenly found no breath.

I circled him then, giving him a chance to get his breath back, but I hurt him and he knew it. Slowly he got to his feet and turned to face me. He didn't rush me this time. He put his fists up and started at me with caution born of experience. We circled twice in the street, each looking for an opening. When I saw my chance I stepped forward with a left hook that bloodied Callahan's lip. He stepped back and tasted blood. Suddenly his eyes turned to pure hatred and he lunged forward swinging a roundhouse right that almost caught me sleeping. I ducked just in time and came up smashing his lips before he could reset first a left then a right and then I backed away.

Callahan was unsure now. He expected to wipe the ground with me, and suddenly the thought occurred for the first time he might not win. Maybe it was the first time he saw his own blood, but it shocked him sober. It angered him too. He walked in on me then swinging both fists, but the captain misjudged me. I was mad too for once again I was set upon unjustly. Those fellows watching were not cheering for me, but for their captain. Looking at their numbers I began to fume. It was no longer four or five, but a dozen!

I backed away from his swinging fists making sure nothing happened then suddenly I changed direction and broke his nose with a left hook. He staggered and almost fell so I hit him again with everything I had. I felt the bones in my hand snap the instant I connected. Callahan hit the dirt unconscious.

I stepped back to catch my breath and two men rushed me. A gun went off behind me and suddenly they brought up short. It was Abigail.

"The first one of you boys lays a hand on my man for winning a fight fair and square is going to cash his ticket, straight to hell," she said waving my gun at them.

I was struggling to catch my breath, but my wife had me covered.

"Now, pick up your captain and get out of town. If you bother us again we won't be so friendly," she said.

Half the town was watching now, folks I knew from way back. Even the sheriff was there and I heard him whisper to someone behind me. "Why them dumb Yankee's picked the only man in town who fought every day of his life just to grow up. Serves them right."

I heard him spit his chewing tobacco on the ground and walk away. I didn't have to look to know what was going on behind me. I smiled as I watched the Yankee's pick up their captain. He was still out cold.

"As much as I hate to offer my services to a Yankee, you'd better get that man to my office," Doc Webster said.

I watched as he led those men down the street carrying their captain. I felt good, but I knew this wasn't the end. This was just the beginning. Now Captain Callahan had been embarrassed in front of his own men. That's what a man gets for fighting drunk, but he wouldn't see it that way. He would want revenge. Revenge, the lowest form of human behavior on the planet.

Abigail took one look at my hand which was already swollen twice its normal size and knew without asking I had broken it. Doc was busy doing what he could to help Captain Callahan, so I didn't have anyone I could see about it until later. It was my right hand and I was right handed. How could I draw my gun and get it into action now? I was suddenly in trouble!

We sat down on the boardwalk and figured what to do next. I couldn't even harness the wagon. Saddling Regret might be possible, right up until it was time to pull the cinch tight. Suddenly I felt like a woebegone creature. I wanted to crawl into a hole and lick my wounds, but I had a wife and friends who weren't about to allow me that kind of behavior. To this day I'm thankful for that much.

A few minutes later I saw Doc Webster walking up the street by himself. He got to where I was sitting and stopped.

"Let me see that hand, Mr. Ware."

I held it out to him and he shook his head. "That's what I thought. You killed him you know, deader than a possum at suppertime and that was the blow what done it," he said while examining my hand. "Them Yankee's are some bent out of shape, talking murder and such nonsense. I know it wasn't murder, but they're going to raise a stink around here just to see if they can hang you."

"I killed him?" I asked in surprise.

"In a fair fight, but that makes no difference. They're calling it murder. If they ever get the ear of the right person to hear them, you'll be hunted like a dog."

"That's what they want, Doc."

"I'm going to have to set your hand, but the swelling has to go down first. You two got somewhere to stay here in town?"

"We need to get home."

"All right, but first I'm going to wrap your hand so you can't injure it any further. I'll give you something that should help reduce the swelling. When that swelling goes down you get right back here so I can set your hand and put it in a cast. Otherwise you may lose it."

"I sure don't want to lose it," I said biting my lip to the pain.

"Come on, let's go to my office," Webster instructed.

"Won't those men be there?"

"They left already. They left when Callahan cashed in his chips."

Doc Webster wrapped my hand, gave my wife instructions for keeping it wrapped tight and sent us about our business, business which was nothing more than getting our wagon back. I wasn't much help in removing the saddles and harnessing the animals, but Abigail knew what she was doing. While I watched her hook up our horse and mule team I began to contemplate the mess I was in.

How could I get my gun into action with a busted hand? I knew the answer and I didn't like it one bit. I was left handed now. I never used my left hand for much of anything, but I was going to have to learn how to use it or die. I cringed at the work necessary in order to create a fluid action when retrieving my revolver. If I was slow before, I was a turtle now. My only saving grace was the fact a fast draw had not yet been invented.

Men fought in those days with dueling pistols or swords, and I knew deep down in my gut such a time honored tradition was no longer good enough, not if I wanted to live. I pulled my gun and held it in my left hand then, a feeble and uncomfortable hold, but I knew it was just the beginning. I was going to have to practice like never before. I was going to have to be able to get my pistol into action in any sort of manner with my left hand.

When Abigail finished harnessing the team I weighed the gun in my hand and dropped it back into the holster.

I stepped up into the wagon and she started for home. Suddenly I realized I needed my gun out, and I pulled it back out to hold in my hand.

"Are you going to do that all the way home?" she asked me.

"Yes, I am. I won't get a chance to draw my gun if Holloman appears. He'll just shoot me dead."

"He wouldn't."

"Yes he would, and he'll be leading them now," I said.

We rode in silence after that. Thoughts were racing through both of our heads. Me wondering how I might draw my pistol and get it into action, and my wife, I later learned, was wondering if we would live till the end of the week. With Captain Callahan gone, there was no one to rein in the men. Holloman would be one to urge them into despicable low-down evil deeds. He was their leader now.

As we rode into the yard, Conrad met us out front. "We were fixing to come and get you. Is everything all right?"

I lifted my hand and he whistled. "Now that's not good. Can you still handle a gun?"

"With practice," I said.

"He killed Callahan, with his bare hands," my wife explained. The other fellows were gathering around now and they didn't miss Abigail's statement. "Callahan set out to beat James Le Roy half to death, but I don't think he ever landed a punch."

"I wish I could have seen that," Darnell said.

252

"Me too," Butch said nodding in agreement.

"Holloman will be leading them now. He's a mean one so we need to be ready for anything," I said. I glanced down at my left hand because I suddenly felt a stabbing pain shoot up my left arm and I saw instantly it also was beginning to swell. I was in trouble, but good. If I was attacked now I would have no way to defend myself.

"Darnell, would you put the animals away?" I asked.

"Don't fret over that, come on Butch, let's put them up."

Chapter 35

I know we all start from a different place in life with different parents, different beliefs and different incomes. So it is that all men are created equal, ends at birth! No human being has the right to take the life of another, yet I'm reminded that we're all headed for the grave from the moment we're born. I don't understand hastening the matter, but some folks just don't know when to let well enough alone.

Since arriving home them Yankee's over Belle Grove way were whittled down to size. You'd think at some point they'd begin to wonder who might be next. I know I would have if I was one of them. But as I learned the next morning, they were hell bent to be the first ones to shake hands with Satan himself.

The attack was unprecedented. We were civilians wanting nothing more than to be left alone. I didn't want to fight, but as the first hint of gray began to usher in the morning they attacked. It was a pre-dawn attack designed to burn us out. We heard them coming before we saw them, riding hard at the house and barn. Then we saw the torches for it was almost still dark. I was not yet dressed, but I ran to the gun barrel to pull out a rifle left handed like, but before I could get to the front door and get it open I heard a rifle shot.

When I did open the door I saw a Yankee soldier in the throes of agony lying on the ground, his torch beside him. He was struggling to sit upright. His horse was dancing around in the front yard not knowing which way to run. I cocked the rifle in my hand awkwardly, but just in time to see another soldier with a torch in his hand riding hell bent on burning us out.

As he neared the barn he drew back to throw his torch and a bullet lifted him from the saddle. He hit the ground already dead. Three more came down the road then, but they weren't bearing torches, they had rifles and they were shooting. As they entered the yard they noted the situation and did a complete about face. We didn't shoot at them for long because in the dark there simply wasn't a good target unless they were wielding a torch. Those three at least had enough sense to turn about and get to safety.

There was a lot of shouting in the woods which didn't make sense to me, and then Cajun squalled loudly. Suddenly you could have heard a pin drop. Them Yankee's were afraid of that cat and for good reason. There was dead silence for a while before we heard a skirmish going on out in the swamp between Cajun and one of them Yankee soldiers. Another one of them was dying.

It wasn't long after sunup when Cajun came dragging what was left of the fellow up to the front porch. I was horrified at the sight, but the fellow had been warned. It was then we heard the rest of them mount up and high-tail it out of there. They lost three more men, but one of them was still alive. He'd been laying in the front yard groaning for the last half hour. Cajun started toward the one live soldier who lay on the ground and I called him back.

"Cajun, come on back, boy," I said saving the man's life.

I patted Cajun on the head and talked to him while the others tended to the wounded soldier. He was hurt, but he would live. I never got off a good clean shot myself, but I did manage to pull the trigger on my rifle once during all the action.

I realized then I was stove up pretty bad. My very life depended on my friends and their ability to fight. I was completely at their mercy. I couldn't handle a gun at the moment, and any moving I did started my right hand to hurting like it was on fire. The pain was almost unbearable at times. I wanted to scream, but I wasn't about to. Others were depending on me and they needed to know I was a stable soul.

My friends set about laying traps, preparing for the worst. Cajun disappeared into the woods and I sat in the rocking chair on the front porch. Chin and Conrad took the buckboard to town with the wounded Yankee riding in the back. Abigail was cooking and I started practicing getting my pistol into action with my left hand but it hurt like the dickens.

My action was clumsy and useless as a puppy with its tail tied to a cat. Why I had no more chance of beating someone to the draw than I had of dying a millionaire.

There was no way I could defend myself with a pistol at that time, so I shucked my rifle and practiced with it for a while.

The result was much better. For one, the rifle was already in my hand. I didn't have to draw the weapon. I also had a better feel for the rifle, it had a better balance. I laid it across my lap in the chair whenever I got tired, but I never let go of it. I wasn't going to hit anything with it for sure, but it would feel good to at least get a shot off.

I could smell the cooking of breakfast in the house and I thought to myself, there is an upside to being married. If my wife was going to cook for me even once a day, I was going to become a spoiled man. I hadn't been waited on like this since I was a youngster. In fact, I struggled of late to eat a good well-balanced meal. Usually it was a rabbit or a squirrel over an open flame.

I watched then as Butch and Darnell came out of the barn, walked over to me and sat down.

"The traps are set. If any of them Yankee's get close to the house, they'll trip a wire," Darnell reported.

"Cajun won't know about them, make sure you don't shoot Cajun," I said.

"Cats can see in the dark. That's why he's so dangerous. He won't trip over it at all," Butch promised. "He'll see it and step right over."

"Cats can see in the dark?"

"Yes, don't you remember learning that in school?"

"I guess I forgot, but now that you mention it, I do seem to remember something about cats being able to see better at night than we can in the daylight," I said.

"I wouldn't worry about that cat if I were you. He knows more about how to get around than we do," Butch said.

"Sure, but we're carrying guns and I don't want him shot!"

Conrad returned with the Chinaman a little after noon. The two of them acted like two lost friends who hadn't seen each other for years. I watched as they put the wagon away and took care of the horses. It seemed strange to me, but who knows what's in a man's heart. They were getting along like a couple of old pals from bygone days. I had the feeling then, if Conrad lit out the Chinaman was going to be right on his heels.

Conrad walked up to me and said, "The two of us are going over to Belle Grove and get some of the stock back. We don't want any help. It's best the rest of you stay here in case there's trouble."

"We take soldier horses," Chin said.

"What he means is, we're going to take two of them U.S. branded horses and ride over there to get what's ours."

"You think that's wise?" I asked.

"I think it best. They won't give us any trouble," Conrad promised.

"Well, watch out for Cajun. He headed over that way a while ago."

"We'll be mindful. You get some rest, keep the roof on the place and we'll be back before you know it."

"By the way, how many horses are in the barn?"

"We have nine all told. A few ran off when those Yankee's left out."

"I'm going to pick two and start breeding them with Penny. You can divide up the rest any way you want," I told him.

"We'll do that later. Right now I want to get our food recourses back before them Yankee's eat everything around here."

"Good luck," I said.

Conrad turned and headed for the barn with Chin on his heels. A few minutes later I watched as they rode out on the wagon behind two stout Union mounts. They were begging trouble by doing such a thing, but I wasn't about to argue with either of them. Right now I couldn't whip a wet pup.

They left behind no dust as they rode because the ground was still damp from recent rains. That was the thing about this part of Louisiana; it rained all the time seemed like. You could plan for it, and not be disappointed. If a man couldn't grow a crop down here, he'd better find another line of work.

Chapter 36

Along about dark I looked up to see Chin and Conrad coming down the road with milk cow in tow, goats, and chickens in the crates lining the back of the wagon. Neither man looked worse off for the wear leaving me puzzled.

How could they have gotten all that livestock back without a fight? Had they just waited for the soldiers to leave? What I was seeing didn't make a bit of sense, but they sure enough had the animals which proved their worth. Abigail came out onto the front porch to watch them as they came into the yard. She had been inside playing with her dolls all day it seemed. I knew one thing for sure, if she was going to be my wife she was going to have to stop playing with dolls. That's what I thought at the time, mind you.

Everything went to the barn except for the goats. They were left to run amuck in the yard in order to keep the grass trimmed low. Some of the prettiest yards I ever saw used goats to trim the grass. They did a nice even job and they were efficient. As long as you had the number right, there was almost no sign they were even around. Now and then one of them would stray, but it wasn't too hard to herd them back onto familiar ground.

The swelling in my hand went down enough by then so Abigail and I saddled up with help from Butch and rode to town. I had to get my right hand set. When we left the yard it wasn't long before Cajun fell in behind us. This began to worry me, because we were headed for town. I didn't think the folks at White Castle were in any mood to have a cat such as Cajun amongst them today.

"He can't come to town with us," I told my wife.

My rifle was in my left paw as we rode, my wife wore my holster with my pistol in it. In those days, everybody went armed.

"He's come with me before," she said.

"What happened?"

"Nothing, folks just don't go outside."

"I'll just bet they don't." I shook my head.

I took some comfort in the fact we were riding Penny and Regret. Otherwise the outcome here would have been in question. Some of those Union horses weren't exactly adjusted to our cat yet. If we'd been on one of their horses when he came out on the road behind us, I'd have had a hard time hanging on.

"I have a question for you, dear. Just what are you doing with those dolls of yours when you are playing with them?" It was in my mind to put the practice of playing with dolls to rest once and for all.

"I'm not playing with them," she said as we walked the animals down the lane.

"All right, what are you doing with them then?"

"I'm blessing some, cursing our enemies and protecting the ones I love."

I stopped Regret right in the middle of the road. I stared at her for a moment and then at a loss for words, I nudged Regret forward again.

"You thought I was playing?"

"Well, I thought that was what dolls were for."

"I'm doing my best to protect you, our friends and our home. Those Yankee's are the only problem we have. I figured out how to get Cajun to help us and I've been making sure every night that nothing happens to him, and that he helps us in some way. That's what those dolls are for."

"You can do that?"

"Yes, I can do that."

We rode down the lane toward town and I realized I really didn't know my wife or her limitations. I didn't understand her practice of Voodoo and I didn't know what to think at that point.

While Cajun wondered to and fro on Main Street of White Castle terrorizing the local citizens, Doc Webster took a few hours to set my right hand. He checked my left to make sure I hadn't broken it as well. This was something I fretted over for several days. He told me to limit the use of it until my hand had a chance to heal some, but thankfully, my left one was not broken.

We left town mid-afternoon and started home down the long winding narrow road which was the main road. We crossed the small bridge which was built as a creek crossing many years before and here we picked up Cajun once again. He must have gotten bored with waiting for us to appear in town and decided to wait for us at the bridge. About six miles out we turned onto the home route and started up the lane toward the house.

There was no thought for what happened next. A neighbor was waiting for us as we neared the house, a neighbor from about ten miles farther on. It was a young lady a few years younger than my wife. She said her mother was about to have a baby and would Abigail come and nurse her through. There was no discussion, my wife grabbed a few things kissed me goodbye and they rode away.

Nothing seemed out of place and nothing was, not until my wife attempted to return home a few days later on her own. She was detained by the Yankee's who were now being led by Tope Holloman. I know this because they sent me a note. Obviously they were no longer at Belle Grove Plantation. The note said they were hiding out in the swamp that they would be in touch when they were ready. There was just one problem. They had my wife. I wasn't about to wait for them Blue Bellies to do to my wife what they had done to Abigail's mother.

I saddled up Regret and started for Belle Grove. My friends rode with me. When we arrived we found the place empty. Cajun was in the woods nearby, but he was remaining quiet as if he knew something was wrong.

"You fellows stay at Belle Grove, don't give her up without a fight," I told them.

"Don't worry none about that," Butch promised. "I'm home now. Them Yankee's are out in the cold."

"I plan to take Cajun hunting with me. I've got to find my wife," I told them.

"You be careful, you don't have but half of one good hand," Darnell cautioned.

I stepped back into my saddle then and circled Belle Grove looking for the most recent tracks. Once I found them, I picked up my cat about one hundred yards from the house. He seemed to know what I was about, but I couldn't say how. I heard a cat has nine lives, but what about senses? Did he understand what was going on? I was handicapped, but I wanted my wife back. I was going to free her or die trying. I was thankful my friends respected my stance enough not to argue with me busted hand or not.

I carried my rifle in my left hand cocked and ready. I still probably couldn't hit anything, but that wasn't going to stop me from trying my best. Cajun seemed to be almost sniffing the air at times. Could a panther smell a trail like a dog? It seemed so. I watched in amazement, realizing I really didn't know anything about my cat, or was he Abigail's?

It was my hope whatever protection she conjured up for us, she included herself in matters. I heard some of what Tope Holloman was capable of out in the Indian Nation land in Oklahoma. He was a mean one. He'd killed two squaws and their children figuring white men didn't go to jail for killing any kind of an Indian. It was said he raped the squaw's before he killed them.

I made up my mind then, if he laid a hand on my wife he was a dead man. Cajun was purring as he walked beside me and Regret. I knew once we got close to them he would become silent. My hope was he would stalk them in the night and kill them all one by one. If Cajun would do that, he would terrorize those men into some form of surrender and my wife would go free. What I couldn't figure was why they wanted Abigail in the first place.

Riding along the trail like I was my mind failed to notice when Cajun slipped off into the woods. My thoughts were so preoccupied I never even noticed he was missing. Suddenly with no warning I was removed from my saddle by a man swinging on a rope. I never saw him coming until it was too late. His booted feet hit me dead square in my rib cage sending me flying to the ground. My rifle clattered on the ground next to me and before I could recover I was pinned helplessly to the dirt.

"I got him Tope," the man yelled into the woods.

I struggled to get free but my efforts were futile. It was then I saw Cajun leap from a nearby tree and take the man by the neck. He screamed as the cat literally had him in a death grip. Cajun didn't let go until the man was limp in his grasp. Then he dropped the soldier and let out one of those hair curling growls. I heard men running through the woods, but suddenly there was dead silence.

I picked up my rifle and stepped back into the saddle. Then I yelled at them.

"Let my wife go or you'll all die just like this man."

Cajun took off back into the woods and growled some more. He was moving around out there, but he had a way of blending in with the trees and he made absolutely no noise when he was stalking. They weren't going to spot him so easy.

"You call that cat off," I heard Tope yell from deep in the woods.

"You send my wife out," I yelled back.

I was answered by silence. Where we were was about ten miles south of Belle Grove near the big thicket. I didn't think them Blue Bellies knew about the big thicket so I figured they were all strung out along here in the woods just waiting for Cajun to pick them off.

By my count, there were seven men and my wife. Now it was six. I knew Holloman's mean streak was a mile wide, but so was mine when it came to personal matters and this was a personal matter. Here I was trying to start a nice family and those fellows were doing their best to plant me six feet under. I wasn't having any of it. With Cajun on the loose I had the upper hand. The only thing I could figure is, those fellows could write a report explaining things the way they wanted them explained and they didn't figure anybody up north would care what went on this far south.

Callahan set the army against me or was it Tope? How long had he been in the area? I wasn't sure about the timeline, but I knew Tope could get other folks to fight for him, as he was doing now.

Giving those Blue Bellies a wide girth I rode for the big thicket. It was coming onto dark and I knew how to make myself comfortable there. I didn't want those Yankee's getting cozy at all. Cajun would know where to find me so I didn't worry about him even a little bit. Besides, he was not finished if my guess was correct. He wouldn't be finished until Abigail was free.

What had she done to him? Was he so much under her spell that he was an extension of her will? How did she control him, because I'm certain that was exactly what she was doing. Somehow she had complete control of our cat. How? What part of Voodoo allowed her to control his animal instinct in the forest? Was this the dark side of Voodoo? Was there a dark side? I had many questions, but no answers. This then was living by faith.

I was living by the simple faith, but my wife knew more than I ever would about the spiritual realm. This was the only place where you could get control over the animals. Something like that didn't happen in the physical world, unless by force. What she was doing required a greater manipulation in the spirit world. At the age of seventeen she must just be getting started. If her power was this strong already, what might it be in thirty years? I shuddered to think.

Unexpectedly I heard a man scream nearby and then a short struggle. Abruptly it was five. Five men left. I was almost to the big thicket when the attack took place. As I arrived I unsaddled Regret and turned him loose in the grass. He seemed to know men were dying around him, but he gave no care. Oh, he would raise an ear or turn his head, but he just didn't worry about all the commotion going on. I spread my blanket roll and lay down.

The night was going to be a long one. I knew deep down more of those men would die. I didn't feel sorry for them. Some of them were young like me, but still I felt nothing for them. They set out to destroy me for no reason at all. Young or old it didn't matter, once a side was chosen, right or wrong a man was destined to see the fight through to the end. That was something I learned the hard way aboard the *Carondelet*.

I closed my eyes and tried to remember the faces of the men I fought with on the *Carondelet*, but I could no longer see them clearly. Where were my shipmates now? Were they all still alive? How many of them were enduring the type of trouble I was having at the moment? I tried then to remember them all, but I could only remember a dozen or so. I had been so young; I guess my memory was fading already. Maybe it was because I didn't want to remember the war at all.

Eventually I got up and led Regret into the thicket then lay back down. Soon thereafter Cajun came up to me sniffing to see if I was all right. I reached up and petted his ear so he turned and lay down beside me. I went to sleep just like that. I was so tired I had no thought of getting up.

I awoke in the middle of the night to find Cajun gone. I looked over to see Regret was doing fine and I lay my head back. I thought about riding into their camp and getting my girl, but then I considered the shape my hands were in and I knew my idea was a foolish one. I would be better off to wait and let Cajun thin their ranks. I never felt so close to an animal as I did Cajun at that moment. It seemed bizarre, yet at the same time I knew our relationship to be real. Made possible by Voodoo?

I gazed up at the stars through the brush and wondered what chessboard I was playing on. Since marrying Abigail all sort of new possibilities seemed to open themselves up to me. Was I the leader with the pet cat in the old Indian legend?

When she first told me about it, I thought she was crazy, but now I could at least see where I had a rather large cat. My chessboard of life seemed to have some type of magical property to it suddenly. The pieces aligned themselves like the stars up above, awaiting their orders from yours truly.

I fell asleep again and when I awoke it was morning. I looked over at Regret and he was standing where I left him. He was staring at me this morning. The look in his eye said, "Can we go home now?" We couldn't of course, but I couldn't tell him so.

With fumbling hands I rolled up my blanket and then I saddled my mule. The task wasn't easy and I knew it wouldn't be. My left hand wasn't that strong, but eventually I got the saddle in place, fumbled with the strap and pulled the cinch tight. I saw Regret when he inhaled and didn't let go so I stepped back put my knee hard to his rib cage and he let go the air he was holding. I yanked hard and fast on the cinch one last time. He was being stubborn this morning so I had to outsmart him.

The last thing I needed today was a loose saddle dumping me in the middle of the swamp somewhere amongst the water moccasins and alligators.

Chapter 37

I led Regret out of the thicket and stepped into the saddle. This was no easy task as my rifle was in my left hand, my only good hand and it wasn't that good. I reached down took up the reins and eased him toward the swamp. Five men still stood between me and Abigail, five men whom I had no sympathy for. I hadn't thought of eating since I got the note and I didn't think of it now. All that was on my mind was separating the wheat from the chaff.

There was a slight chill in the air as I rode from the thicket and a woodpecker began its stuttered drumming on a hollow tree. I didn't know if woodpeckers only picked hollow trees, or if they just liked them better, but when I looked his way I saw it was a Yellow bellied Sapsucker. Regret paid him no mind as he stopped his drumming long enough to scavenge some of the sap he just uncovered, though I watched him with interest until we were out of sight.

My direction was to the east toward the Mississippi River. The sun would rise above the trees soon and I would have it in my eyes. A faint mist still drifted in the lower reaches below the tree limbs in the swamp. There were hammocks here and there raising up above the land, but generally anywhere you set a foot in this part of the country you sank eight to ten inches straight down before anything solid offered itself up as footing.

Regret was knee deep this morning as we skirted the area where I believed the men holding my wife might be hiding. There were only a couple of places besides the big thicket where they could find any elevation or solid ground, so that's where I concentrated my search.

The first knoll was the smaller and it was vacant. There was no sign anyone was in the area. My discovery left only one place so I headed in that direction. I checked the load in my rifle to make sure it was ready because I had a sneaking suspicion there just wasn't going to be any other way to handle matters.

I had been around Yankee's enough to know they couldn't be quiet even if their life depended on it. They would be talking about one thing or another which meant they would never hear me coming. I just hoped my wife was unharmed, because if she was hurt in any way I was fixing to get myself killed. I gave plenty of thought to our difficulties where my wife was concerned. She was worth fighting for even if I didn't understand her Christian enhanced Voodoo religion. I said some vows and if a man's vows didn't add up to anything, the rest of his word wasn't worth much either.

As I neared the second location where I guessed they might be, I heard something rattle deep in the woods which sounded like a tin cup or plate landing hard. I reined in my mule and sat silent listening. I heard more sounds, the sounds men would make around a campfire, and then I heard Abigail.

"You'd better let me go or you will all die," she said.

"Listen to you. We're ready for that cat. Why, if he comes anywhere near us he's dead meat," Holloman retorted.

"If you touch my cat, you won't live out the day," she promised.

"And just what are you going to do all tied up and helpless like you are?"

"Mister, you're going to get it," Abigail swore.

"I might, but it won't be today," Holloman laughed.

I continued to sneak closer all the time they were talking. It wasn't easy, but those Yankee's were busy in the other direction so I got close enough to see what was going on. My wife was tied up with her back to a tree and Holloman was tossing another stick on the fire. With malice in his eyes he removed a long hot burning stick and held it up to my wife's face.

"I'll have my way before we're through," and then he lit a cigarette which was dangling from his lips. He turned back to look at her and dropped the hot burning stick back into the fire.

"When my husband catches up to you, he'll..."

He backhanded her across the face drawing a bit of blood to her lower lip. I started to jump up and run in there without thought, then realized such a move wouldn't be prudent. Calming down a mite I checked my position further. This was in close, too close. If I was discovered here I would be killed without a second thought. Abigail would have to mind her manners for a little while longer.

I eased away from my position near the knoll and retraced my steps back to Regret. He gave me his look which said he wanted to be anywhere else but here and you know what, I felt the exact same way, but I couldn't do anything about it. My wife was in there on that knoll, and she needed me to help her escape.

I lifted his reins and stepped up into the saddle, again this was no easy task.

Once in the saddle I eased Regret away from the wooded knoll and started to circle. The idea in my mind was to flush them out. I didn't know how, I wasn't a military tactician, but I had to do something. As we circled I saw what appeared to be a Yankee blouse laying high up in a tree and I pulled rein. It was a Yankee blouse and there was a man in it! I turned Regret so I could get a better angle with my rifle and lifted the weapon to my shoulder. Taking aim with the rifle in my left hand, using my left eye, who knew if I could hit anything, but I was going to wake him up. If I was lucky I was going to put a bullet in him.

Slowly I squeezed the trigger. My rifle leaped in my hands and the hammer punched me right beneath my eye. Jerking the rifle down I saw the man jump, he went straight up for a moment then he came straight down. I didn't think I hit him, but as he fell toward the ground bouncing off this limb and that I saw what looked like blood. Then he landed in a heap on the ground in front of me and let out a grunt. He started to lift up, but dropped back dead. I cocked my rifle and walked Regret up to where he lay.

Another one bites the dust, I thought to myself. I didn't bother with last rights or seeing if he was rich, I left him lay right where he landed. I still had a few more of them Blue Bellies to deal with. What pained me was the fact I wasn't getting my fair share of them. I nudged Regret and we ambled on. I knew what I was looking for now, so I moved cautiously to be certain I didn't ride straight into one of those sinful varmints. Guiding my mule we walked about thirty paces and paused. Looking around it became obvious my task would not come easy.

Once I was certain of not being watched I moved another thirty yards or so turning north as I went then I pulled up. I spotted some brush off to my right so I took Regret in that direction. It would do well to keep him under cover until I could root around the knoll some more and see who was where. I still needed to find three more soldiers and Tope Holloman. Holloman would be easy to find, he would be right beside my wife, probably with a knife to her throat just like the coward he was.

I left Regret behind and slipped away. My boots were soaked through and through, but that's the swamp for you. At least it wasn't freezing cold. It was springtime coming onto summer. I wondered suddenly what kind of flowers the Rost family had blooming right then. It would be an incredible display of Gods hand. What we saw while there was incredible, and it wasn't yet summer, many of her flowers had not blossomed.

Looking around to make sure I couldn't be seen, I dropped to my knees and said a short prayer. Abigail insisted I needed to give more respect to God by dropping to my knee's to pray. I did so now.

"Lord, I'm not a praying man, but I ask you here and now to spare my wife, to keep me safe and to send those wicked Yankee's back home, running or in a box makes no difference to me, but please Lord, take care of them for us. You see how stove up I am, I'm no good to anyone in my current condition. Give us a chance Lord, Amen."

As my prayer ended there was commotion off to my left. A crow cawed from a treetop in the distance, a man screamed, gurgling his last breath. Cajun struck again. Now there were two men left besides Holloman. I shuddered at what I would find next, but they asked for it.

I heard shouting then, someone was arguing back there on the knoll and it wasn't Abigail. My wife had a distinct female voice and the argument was between two or three men. Not close enough to make out what they were saying, my ears strained to listen. Suddenly a gun went off somewhere in the woods and there was more shouting. The gun boomed again, then all I heard was silence.

I left Regret tied securely, but suddenly the urge was on me to retrieve him, to mount up and get my mule under me. I didn't know why the feeling was so strong, then suddenly with no warning I saw Holloman in the distance leading my wife on her horse. They were both mounted heading away to the south. Instantly it was apparent why such a feeling was on me. I needed to get back in the saddle. I turned and went back to my mule, pulled his reins loose from the tree limb and climbed back into the saddle.

It was clear to me Holloman just killed his two companions. He took my wife hostage and was now running. There was no one to protect her. I was all she had in the world right then, me and Cajun, I couldn't forget about Cajun. He was probably more effective than I could ever be.

Obviously the Yankee's were through in this part of the country. There was nobody left. Tope Holloman was the last vestige or remnant. Of course, Tope wasn't really a Yankee, he was a selfish opportunist. He wanted to build his wealth on the ash heap of a war which ended twelve months ago. He wanted to steal that which was not his while no one was looking. If I wasn't careful he was going to get away with his diabolical little plan too.

It suddenly became clear to me that Tope and Callahan were working together to accomplish a means to an end, I just wasn't sure to what end. Had it been Belle Grove Plantation? What for? What had been their intentions? They obviously commandeered an entire Yankee troop. What for? Those men along with Callahan were now dead. The Yankee's had been expendable from the beginning, I knew now they were gone.

Chapter 38

When you grow up in a swamp you learn things. You learn how to track a man or a beast through the worst conditions. As Holloman ran with my wife in tow, I had no trouble following the trail he was leaving. I could see it plainly, even when he entered the black water to try and throw me off.

If my guess was right, I wasn't the only tiger on his tail. Cajun would be stalking him just the same. In fact I was certain of it. Cajun would be up ahead somewhere waiting for him to let his guard down, but I knew Holloman's type and he would not wait much longer before taking certain liberties with my wife. Certain liberties which would get a man killed. In his little mind he figured he could just kill me and have my wife for as long as he wanted. I had other ideas.

The shadow of a bird crossed my path and I shielded my eyes against the sky. A lone Blue Heron swooped down low and landed in the water's edge about three hundred yards off to my left. As I watched him land I saw a gator slip into the water and disappear. A moment later the heron flew up, unsatisfied with the spot chosen. Good thing too, because that gator was hungry.

Looking down I studied the tracks on the ground. They weren't tracks, just a place where the water had been disturbed by horses. Water here was maybe six inches deep. One of the biggest dangers to a horse or mule was getting greased hoof in a swamp like this. It made their hooves so sensitive they could no longer walk. It would take time for something like that to heal. We were off the roads, off the beaten path and all of the mounts involved in this chase were susceptible to the disease. All day and into the next I followed them.

I led Regret along the same trail Holloman painted for me. He wasn't going anywhere at all. In fact the direction he was going was fixing to dry up real fast. He was only a few miles from the gulf waters. Once down there he had to turn right or left, unless he had a boat. I panicked at the thought. If he managed to get Abigail aboard a boat they would be gone.

I dug my heels into Regret in order to get him moving. I couldn't lay back and wait for the right time to overtake the man, I had to move now. In fact I must beat him to wherever he was going. This was not an easy task, because first I needed to know where he was going in order to beat him there. I studied on him then, following his trail all the while.

He wasn't swamp savvy, he never grew up in one and it showed by the mistakes he made. He had my girl and I was not happy. I couldn't fight him with my bare hands; that was out, I had to get him cornered and put a bullet into him.

Suddenly I broke off from the trail I followed and turned southwest in order to swing around and get in front of him. He was heading straight south since leaving the knoll and I suspected he wasn't going to deviate from his general direction. I swam Regret through some deep water then we climbed back up onto another knoll. There was a land bar here and if I hadn't grown up in these parts I wouldn't have known about it. Once on land I galloped southward until I ran out of terra firma about three miles south.

Turning back to the east I let Regret have a blow. Here I pulled my rifle out of the scabbard and held it to the ready. I was on the beachhead. Suddenly I drew up. I saw them come from out of the woods in front of me. The sawgrass was high, waving in the wind, so there was plenty of motion around. This, I thought, was the only reason I hadn't been spotted yet.

Stepping down I led Regret in the direction which would allow me to intercept them. Holloman was a mean one, so I would likely die, but I wasn't about to die without trying. The man had ten to fifteen years on me, so I wasn't in the best of positions, but I had guts and determination.

I led Regret forward carrying my rifle in my left hand. The sawgrass was as tall as me, so I wasn't providing a silhouette the man might see. I kept an eye on him watching as we walked. Soon we were going to meet and when we did all sort of commotion was going to break out.

Abigail locked eyes with me first and I thought she was going to give me away, but she swallowed her surprise and resumed her posture. Whatever she'd been about to say, she swallowed that too. I'm thankful she did, because otherwise I probably would have died.

Holloman saw me then, his eyes flared in disbelief and he charged straight at me. I lifted the rifle and tried to pull the trigger, but I was not left handed and I missed in my attempt. His horse hit me and threw me back onto the sand. Before I could get my feet under me, Tope Holloman was on top of me beating me with his fist. He jerked my head up and hit me again. I could hear my wife screaming at him to stop. Her screams only made him more vicious.

Suddenly he jerked me up and tossed my rifle out into the water. He walked over to his horse and pulled out my pistol along with the gun belt. Throwing the weapon at my feet he yelled at me, "Buckle it on, pretty boy!"

"My right hand is in a cast," I argued.

"Use your left. Now buckle it on."

I stared in disbelief. So, this was how it ended. I knew I would never be allowed to actually get the gun into action. This was not going to be a fair fight. I had virtually no ability with my left hand. Not yet anyway. What I was going to need was my right hand and that wasn't about to happen.

Reaching down I picked up the belt and unbuckled it so that I could strap it on. When I tried to buckle it, I winced at the pain in my right hand. Somehow I injured my hand again. I eventually got the contraption strapped on, but the gun was on my right hip and I said as much.

"I can't fight you like this, the gun is on the wrong hip," I said.

Holloman walked over to me and spun the belt around then pulled my gun and spun it around backward in the holster. "There, now it's by your left hand."

He stepped away and started to back up slowly.

"I'm going to kill you boy, and then I'm going to have your woman for as long as I want," he sneered.

He backed up a few more steps and spoke again. "I've been looking forward to the day I got even with you. That little trick of yours out in the territory cost me ten thousand dollars. Now you're going to pay."

"What trick," I asked incredulously.

"When you slipped McDonald those two aces, you thought you were slick."

"I brought drinks to the table, I didn't have any cards," I protested.

"Don't lie to me boy. I know good and well what you did. The two of you were in cahoots." He kept backing ever so slowly. There was evil in his eyes, an evil I rarely witnessed. He was mistaken about me, but it didn't matter now. No one would convince him any different.

"Now draw!" As he yelled the command Cajun leaped from the tall sawgrass and attacked. His gun went off into the air because the first thing Cajun latched onto was his arm. Holloman scrambled to get in a shot, but suddenly the gun was gone and Cajun grabbed Tope Holloman by the throat and ripped. It was an ugly death. Blood spewed everywhere on the beach, and Tope Holloman gave up the ghost within a minute. I was reminded then; no man could overcome his own appointment with death. I don't remember where I heard it, maybe it was my mother's teaching or the Whipple's, but the thought was there. No man could place his soul back into his body, no one but Jesus Christ, the son of God had ever done so.

I walked over to Abigail and untied her. She dropped down from her horse and threw her arms around me. "James Le Roy Ware, you are my hero," she said.

"What happened back there on the knoll?" I asked pointing north.

"Holloman killed one of his men. He tried to kill them both, but one of them was only wounded. He may be in bad shape. We should check on him," she said.

"You think he's still alive?"

"I think so. He was trying to save me, to let me go."

"Then we will make sure and check on him."

"Here, you'll want this back in your pocket," she said handing me my rabbit's foot.

"How did you get that?" I asked.

"I needed it in order to protect you. I took it while you were sleeping. Oh, Le Roy, is this crazy situation finally over?"

"I think so, but I thought I was protecting you. That's why I came after you."

"Le Roy, you certainly have a lot to learn," she said staring me in the eye.

I kissed her. When I pulled back I said, "Let's go home."

Cajun walked up beside us and purred. We mounted up and rode away leaving Holloman on the beach. The way I figured, a man like Holloman deserved to have his blood spilled over the shifting sand. He wouldn't be the first man to never have a grave dug for him. The vultures would clean his carcass to the bone in a few days. I was not going to worry about him.

I didn't do what Holloman claimed. I remember working at the Hotel How-De-Do in Oklahoma territory for a few days to earn some money, but I never done anything of the kind. If McDonald had an ace or two up his sleeve, it was purely his own doing. I only served the drinks to the poker table as requested. I knew way back then Holloman was a bad one and wanted to do nothing to attract his attention toward me.

Two days later when we reached the knoll where Abigail had been held hostage we found the soldier still breathing. I loaded him onto Holloman's horse and headed for town. It was pushing midnight when we arrived, but Webster was up in a jiffy. He went to work on the man and we went to get a room at the hotel. I took the stock down to the stable and put them up for the night and then went back to our room where Abigail was sound asleep.

Chapter 39

Noon was breaking when I finally woke up. White Castle was all hustle and bustle with people, because more Yankee soldiers had arrived. I cursed my luck and got dressed. That was the last thing I wanted to hear. I wanted the killing to stop. It made no sense for men to die in such a way. I believed that when Holloman's men got their fill the charade was over. Now this conflict would continue with no end in sight.

"What in the world," I asked. "When will the Yankee's leave us be?"

"They arrived while you were sleeping. The major wants to speak with you," Abigail told me.

"Did you tell him anything?" I asked.

"No."

"Well, why not?"

"Because, he didn't ask me anything," she said. "I want to speak to your husband; that was all he said."

"That's just great. He's going to want to lock me up for the killing of Callahan and his men."

"I think you ought to speak with him, he seems to be a nice man, not at all like the ones we have been dealing with. He seemed sympathetic."

"Well, if he's anything like the others, we're in trouble."

We opened the door to our room to find a rather large cat lying in front of our door. We brought Cajun inside, left our room and went downstairs. At the desk was a soldier, he was there to escort us to see the Yankee major. I didn't argue with him, I just fell into step with my wife beside me.

"It will be all right honey," my wife promised.

The sheriff was sitting at his desk when we walked into his office. "There's a whole new troop of Yankee soldiers in town," Cobb said.

I could see that. As I looked around the room I felt surrounded. "We can't go on like this," I said. "Sooner or later it will be us who dies or maybe all of us and then what?"

"I don't know. Maybe it's time to move on. Go out west somewhere and leave all this killing behind," Sheriff Cobb suggested.

"This is our home, sheriff. As much as I would love to oblige, Abigail and I are staying right here."

I eyed the Yankee sitting in the corner who hadn't opened his mouth, but I knew by instinct he was in charge here, he was the major. He was listening like a canny old wolf just waiting for someone to slip up or make a mistake, but he was ready. He was the man in charge, I'd bet my life on it.

"The name is Major Poindexter. I know some of your troubles here young man, but I want to be the first to apologize."

My mouth dropped open because I couldn't believe what I was hearing. "You want to apologize," I stuttered.

"Yes, I want to apologize because there is no Captain Callahan and never was. I don't know the man's real identity, but he was not a real Yankee soldier."

"But he was here, he wore the Yankee blue."

"He wore the uniform, but he was never a Yankee soldier. I was sent down here to investigate recent events to include the theft of a captain's uniform from the first Illinois. We found Captain West stripped of his uniform and left for dead. Now it appears I can't even locate the troops who were assigned to Captain West at White Castle."

"Sir, I believe they may all be dead, but for one."

"They're all dead? Where might I find the one live soldier?"

"He's down at Doc Webster's. I think he might be able to tell you a thing or two."

Major Poindexter stormed out of the room taking his soldier with him. He didn't wait for any further explanation, he didn't say excuse me, buy your leave or anything else, he just left.

"Well, Le Roy it seems there may finally be some peace around here," Cobb offered.

"I hope you're right sheriff, because I sure need to heal up some."

We vacated Jessup Cobb's office and went back to our room post haste. Neither of us had any idea what Cajun might do if left alone in a strange place for too long. He was spread out in the middle of our bed like he owned it, so we gathered our things and went to the stable to mount up, our cat lumbering along beside us. The feeling was upon us to be getting home. I knew Major Poindexter's investigation was just beginning, but I wanted to rest in my own bed this evening.

We rode out a few minutes later, but I couldn't help noticing the looks we were getting from the local folks and soldiers. It seemed every eye in town was on us, but I couldn't grasp why. Why should anyone here in these parts care about James Le Roy Ware? All I wanted was to be left alone. Something told me that wasn't about to happen, not in the near future anyway. We headed up the lane to Belle Grove Plantation first, because that was where we left our friends a few days before and suddenly I realized, it wasn't me drawing folk's attention, it was Cajun or maybe my wife, but I was the least of their concern.

When we left the stable in town I took Holloman's horse and saddle. He sure wasn't going to need them anymore. The horse was a well-bred sorrel with four black stockings. I knew a horse with four stockings was taboo, but the horse was a good one. I didn't care what everyone else's superstition might be. I was going to use him for breeding purposes anyway. Today however, I was giving Regret a well-needed rest leading him by his reins while riding the sorrel. My decision to rest my mule almost got me killed.

As we neared Belle Grove my horse kicked a tripwire my friends set to warn them of coming riders. If I hadn't realized immediately what I'd done, we would have been blown from our saddles. As things worked out I yelled. "Don't shoot. It's me, Le Roy Ware."

We rode forward enough for them to see us and my friends were ready. All four of them had a gun in their hand. Darnell was up on the top of the big stone staircase, Butch was at the bottom, Conrad was around to the near side and Chin was across from us near the woods. For the first time he carried a gun.

The yard was full of animals. There was no doubt in my mind my friends brought them all back. Such a move made sense. If they were going to be here, someone needed to feed all those animals, all but the goats that is. They could forage for food pretty good on their own. I noticed a few unfamiliar ducks and when Cajun entered the picture behind us that yard emptied out like Ford theatre after Lincoln was shot. Suddenly, the animals were scarce.

"We didn't expect to see the two of you back, but I'm glad you are here," Butch said greeting us.

"Yeah, we didn't figure you had much of a chance all stove up like that," Darnell said from the top of the staircase.

"Some kind of friends I have, I bet you didn't worry about us one bit."

"Well, you wouldn't want us to get an ulcer now would you?" Darnell said.

"Is everything all right here?"

"Sort of. Your other place was burned to the ground right after you lit out."

I looked at Abigail and I could see she was beginning to get emotional. We were suddenly homeless. I had a few feelings myself. Could a man not have anything without someone wanting to take it from him? When was I going to get a reprieve? I couldn't get up in the morning without worrying if I would live through the day or not.

"I thought the two of you might care for Belle Grove in my place," Butch said. "Conrad and Chin are fixing to go sail the high seas. Darnell and I thought sailing might be fun for a year or two. So we thought if the two of you returned you could watch Belle Grove and live here until Mr. Andrew's figures out just what he wants to do about the place."

I looked over my shoulder to see Cajun sniffing around beneath the live oak where the Yankee's strung up their cat kill. He seemed disturbed about what his senses were telling him. I had an idea the cat was Cajun's female companion, but I would never know for sure.

"Honey, you want to go calm Cajun? He doesn't need to be over there sniffing around just yet."

Abigail turned Penny and rode over to Cajun circling beneath the tree. I knew I could never afford a home like Belle Grove Plantation, but to live here, even if for just a little while would make me feel like a king. I had nothing left, nothing but a few horses and a mule. Of course there was my wife and cat. I did have a rather large cat and my wife seemed to be the cat's meow, if I might inject a bit of humor.

"So the four of you are going sailing?" I said.

"Just as soon as we can." Butch grinned at me.

"We're going on a trip around the world," Conrad said as he walked up.

"Well, you're welcome here at Belle Grove anytime."

I stepped down from my horse and shook his hand.

"You know, it'll require a good deal of money to care for such a place properly," Conrad said.

"Well, money is one thing I don't have much of."

"Before we leave, I'll transfer some more money into your account at Dix in New Orleans. A place like this deserves to be cared for. I'm certain you'll do a fine job in our absence."

"I don't know what to say."

"Don't say anything for tonight we celebrate. In the morning the four of us shall leave the place in your capable hands."

Chin walked up then and said, "Every man shall give as he is able, according to the blessing of the Lord which he hath given thee."

"Chin, I'm going to miss having you around."

"Chin miss too."

"You fellows help him with his English, it could stand a bit of work," I offered.

"You ready eat?" Chin asked.

"I am," I said. Looking over at Abigail she had Cajun calmed down, but he seemed sad. She stood up and walked over to us. We entered the home and for the first time Abigail saw the grander of Belle Grove Plantation. We walked the halls with Butch showing us all seventy-five rooms, then we returned to the dining room for supper. Chin fixed us a fabulous feast he called Chinese stir fry. This meal came with plenty of rice.

We talked of Captain Callahan and his men, Tope Holloman and the Yankee's until we were all reassured they were taken care of. The new Yankee detachment was an unknown element, but we were reassured in that Major Poindexter had apologized to me earlier that morning. Also the fact Captain Callahan was an imposter was in our favor.

I cannot describe the feeling that came over me while we were eating. The fact Abigail and I would be sharing such a big home all by ourselves. A haunting thought occurred to me, but I dismissed such thoughts immediately. I only said those things to scare the Yankee's, not to scare me, yet the halls of Belle Grove were large and foreboding. We lit the candles as the sun went down and continued to discuss matters into the late evening hours.

Abigail continues to play with her dolls, even today. We have ten children and twenty-nine grandchildren. Our home is full of laughter and joy. I began breeding my horses and in 1876 a fellow named William Astor partnered with me to run the Kentucky Derby which Vagrant won going away. I only ran the one race, for I had all the proof I needed to place a proper value on my stock.

Many of the former slaves returned to work in the sugar cane fields, but this time as paid workers. I bought Belle Grove in 1867 for the taxes owed. John Andrews found a new love in Paris, France and would not be returning to America. Even now all these years later, I wonder what happened to my friends. There was never another word from them, but Conrad Lafitte did as promised and transferred money into the existing account for Belle Grove Plantation, all of it!

To the Chawasha tribe and Chief Eagle Feather I became known as the peacemaker, the one who ruled from the great castle, the leader of many people. I never saw it coming, not in those days, but as time marched on I became a man, a man to reckon with, but a man cannot become a real leader if he does not build a family of his own. Those who refuse to do so will never become leaders. By the way, I do have a rather large catamount!

Power in the Blood

I wrote *Blood Once Spilled* because I don't think people realize just how easy it is to get killed in today's world, and I don't think people understand Jesus Christ spilled his precious blood on an Old Rugged Cross so God could redeem us from our sin. I'm no preacher, I don't expect to ever be one, but I do know that God loves every one of us. I have what many people would consider a personal weakness, I believe in our Lord and Savior Jesus Christ, I believe in God and I am not ashamed of my heritage.

I know there have been many times in my own life where I could have died in an instant, yet by the grace of God I have lived in spite of those situations. I know where my bread is buttered. Jesus Christ shed his blood, and that precious blood once spilled can never be put back into its human vial. It was shed for your sin and mine, but if you choose not to partake of his blood what happens when you die is nobody's fault but yours. I have chosen to accept what he did for me, because I'm telling you I am not perfect, only through the shedding of his blood I am made so. Not any work I might have done, but His blood once spilled is all anyone needs.

Author's Note

Once again our nation is divided against itself so vehemently I shudder to think of what might happen. One of the reasons I have been writing my books, *The Gaslight Boys*, is because I would like to heal some of the old wounds through understanding. If Harriett Beacher Stowe is known for dividing a nation against itself (*Uncle Tom's Cabin*) I want to be known as the man who brought it back together through understanding.

---John T. Wayne

Seven men who died fighting for the rights of all Americans to remain free upon the land. They lost, yet they are no less the hero. It is becoming quite evident one hundred fifty years after the fact these men were fighting for state sovereignty and the right of a state not to bow down to the federal government. While the north won the war, every northern state lost their sovereignty as well. In essence, everybody lost. I am dedicating this book to these brave men who knew what federal over-reach was one hundred fifty years ago and fought so hard against it.

Dr. James B. Cowan Surgeon Forrest, Cav.
Pvt. Joseph Ranson Edwards
Pvt. R. F. Balthrop 22nd Tex Cav, 1st Reg
Pvt. William A. Page, 9th Tenn. Inf. A Co
Joseph B. Dodso,n 6th Cav. A Co
Henry H. Liles, 7th Georgia Cav.
Capt. William H. Holloman, 47th Tenn. H Co

About the Author

John T. Wayne was born in St. Louis, Missouri in August 1958. He attended numerous schools all around the show me state while growing up, eventually settling in Hermann, Missouri. He graduated and joined the U.S. Marines in 1976 then attended the University of Oregon on his G.I. Bill. Upon the death of his daughter, Kimberly Marie in December 1985 he began writing. In time he settled into writing the Civil War and Wild West stories you are reading today.

CPSIA information can be obtained
at www.ICGtesting.com
Printed in the USA
LVHW04s2239210618
581511LV00004B/786/P

9 781635 352627